Eyes of the Beholder

Rick Ludwig

Praise for Rick Ludwig and Eyes of the Beholder

"In his latest book, *Eyes of the Beholder*, must-read author Rick Ludwig brings us a world that will have you questioning what is right ... and what is left."

— R.J. Johnson, award-winning author of *Dreamslinger*

"An auto accident destroys Detective-Sergeant Keone Boyd's roadster, plunging him into an unexpected realm as he grapples with a suspect's alternate reality and unexpected plot twists. This is not your typical investigation. *Eyes of the Beholder* is a gripping read that will leave you wondering what comes next."

— Kenneth Andrus, acclaimed author of *Arctic Menace*

"If you're yearning for a page-turning tale of suspense and skulduggery, look no further. If you're hoping for some crackling dialogue and vivid descriptions, you'll find them here. And if you're yearning to go that land of myth and mystery in the middle of the Pacific, let Rick Ludwig take you. Along with the beauty, he'll show you the dark side of paradise. Don't miss it."

— William Martin, *New York Times*-bestselling author of *The Lincoln Letter* and *December '41* (for *Pele's Fire*)

"Ludwig brings this crime-fiction reader full circle from the Hawaiian Islands to the Italian Coast and back again. He has not only created believable characters and complicated crimes, but also he's introduced me to a detective I hope resurfaces in the future. "

— Elaine Gallant, author of *The 5th C: A CIA Novel*

Eyes of the Beholder

For Christy

A Note on the Spelling of Hawaiian Words

After moving to Maui, I learned a great deal about the history and culture of the Hawaiian Islands. I respect this ancient and vibrant culture and have tried to reflect this in everything I've written in this beautiful place. But I am neither a native Hawaiian nor a speaker of the language. Though I have learned a few phrases that I am not too embarrassed to speak aloud, I faced a challenge in spelling Hawaiian words.

Two characters are used in proper Hawaiian spelling that may be unfamiliar to those new to the language. These are the *'okina* and *kahakō*.

The 'okina can be approximated by an apostrophe but is an actual consonant and represents a glottal stop. It may occur at the beginning or in the middle of a word and changes the pronunciation and meaning of words. An example familiar to many non-Hawaiians is the name of the island Lāna'i (Lah-nah-ee), which is very different from the word for a veranda or covered patio, lanai (Lah-nigh). Throughout the novel I have used a reversed apostrophe to represent this important consonant.

The kahakō indicates vowel length, which changes meaning and the placement of stress. In other languages it is referred to as a macron and represented by a line over a vowel. An example of how these can impact meaning in a Hawaiian word is the word kāne (kaa-nay) which means male, while the same word without the kahakō, kane (ka-nay), means skin disease.

In this trilogy, I have elected to use both the ʻokina and kahakō. I apologize to Native Hawaiian readers for my other limitations.

I have also attempted to use the standard method for distinguishing non-English words, using italics for the first occurrence of such words, except for place names.

Another characteristic of the islands is the common use of pidgin in friendly banter. I have learned that there are subtle differences between the pidgin used on each of the Hawaiian Islands. What I have tried to capture, on occasion in this novel, is probably closest to the pidgin I heard on Maui. I have tried, phonetically, to capture the essence of this joyful and constantly evolving language as I heard it spoken. Born from the desire of each wave of immigrants to this lovely place to communicate with each other, despite vastly different native tongues, Hawaiian pidgin is an essential component of daily life here in paradise. One very common aspect is a tendency to end most sentences with, *yeah?* It's kind of like ending a sentence on the mainland with, *right?*

1. Left Isn't Right

"If you don't know where you are going, any road will get you there."

— Lewis Carroll

Chapter One

Friday, March 15, 2013 – 4:30 p.m.

Sport Green. That was the official designation. But to Keone Boyd it was the color of freedom. That first look at his new Morgan Roadster on the dockside in Kahului triggered memories of another green Morgan, his dad's.

When his father was young and single, he'd owned a Morgan. Keone had only seen pictures and heard stories of his father's many adventures in the fabulous car. He wasn't as young as his father had been but was still single. On a Maui PD salary, many things took longer. He'd spent months on a waiting list, then waited another eighteen months for his brand-new roadster to be constructed in England and delivered dockside in Kahului. Now it was his. Both of his grandfathers had owned Morgans, too, but those were horses.

Paperwork signed, keys in hand, it was time for Keone to fulfill a lifetime dream. He eased himself into the specially designed front seat, custom made to handle his unique physique. No further adjustments were needed. He turned the key and the three-liter, Ford Duratec V6 engine roared to life. He couldn't wait to hear it sing.

He gunned the engine once, then eased out of the dock area and onto a surface street. He kept it close to the speed limit until he was on Kuihelani Highway. Time to open it up. He blew through eighty miles per hour on the one stretch of road on Maui where that was practical, knowing no cops would be patrolling his route at this particular time on this particular day. There were advantages to being one of Maui's finest.

He sailed through the cane fields of central Maui with the cream-colored, cloth top down, wind tossing his thick mop of black hair. He knew he'd have to slow down to make the turn onto Honoapi'ilani Highway but savored this first, short burst of freedom.

Keone missed the light, which allowed the traffic from Kahului airport to catch up and fill both westbound lanes. A glance in his side-view mirror revealed twenty other cars waiting patiently for the light to change. A luscious, tanned island girl in the lane to his right seemed fascinated by the trademark leather strap across the Morgan's hood—what Brits called the bonnet. Filing away the girl's smiling face in his impressive memory, he focused on being first in line at the next signal.

The second the light turned green, he matched the specs of zero to sixty in four-point-nine seconds, leaving all the other cars in the red dust of Maui. Unfortunately, the light at Kapoli Street changed to red before he could get close enough to pretend it was still yellow. Keone drummed his fingers on the leather covering his steering wheel while the long line of cars caught up. Four pulled up behind him into the left turn lane, and the rest crammed the lane to his right. Looking left, he saw the green roofs of his condo complex. He and his Morgan were almost home.

Out of the corner of his eye he caught rapid movement.

What the hell?

A black Hummer approached at full speed, aimed directly at the cars stopped beside Keone. When the wrong-way driver saw the cars, he tried to swerve to his right and turn onto Kapoli. But the Hummer couldn't handle the sharp change in direction and began to tumble sideways into both lanes of stopped cars.

Time stopped long enough for one thought to coalesce in Keone's brain. *Not now.*

Then a crushing weight.

Then nothing.

Chapter Two

The two firemen who carved Keone out of the wreckage found him not only alive but conscious. A brawny arm reached in to help him crawl out.

Keone glanced at his watch to find it had stopped, retrieved his notebook from his hip pocket, and wrote: *Time of collision 4:49 p.m.*

"What time is it now?" he asked a fireman.

"Five-fifteen. Sir, we need to take you to that ambulance to evaluate your injuries."

"I know the drill. I'm MPD."

The fireman's partner spoke up. "We know Detective Sergeant Boyd, Kel. We've worked together before."

Looking more closely at the two firemen, Keone smiled. "Kimo Kelly and Jimmy Mahoe. Sorry I didn't recognize you at first. Howzit?"

"Busy. And don't apologize. You had your bell rung pretty good. Better check in with the EMTs, Sarge."

EMTs were standing around an ambulance that Keone was not about to take a ride in. He recognized one of them, Eldon Miranda, pressing a thick layer of gauze against a young woman's lacerated cheek. The same young woman who'd caught his eye at the signal

Miranda looked up. "Hey Sarge, you okay?"

"Yeah, I was only out a couple minutes."

Miranda glanced at what was left of Keone's car and back at him twice before saying, "Yeah, right."

The efficient EMT finished with the young woman, then smiled and indicated she should get into the ambulance. Keone smiled at her, too.

She rolled her eyes. Keone translated, *Even in emergency situations, men are pigs.* She was probably right.

Five minutes later, Miranda completed his examination of Keone. "You should be dead, you know. I'll cut you loose, Keone, but ya gotta promise to stop by the hospital to get checked out. And I mean before you go anywhere else, even home." A doctor in the Philippines, Eldon worked as an EMT on Maui while studying for his U.S. license. Keone had worked numerous cases with him and respected his expertise.

"Don't worry, Doc. I'm going straight to the hospital. I need to see a man about a Hummer. I assume you guys sent the occupants of the Hummer directly to the hospital."

Miranda looked at his own notebook. "Yeah. Guy named Loftus was the driver—first name Samuel. The passenger was... uh... Marder—first name Leroy. They were both unconscious."

"*Mahalo*, Eldon."

Keone walked over to three patrolmen investigating the scene and asked the nearest for the keys to his cruiser.

"Sure, Sergeant Boyd. I'll catch a ride back to the station with Manolo. You headed for the hospital?"

"Yeah. Hey, Keali'i, while I'm there you want me to take care of some of the grunt work for you?"

"Hell, yes. We're up to our asses here."

"No worries. I'll square it with my LT and your watch commander and shoot you a copy of my supplementals."

"Mahalo, brah."

"Don't worry. I'll take good care of your ride." They both glanced at the scrap metal that used to be Keone's ride. "Better than I took care of mine."

~

WHEN DETECTIVE SERGEANT KEONE BOYD BURST through the automatic doors into the emergency department of Maui Memorial Hospital, he saw *utter chaos*. The island hadn't dealt with an accident of this magnitude in years, if ever. The wrong-way driver not only totaled one pristine Morgan roadster but also disabled fifteen other cars on the island's major east-west artery. Keone was going to find out why.

He flashed his badge at the first person who approached him in the ER. The expression on the pissed-off, six-foot-seven, two-hundred-seventy-five-pound Hawaiian's face must have clued the young nurse that he was not up for polite conversation. She halted mid-step and wisely turned around.

Keone's eyes swept over the gurneys in the hallway. From what he could see, most of the injuries were minor. A few elderly patients seemed to be having more trouble than the rest. Probably the shock of the collision set off existing heart, circulatory, or lung conditions. One kid, about three years old, had severe facial lacerations. The kind caused by flying head-first through the windshield.

When would people quit ignoring the seatbelt laws?

He passed the third treatment cubicle on his right and noticed a wall clock. Six-thirty-five. He'd made good time. A conversation coming from the cubicle caught his attention.

"Sammy was driving just as normal as can be, griping about all the crazy tourists coming from the airport. He got this weird look on his face—like he was about to hit a brick wall or something. I remember him saying, 'My God, everything's changed.' Then he swerved to the wrong side of the road just before the stoplight at Kapoli. He tried to swerve back at the light to miss all the cars. But the Hummer started bouncing down the road sideways. I didn't know whether to shit or go blind. I saw the front half of the car headed for the left turn lane. That first car in line was sure a beaut'. It looked brand new. My half of the windshield was pointed right at the driver before the Hummer bounced up and steamrolled the back half of his car. I'll never forget the look on his face. I sure hope his airbag worked. Sam's knocked me silly, but it saved my life. Next thing I knew I woke up here."

Keone pulled the curtain aside to find a man of about sixty propped up on the bed. A grey-haired, no-nonsense nurse that Keone knew well from previous visits to the ER was cleaning abrasions on the man's face, chest, and arms with disinfectant.

He identified himself, flashed his badge, and flipped open his notebook. "You're Mr. Marder—Mr. Leroy Marder?"

"That's me. But call me Lee, okay?"

"You were riding in the car with Mr. Loftus when the accident occurred. Is that correct?"

"Yes, I was. Scariest damn thing I ever saw."

"Could you tell me exactly what happened?"

"Well, like I was telling this lovely young lady here, we left work at four-thirty, like we always do on Aloha Fridays. Most of the trip from Lahaina was as normal as could be. Sam had his usual Friday CD playing. He has a different CD for each day of the week. This one started with the Aloha Friday song. You know:

It's Aloha Friday,
No work 'til Monday,
Doot de doo,
De doot de doot de doot de doot de doo."

"Yes, I know the song. What happened next?"

"He played some Bruddah Iz, some Keola Beamer, some Keali'i Reichel—"

"No, I mean when did the drive get...less normal?"

"Oh, right. When we passed the harbor entrance, just before

that big old restaurant... uh... used to be called Buzz's, everything got wonky."

"Wonky?"

"Well, this thing happened, then Old Sammy swerved into the wrong lane. I call him Old Sammy cause he's so much younger than me, get it?"

"You say he swerved?"

"Yeah, but when he saw all them cars at the signal, lined up in his lane, he tried to swerve back to miss 'em. His big old Hummer had too much mojo and started to roll. Damned if we didn't end up hitting both lanes."

"What thing happened?"

"Huh?"

"Before he swerved the first time, you said 'this thing happened.'"

"I'm not exactly sure, because it only happened to Sammy."

"Did he say anything?"

"Sorta cringed at first. Then he said he was on the wrong side of the road, which he wasn't. Then he swerved into the wrong lane."

"Did he say anything else, Mr. Marder? Think carefully."

"Y' know, now that you mention it, right after he cringed, he asked me, 'Did you hear that pop?'"

"Did you?"

"No, not a sound."

"Can you remember anything else?"

"Well, Sam said, 'Did you hear that pop?' Then he started talking weird like."

"What did he say?"

"Uh... something about a soap bubble. Then he swore and said, 'Everything's changed. I'm on the wrong side of the road!' Then he swerved onto the wrong side and.... Hey. Weren't you the guy in the first car we hit?"

Keone nodded.

"Your face was the last thing I saw before I woke up here. Thank God you're okay."

"I'm fine, Mr. Marder, here's my card. If you think of anything else, give me a call."

Marder studied the card. "A detective? Boy, is Sammy screwed."

Chapter Three

After his interview with Marder, Keone asked the nurse to direct him to Sam Loftus.

"I have to stay with my patient, Sergeant. You'll need to ask at the desk. By the way, does Dr. Lloyd know you're here—again?" She thrust open the curtain and waved Keone out.

The last person Keone wanted to run into was Lloyd, the annoying bastard that ran the ER.

He grabbed the arm of the next doctor to walk by. Glancing at his nametag, he said, "Excuse me, Doctor Wayne?"

Wayne glared at the large man grasping his arm. "Can I help you?"

"Sergeant Boyd, Maui PD. I need to speak with Mr. Samuel Loftus," he said, flashing his badge.

"No problem. I'm Sam's family doctor. Just got here myself. He's supposed to be in the fifth cubicle on the left."

He kept hold of Wayne's arm. "Anything I should know about him? Medical conditions that could be relevant to the accident?"

Dr. Wayne ran his fingers through his thick, brown hair, pushed his glasses up on his nose, and cleared his throat before speaking. "I've been Sam and Janet's doctor ever since they moved to Maui."

Keone wondered if the doctor was stalling for time. "Janet?"

"Sam's wife."

"I see."

"To answer your question, I just gave Sam his annual check-up last month and his results were all within normal ranges."

"Emotional problems, odd habits?"

Wayne hesitated. "No, not really. He's relatively reserved and very meticulous, but that comes with the territory when you're an accountant."

"Medications?"

"Nothing unusual for a man his age. You must realize I won't disclose confidential patient information."

He did, but it was his job to ask. "Any idea why he would cross into on-coming traffic?"

"None. May I see my patient now?"

"Yeah. Let's go." Keone knew he wasn't going to get anything else of value from Wayne. The doctor was clearly worried about his patient, but Keone's detective instincts sensed something else.

He followed the doctor into the designated cubicle to find an attractive, impeccably dressed woman, early thirties, standing at the side of an emergency room bed. *Sam's wife?*

Keone guessed the man in the bed was just a few years older. *Mid-thirties?*

The man had a lump on his forehead, appeared confused, and looked about the room anxiously. "How did I get here?"

Keone guessed Sam Loftus had just regained consciousness.

The woman at his side leaned over and kissed his forehead. Her honey-blonde hair fell across his cheek. "It's good to have you back, Sam."

Sam stared at the woman for a moment, then said, "Janet, how nice of you to come. I had an accident, didn't I?"

"Yes, but you're in the hospital now." She squeezed his hand. "They'll fix you up as good as new."

"How long was I out?"

Janet glanced at the nurse in the cubicle, then her watch. "They told me the crash was right before five o'clock. It's nearly seven now."

"Two hours. Everything's so strange. Has anyone told Julie?" Sam glanced around the cubicle.

"Uh... no, I came here as soon as they called. I'll call everyone as soon as I'm sure you're okay." She glanced at Dr. Wayne, who shrugged his shoulders.

Sam laughed. "Well, I think my wife should know about this, don't you?"

"I *do* know. I'm right here."

"And I'm very grateful, but you're not my wife. I need to see Julie."

Keone watched Janet's concern change to fear, then anger.

"You stop this right now, Sam Loftus. If you think this is funny, it isn't—"

Dr. Wayne touched Janet's arm. "Sam, do you know who I am?"

"I ought to, Bob. I beat you at poker once a month, let you deliver one of our babies, and very occasionally let you treat me when I'm sick. I guess around this place I should call you Dr. Wayne, sorry."

"I'm glad to see that you know me, but you're talking kind of strangely. What baby did I deliver?"

"Our son Timmy, of course. Cindy was born before we moved to Maui."

"You and Janet don't have any kids."

"Of course we don't. I prefer to make babies with my wife, not her sister. That would be highly inappropriate."

"Have you been taking your medications as prescribed?"

"Ah, a trick question. You know I don't need any magic pills, at least not yet. Hell, I'm only thirty-six."

"Yes, you are. Just rest for now, Sam. I'll be right back."

"Okay. But bring Julie next time. I really need to let her know I'm all right."

"I'll let her know right away." Dr. Wayne motioned to Janet Loftus and Keone, guiding them out, whispered something to the nurse as he left the cubicle, then walked Janet and Keone to the far end of the ER.

The congested ER hallway seemed like a breath of fresh air after the surrealism of Sam Loftus's bedside. Janet slowly raised her hands to her face and began to cry.

Dr. Wayne cupped her shoulder with his hand. "Janet, Sam suffered a head trauma. On initial examination, the ER doctors thought his injuries were minor. His behavior just now suggests it's a bit more serious. But I don't want you to worry. Disorientation and even temporary amnesia are quite common in injuries like this. Remember, he's conscious and able to speak, so his prognosis is good. The fact that he recognized you and me, even though he confused you and Julie, is actually a good sign."

"A good sign? He says I'm not his wife." She glared at the doctor through tear-glazed eyes.

"He's disoriented. I'm sure twenty-four hours from now he'll be back to his old, annoyingly accurate self. In the meantime, I'm going to get him up to a private room and give him a mild sedative. I'll perform a complete exam tomorrow and schedule a battery of tests—if he still needs them. After a good night's sleep, he may well snap out of this temporary disorientation."

"I pray you're right. Can I go back in with him?"

"I need you to hold off until tomorrow. I know you want to be with him, but we can't risk upsetting him. It's critical we do nothing to enhance his disorientation. The best thing you can do right now is go home and get a good night's sleep. Do you still have those blue pills I prescribed last month?"

"Yes, but I—"

"Take one—just to take the edge off—about a half-hour before your regular bedtime. Trust me, Janet. I'm the doctor." He gave her a hug before placing his hand on her back and gently guiding the devastated woman toward the exit.

Keone watched with increasing interest. When the wife was gone, he spoke up. "I understand why you wanted her to go. But I need to ask you and Mr. Loftus a few questions—for my report."

"I understand. I've worked with the police before"

"Who's Julie?"

"Julie Walden, Sam's sister-in-law and Janet's sister."

"Do they look alike?"

"They're twins, but not identical—fraternal."

"Do they look alike?"

"They both grew up on a farm." *Is he stalling again?*

"Do they look enough alike for Sam to confuse them?"

"Well, no. Not really."

"Does Sam Loftus have children?"

"No."

"I'll need to talk to Sam now."

Dr. Wayne's confidence seemed to slip a bit. "I'm afraid that will have to wait until tomorrow. He's already been sedated."

Keone remembered the discussion Wayne had with the nurse as he ushered them from the cubicle. *If he's worked with the police before, why would he—*

"Let me get him moved to a private room and through the night. Then you can ask him any questions you want, as long as you keep it brief."

Although not satisfied, Keone held himself in check. He could understand Wayne's concern about his patient's ability to get through the night with what remained of his sanity. But his detective side suspected Wayne had another reason for isolating Sam from interrogation.

"You're concerned about him."

"I am. His physical condition doesn't explain his confusion."

"I thought he was surprisingly lucid, considering."

"Every patient is different. Sam's world is very ordered. And he was just confronted with the ultimate in disorder. It's essential he avoid facing additional challenges right now. I'm sure his neurons will be firing more normally in the morning."

More excuses. "Aside from the obvious, what else suggested confusion?"

"Well, he seemed more gregarious than usual, and wittier. It could just be the adrenaline rush associated with accident. He also seemed more muscular than when I saw him for his check-up. I'll have to ask Janet if he's been working out."

None of which suggested confusion. "You said you've worked with the police before?"

"Yes."

"My lieutenant expects an interview of such a key witness within twenty-four hours of the incident." Keone's expression left no room for argument. "I'll be back tomorrow morning at ten to question him."

"Agreed."

Wayne re-entered his patient's cubicle, leaving Keone no choice but to head for the exit. He'd almost reached the doors when a hand grabbed his shoulder.

"Detective Sergeant Boyd. Why am I not surprised to see you once again in a restricted area where you have no business?"

"Dr. Lloyd. Nice to see you again."

"Wish I could say the same. You cannot be here."

"I'm just leaving."

"That's not good enough. After your last escapade, Lieutenant Alcala promised me you would never again disrupt the critical activities of this emergency department. I'm reporting this."

"I was just in a car accident. The EMT told me to get checked out in the ER before going home."

"I didn't see your chart in the rack."

"The doc looked me up and down and said I was fine. Given the number of other patients you have in here tonight, I didn't want to keep him." Keone wasn't anxious for another negative report to reach Lieutenant Tony Alcala's desk.

"Oh. Well, just see to it this doesn't happen again." With that Lloyd walked off. Keone hoped he'd talked his way out of another reprimand.

Chapter Four

Saturday, March 16, 7:25 a.m.

Sam Loftus opened his eyes to discover he was lying on a cool, firm bed in a sparsely decorated room. He recognized the odd flat shape against his right upper arm as a blood pressure cuff.

Okay, I'm not in a cheap hotel.

As the pale dawn light crept through a gap in the window blinds, scattered memories from the day before crept into his awareness. A wild, spinning sensation. A man's face filled with surprise in a shiny new car. A loud crunch. Severe pain.

He reached for his forehead and touched the tender lump above his right eye. His chest hurt, as well. Pulling down the sheet, he saw a diagonal bruise.

A car accident?

More memories. In the ER, the same face from the shiny car studying him while Bob Wayne talked foolishness. Julie's sister Janet acting like she was his wife.

The pieces slid together at last, but the image they created was too bizarre. It must have been the drugs they gave him. Today everything would return to normal. Order would be restored.

Sam's eyes surveyed the room, pausing on individual objects. A bedside table stood solidly to his left. One of those little over-bed tables was on that side too, turned away from the bed, waiting patiently on its wheeled base. His eyes followed the U-shaped track for a privacy curtain, which was pulled all the way back to his right. Beyond the curtain, adjacent to the door, a chart hung on the wall, marked with scribbles he couldn't read. The pale round face of a clock glared down on him from across the room. When he focused on the numbers, he flinched.

"What the hell?" His voice echoed in the empty room.

A nurse appeared, as if in response. "So, you've decided to join us this morning. Can you tell me your name?"

"Samuel Loftus."

"Good morning Mr. Loftus."

"Good morning. Are you my nurse?"

"I'm one of them. Do you remember why you're here, Mr. Loftus?"

"I seem to recall an accident. A car accident?"

"Yes. You were involved in a car accident. How do you feel?"

"Like my face was crushed by an airbag. How do you feel?" He found this somehow humorous and giggled.

The nurse came to his side, straightened his arm, and fiddled with the blood pressure cuff before sticking her stethoscope's earpieces into her ears.

Sam decided conversation could wait until she finished.

He spotted her nametag and received his second shock of the morning. He couldn't read it.

After a bit of study, he realized why. It was in mirror writing. Slowly he translated, discovering his nurse's name, Gwen Tanaka.

When she finally deflated the cuff and removed her stetho-scope, Sam asked, "Is this backwards day, Gwen?"

Gwen looked confused.

"And where'd you get a clock with the numbers increasing

counterclockwise and a movement that runs in reverse? A friend of mine in college had a watch like that, but it had Goofy on it. It's 7:35 a.m., right?"

Gwen glanced at the clock and back to Sam. "Yes, Mr. Loftus." She removed a small penlight from her pocket. "Could you please look to your left for me?"

Sam did what she asked, which did nothing to allay her confusion.

She shined the light in his left eye. "Now look to your right. Good. Now follow the light with both eyes." She moved the light back and forth.

"You can rest your eyes, now." Gwen switched off the light and walked to the door. She removed the chart from the wall and busily inscribed his blood pressure readings and whatever her penlight had disclosed.

Sam winced. Everything she wrote, and everything else in the chart, was reversed, as if he was looking in a mirror. She continued in this exotic script with no more effort than if she'd been writing normally. He managed to translate the last two words, *extremely disoriented.*

Before he could comment on Gwen's bizarre behavior, she slipped from the room, leaving him flummoxed. *What the hell is happening to me?*

~

About forty miles away by car, near the top of Haleakala Volcano, a young scientist named Brad Carvell prepared to leave a laboratory filled with advanced monitoring equipment after a long night of work. Brad never felt so alive as when he was immersed in research.

"Hey, Radha? Got anything interesting for me from yesterday afternoon."

Dr. Radhakrishnan Rathnachalam, another post-doc in the lab, had just arrived for his day shift in the lab and spoke to Brad over his shoulder. "You know Dr. Hasselbach doesn't like me sharing the terrestrial data with you before him."

"Yeah, yeah, but we share everything at lab meetings to—what does he say—*allow multiple minds to address problems*. Not to mention how many times I've saved your butt. So..."

"Okay, okay, but before you get too excited. The data's very preliminary." Radha walked to a computer monitor and pulled up a colorful 3D display containing large flat areas punctuated with tiny peaks.

"That's it." Brad pointed at the largest spiked peak on the display. "Exactly what I predicted. When and where was this measured?"

"It was at 16:48 HST near Ma'alaea Harbor. Probably just a flaw in the detector. We haven't had a chance to run a complete diagnostic yet."

"Funny, I always thought we'd find it up here on the volcano," Brad said, almost to himself. "Did you copy the data for me?"

"Yes. On this." Radha handed him a portable hard drive.

"Even if it's just a glitch, it should be informative. I'll run a full analysis when I come in this evening." Brad made a show of placing the drive in a drawer at his own workstation. He made sure Radha was focused elsewhere when he swapped it for a blank before closing and locking the drawer.

Brad couldn't wait until tonight. As soon as he got home, he'd analyze the data in his own lab. The one Hasselbach didn't know about.

Chapter Five

A couple hours after Sam's encounter with the nurse, Bob Wayne entered the room, pasting a big smile on his face. Inside he felt nervous as hell. Sam's behavior last night was the strangest he'd ever encountered, and what the charge nurse described this morning wasn't encouraging.

"Good morning, Sam. Welcome back to the real world. I trust that a good night's sleep cleared out the cobwebs."

Sam grimaced as he tried to prop himself up on the pillow. "I don't know about cobwebs, but I'm sore as hell."

"I'm not surprised, after that crash, but I need to do a brief exam before I give you more pain medication, okay?"

"Fine. Just don't take all day. My head's throbbing"

"The first portion of the exam may seem a bit silly to you, but after an injury like yours we have to check everything." Bob said, using his most reassuring family doctor voice.

"I get it. But let me tell you right off that my name is Sam Loftus, and I was born on September 9th, 1976, over thirty-six years ago—if today is March 16th, as I assume it is."

"It is, indeed, Sam. You answer the rest of my questions like that, and I'll have you out of here before you know it. What do you remember about yesterday?"

"I remember driving home from Lahaina with Lee Marder and having a traffic accident. From that point until this morning, I'm not sure what was a dream and what was real. You must have given me some good stuff in this IV." Sam pointed to his arm.

"Let's start with other things you know that I know, all right?"

Sam nodded.

"Where were you born?"

"Newport Beach, California."

"Where did you go to high school?"

"Newport Harbor High School. We were the Sailors."

"Who were your parents?"

"My dad, Joseph Loftus, was a computer systems analyst and worked in Irvine for a medical device company. My mother, Frances, was a librarian—she would say library scientist—who worked at UC Irvine. She was born here in Hawai'i."

"Brothers or sisters?"

"I'm an only child."

"Who is your closest friend?"

"Dave Walden's been my best friend since college. His wife is my wife's sister and the four of us spend most of our time together."

Bob nodded and made an entry in the chart:

Confusion from last night seems to be resolving. Answered all questions about background accurately. Exaggerated a bit about brother-in-law, but consistent with earlier, closer relationship.

"What is David's occupation?"

"David? Aren't we being a little formal? You're Dave's doctor, too. Dave's a lawyer."

"And?"

"And a damn good kayaker, but not as good as me."

"I meant...does he have any other job?"

"Do you think he needs one?"

"No, of course not."

Though the mental status exam could have gone better, Bob

needed to pursue the question that had troubled David Walden enough to call and send Bob rushing to the hospital last night.

"When did you last see David?"

"I think it was Christmas."

Bob paused at that and made another note:

Memory lapse noted, but it's recent—the last six months—not unusual after such trauma.

Walden was worried a disoriented Loftus might disclose information Sam promised to keep secret. That's why he sedated Sam before that nosy detective could interrogate him. Walden thanked him for that when he reported back and told him specifically what to ask Sam today.

"You mentioned that David's a good kayaker. Do you kayak together here on Maui?"

"No. Dave and I white-water kayaked in West Virginia when we were in college in Indiana, and both loved it. I still kayak here in the ocean, but Dave doesn't care for it."

"Did you ever invite him?"

"Yeah, but he wasn't interested. Said those wild days were behind him. Janet has been a great stabilizing influence on him."

This time he made a mental note, not for the chart. *Sam has no memory of taking a kayaking trip with David on Maui.*

Now that he'd addressed Walden's greatest concern, Bob needed to deal with the elephant in the room from last night. "Tell me about your family."

"I'm married. We celebrate our thirteenth anniversary in June."

Good.

"We have two children. Cindy is eight and Timmy will be five next month. I spoil them both, but Julie keeps them in line."

Shit. Bob struggled to maintain a neutral expression and plowed ahead. "Tell me about your wife."

"Julie is brilliant and beautiful. She's a fantastic pediatrician, but you know that. She was recently named Chief of Pediatrics at this fine institution. A well-deserved promotion which I'm sure you helped along."

Bob ignored the comment. "Who is Janet?"

"Janet is Julie's sister, Janet Walden, Dave's wife. They have two children as well, Rain and Mist. They're four-year-old twins. I remember how happy they all were when the adoptions became final. Those two could melt your...What are you writing down? You know all this stuff."

He looked up from the chart, where he had just written:

Delusions include fantasy children for brother-in-law as well as self. Still believes sister-in-law is wife and vice versa. Also believes sister-in-law is a pediatrician instead of a writer.

"I need a comprehensive record of this examination, especially the stuff I already know. Let's get back to you. What's your occupation and where did you receive your training?"

"I got a degree in accounting at Indiana University followed by an MBA at IU Kelley School of Business. An international property management group headquartered in Indianapolis, called Resorts Unlimited, hired me right out of grad school. I moved to the Maui branch seven years ago, where I'm currently CFO. My office is in Lahaina, and we live in Pukalani."

Knowledge of education and occupational situation mostly unimpaired. Dates his move to Maui two years later than it was.

Sam thinks he moved here two years after that kayaking trip Dave was so worried about. "Okay. Let's move on to the physical exam. First, I'm going to touch you in a few places, gently. You tell me if anything is tender."

The poking and prodding went on for a few minutes with no unexpected findings. If anything, Sam was exhibiting less head, face, and neck pain than Bob had expected.

"Now, let's check range of motion. Can you lift your head a couple of inches off the pillow? Not too far. That's good. Now turn your head to the left."

Sam turned his head to the right.

"Ah, okay. Good. Now turn it back to the middle. Excellent. You're moving smoothly. Are you having any pain in your neck?"

"Not much."

"Good. Now turn your head to the right."

Sam turned his head to the left.

Struggling to suppress a frown, Bob said, "Turn your head back to the middle and let it fall back onto the pillow slowly."

Sam did.

"Okay. Let's check your arms and legs. Lift your left arm."

Sam lifted his right arm.

"Point your index finger down."

Sam did.

"Up."

Sam did.

"You can rest your arm now, Sam."

Bob wrote in the chart:

Evidence of Right-left inversion.

Bob was not surprised that Sam showed the same inversion for his left arm, both legs, movement of his eyes, and identification of locations touched on his body.

"Sam, do you see the clock on the wall?"

"Yeah, and what's the joke? Why is it backwards?"

"Can you tell the time?"

"Sure. It's ten, uh a.m., I assume."

"That's right."

"Are we about done?"

"Almost. Let me show you something. I'll be right back."

Bob left Sam's room and went to the nurses' station. He found the item he needed and noticed the police sergeant from last night had arrived. Bob held up one finger to indicate he'd be with him in just a minute.

When he returned to the room, he asked Sam, "Do you know what this is?"

"Uh...yes. I believe it's called a newspaper. Are you all right, Bob?"

"Humor me. Can you read it?"

"Not easily. It's written in mirror writing, you jerk. What kind of test is this?"

"Let me try something," Bob said, as he moved the cross-bed table in place and opened the hinged section on the right to display a mirror. Pointing the paper at the mirror he asked, "Can you read it now?"

"Of course. Maui police baffled by wrong way driver. Numerous injuries, most appear to be minor."

"How about that small print on the bottom...uh...right of the page?"

"Remains of museum destroyed by terrorist bomber. AP photo."

"Point the mirror at the clock and tell me if it looks better."

"No, it looks normal. That's what happens to things that are mirror images."

Another note for the chart:

Patient expresses difficulty reading newspaper, but surprising fluency reading mirror image of the same newspaper and clock in his room.

"Physically you are recovering very nicely. I'm still concerned about your short-term memory. I need to run a full battery of tests just to be safe."

"What kind of tests?"

"You know, MRI, EEG, a few neuromuscular tests, memory and perception tests. They're pretty routine for a traumatic head injury like yours."

"Okay but get on with it. I don't plan to spend much longer in this hospital, or this bed."

"We'll be getting you up by tomorrow at the latest. Today, just relax and let us check you out top to bottom."

"But mostly top, right? Is there something seriously wrong, Bob? Tell me the truth."

"On the whole you're doing very well for someone who just rolled a car and smashed into two lanes of traffic. There are a couple of things I want to look at further, but they may well be gone by the time we test for them. Just concentrate on getting better."

"Okay, but when you're sure, you have to tell me if there's something I need to know."

"I will. I will. You're not just a patient. You're a friend. I have two more questions to ask. I'll tell you if you get them right, okay?"

Sam nodded.

"What hemisphere is Australia in?"

"The southern."

"Where does the sun rise and set?"

"The sun rises in the east and sets in the west."

"Absolutely correct. I'll see you tomorrow. And get some rest."

"When can I see Julie?"

"Very soon."

Chapter Six

Keone Boyd stood at the nurses' station when Dr. Wayne returned. Last night, on a hunch he'd examined Wayne's interactions with the Maui PD, before finally heading home to bed. The good doctor didn't have a serious record, but he'd been investigated twice for questionable prescription practices. His file also contained hints of a flirtation with methamphetamine abuse. He was never charged, but the name David Walden appeared associated with his file as *amicus curiae*.

Keone also discovered from the ER staff that they hadn't called Dr. Wayne last night. The Loftus family doctor just showed up.

"Hello, Sergeant Boyd. I suppose you want to see my patient." Dr. Wayne seemed more collected than last night.

"I do. My lieutenant will have my ass if I take any longer to get Mr. Loftus's statement."

"All right. I'll give you ten minutes before I re-medicate him, but you need to do something for me. He's still saying some things that suggest a...neurological injury. If he says or does anything unusual, please don't do anything to make him aware of his behavior. After you finish, let me know what you observe, okay? That way, I can get unbiased impressions from a second individual."

The doctor's request struck him as odd, but he agreed to the conditions after bargaining to be allowed fifteen minutes with Loftus.

As he entered the room, he heard Wayne say to the nurse, "Fifteen minutes, no more."

"Good morning, Mr. Loftus. I'm Sergeant Boyd of Maui PD. I have a couple questions for you about the accident yesterday." He flipped open his ID and handed it to the man.

"Weren't you in the first car I hit?" Sam replied returning the leather case.

"Yes, but that's not why I'm here." *Or was it?*

"I'm sorry about your beautiful car. It was a Morgan, wasn't it?"

"Yes, but I—"

"My Uncle Bob had one of those. I think he loved it more than he did my Aunt Terry. A beautiful little car."

"Sir, I only have a few minutes. Do you remember leaving for work yesterday morning?"

Loftus closed his eyes and seemed to concentrate. "Yes. I walked out our front door and waved goodbye to Julie before driving off. Just like every morning."

Keone noticed Sam said Julie, not Janet. He'd checked department records last night after he left the hospital. Janet Loftus was Sam's legal wife. "Was it a normal day at work?"

"Perfectly." Again, Loftus closed his eyes. "I parked in my regular spot and walked up the stairs to my office. While I was opening the door, Lee Marder came by to ask me for a lift home. We joked about our jobs before I walked into my cubicle and started right to work."

Keone noted the level of detail in Sam's answer. "And where is it you work?"

"I'm CFO for Resorts Unlimited's West Maui office."

"And Mr. Marder works there, too?"

"Lee's responsible for the entire complex. It includes retail outlets and restaurants as well as offices like ours. He can fix anything. He spent years as a contractor in Denver doing remodeling."

"What happened on the drive home?"

"I was driving from Lahaina to Pukalani, just like I do every day. Lee and I were talking and listening to music when I had the strangest feeling."

"What sort of feeling?"

"I felt like I passed through a kind of barrier, like an invisible membrane, and heard a loud pop."

Story corroborates Marder's observation. "Was it just your body that passed through or the entire car?" As weird as this sounded, Keone acted as if passing through an invisible bubble was the most natural thing in the world.

"Good question. You know, I can only be certain about my body. The bubble seemed to surround me. I couldn't see it, or if it touched Lee, so I asked him if he heard the pop."

"What did he say?"

"Said he didn't hear anything. That's when I noticed everything was wrong."

"What do you mean wrong?"

"We were on the wrong side of the road. I was sitting on the wrong side of the car. The road signs were unreadable. I swerved to the right-hand side of the road. But you were there...and all those other cars. There was nowhere to go. I tried to turn left around the corner, but started rolling over and over..."

Keone looked into Sam's eyes. "You say you swerved to the right."

"Uh-huh. I discovered I was on the left-hand side of the road and moved over to the right."

"Which way did you turn the wheel?"

"To the right, of course."

"I'd like you to close your eyes and imagine you're back in the car, just before you hit the membrane."

"Really?"

"Humor me."

Keone watched Sam put out his hands and grasp an imaginary steering wheel.

"Okay you hit the membrane, now."

Sam flinched.

"You realize you're on the wrong side of the road and turn the wheel."

Sam made a sharp turning motion with his hands. Keone noted he turned the wheel to the left, as he must have to enter the wrong lane. Not to the right as he'd claimed.

"And then you try to turn to miss me and the others?"

"Yes," Sam said, jerking the imaginary steering wheel sharply to the right.

"What way did you just turn the wheel?"

"To the left, just like I told you."

"You can open your eyes now."

"Time's up," the nurse announced upon entering the room. "I must ask you to please leave."

Keone hesitated.

"Now."

Though he refrained from commenting on the nurse's edict, Keone made no effort to hurry. He just said, "That's okay, we were wrapping up anyway. Thank you for your time, Mr. Loftus."

Intrigued by the interaction, he paused outside the room. *Who is Sam Loftus, really?* What was he like before the crash? More important, was he criminally responsible for the crash?

Chapter Seven

Keone drove to Lahaina from the hospital to get answers to some of his questions about Sam Loftus. His years of experience as a detective told him when people were lying. Wayne had lied to him multiple times. But Sam Loftus was telling the truth, or believed he was. The man honestly believed he was on the wrong side of the road when he wasn't. Keone would swear to it. But why?

As he drove through the cane fields again, in a cruiser he'd signed out from the station in Wailuku, his mind wandered back to yesterday. *Was it only yesterday I was zipping through here in my new Morgan?*

His eyes moistened and he blinked rapidly to clear his vision. *Stop it, idiot.* It was just a car. The most beautiful car he had ever seen. Sure, it was insured, but it would take at least another eighteen months for the company to make a new one. Longer since he hadn't notified the manufacturer or his insurance company of the crash. *Better do that.*

The chirp from his cell reminded Keone that there were others he hadn't notified. The call was from his boss, Detective Lieutenant Tony Alcala.

The phone chirped four more times before Tony gave up

calling his cell. They both had today off. But Tony knew Keone was picking his Morgan up yesterday and probably just wanted to kid him about spending so much money.

On the other hand, if Tony had gone into the office on his day off, as he sometimes did, he might have heard about Keone signing out a car last night when he returned Keali'i Matsuda's ride. He might also have heard about the accident. In that case he'd call Keone on the radio.

If he did that Keone would have to answer or pretend the radio was broken. *Unless I'm away from the car on a meal break.*

Keone called in over his radio that he was 10 - 7. Police code for a meal break. He'd explain everything to Tony, soon. Monday, if he was lucky. He just didn't want to try until he knew more.

KEONE REACHED LAHAINA TO DISCOVER RESORTS Unlimited opened at 1 p.m. on Saturdays. *Welcome to Maui Standard Time.* On Maui people were in when they were in.

On the plus side, the complex that held Sam's office also housed Lahaina Coolers—a favorite hangout of his during the time he worked out of District Four with his friend Sergeant Angela Beyers. Angela worked out of Hana these days, but she and her friend Linda still lived in Lahaina. *What a commute.*

From the outdoor seating area of Lahaina Coolers, Keone could keep an eye on the entrance to Resorts Unlimited. Owner/bartender Max Tanikawa was busy behind the bar inside as Keone chose a table with the best view of Sam's place of business. When Keone looked up, he saw the slightly rotund Hawaiian heading his way with his favorite, a mango cooler (non-alcoholic during work hours), in his right hand. "Howzit, Big Guy?"

"Not good. My new car got hammered at Ma'alaea." Max, who'd been a friend for years and knew pretty much everything that went on in West Maui, must have seen him walking in from the street.

"No way. How dat shit go down?"

"Wrong-way driver."

"God damn tourists!"

"No, a local guy. He works around here." Keone said.

"Was it Walden?"

I wonder why that name jumped to Max's lips. "No, a relative of his, Sam Loftus. Know him?"

"Just to say aloha. He okay I guess, but a little boring. And he got, how you call dat, COD." Max sat across from Keone at the outside table.

"I think you mean OCD. I've heard that he's very meticulous. What about Walden?"

"Like you say, he sorta related to Sam. His wife and Sam's are sisters or sumting."

He opened his notebook. "Janet and Julie."

"Yeah. Dat Julie, Walden's wife. Quite da lookah, but real sweet. Walden, he one playah. She deserve bettah."

"What about Loftus? Is he a player?"

"Hell, no. Like I tell you, he one boring haole. Spend evenings at home wid da wife. She pretty, too, but some kind stuck-up. He try an' bring her here once, but she don' like da friendliness of some of da regulars. Give everyone da stink-eye and nevah come back. But that Walden..."

"What about Walden?"

"Big Guy, you and me been friends one long time, so I tell you. I think Walden one made-man. Always here, drinkin' and schmoozin'. And always wid guys from outta town, off-island."

"One particular guy?"

"No. Lotta guys from all ovah. East Coast, West Coast, Australia, even Europe."

"Mob? On Maui? Ever see him with a doctor named Wayne, Robert Wayne?"

"No, but I hear some rumors about that good doctor. No

surprise if he one client, but not of da lawyer business." With that Max got up and headed back to the kitchen to create one of Keone's favorite grinds.

While he waited, he wrote in his notebook:

Dave Walden. Best friend (?) and brother-in-law of driver. Looker wife. Player. Interesting contacts. Mob? Follow up.

Sam Loftus. Boring life. Stuck-up wife (?) Stays home a lot.

Rumors about Dr. Wayne and Walden's other business?

~

IN A FEW MINUTES, MAX PLACED A BURRITO THE SIZE OF a large cat in front of him. Keone knew these babies were not for the squeamish.

"Why we no see you 'roun here so much no more, Keone?"

"Once I made detective, I was assigned to Division One in Wailuku. I'm part of CID."

"Criminal Investigation Division. I got one niece wid dat bunch. Lindsay Kalani." Despite his island boy speech pattern, Max knew what was what. He had degrees from UH and the Culinary Institute of America.

"I know her very well. She's a fine detective, but I didn't know she was your niece." Keone drenched the burrito with a thick layer of Max's homemade hot sauce.

Seeing this, Max returned to the bar and mixed Keone another mango cooler.

Keone smiled as the first, fiery bite reached his tongue. Strong men had been reduced to tears by a drop of Max's hot sauce, but Keone loved it. The secret to survival was to take it slow and savor each bite. He knew he had enough time to do it right.

Still, he appreciated the additional cooler that Max put on the table. "Mahalo. How did I not know Lindsay's your niece?"

"Well, I guess she my *hanai* niece, yeah? Her dad my hanai bruddah, and I help raise her since she was one *keiki*. Her mom died when she was one *pepe*."

Keone liked the way Max mixed the King's English, pidgin, and Hawaiian in every sentence, like keiki for child and pepe for baby. He also loved the Hawaiian concept of hanai family members. Literally the word meant adopted, but generally the meaning was broader. It meant anyone you adopted into your heart as family. No documents required.

Max ambled off to see to his inside customers before Keone could ask about Walden's other business. Taking a long sip from his cooler, he surveyed the area around him. Although it was part of his job, he enjoyed observing his surroundings, mentally taking note of little details others often missed. The outside seating area of Lahaina Coolers took up most of a large atrium and was surrounded by the two stories of the complex. A mild breeze ruffled the umbrellas covering each of the wooden slat tables. Lunch, Maui-style.

His reverie was broken by a loud, female voice. "Hey, Big Guy. What brings you to our neck of the woods?"

Linda Carroll's voice was unmistakable, as was her arm snaking around Keone's shoulder. Angela Beyers, her housemate and Keone's fellow MPD Sergeant and friend, sat down opposite Keone at the table and Linda plopped into the chair next to Keone.

"I was just thinking about you two," Keone said.

"How sweet," Angela said.

"When were you going to tell me about the accident, Keone?" Linda asked. "I am your insurance agent, you know."

How ironic. He'd thought about the need to notify his insurance company on the way over here. "I've been a little busy. As a matter of fact, that's why I'm here, to follow up on the guy who hit me."

"No problem, Big Guy. I'm just playing with ya. I've contacted the Morgan people and the other guy's insurance company. The former will start building you a new Boyd-mobile as soon as you reply to their letter, confirming you want 'em to.

And the latter has already accepted responsibility." She grinned like a Cheshire cat.

"That's the best news I've received since the crash. You may be a blonde wahine from the middle of the mainland, but you're *'ohana* to me. I guess you two are still living in that cool house in Ka'anapali you bought together, yeah?"

"We are," Angela answered. "But I spend four days a week in an apartment in Hana,"

"I figured making that drive every day would be a challenge. Even Wailuku would be better than that. Did you manage to take that detective exam, I suggested, Ange?" Keone was always encouraging his friend to tackle new challenges.

"She took it and aced it, like she does everything." Linda answered for her housemate. "You guys got any openings for her?"

This put Keone on the spot, but he didn't mind. He would love to help Angela with her career. "I knew you could handle that exam, Ange. I knew it when I first met you in California."

Linda held up her hand. "Wait a minute, I never knew you met before Keone joined the force. Were you two an... item?".

"No, Lin. He came to one of my criminology classes at UC Irvine. He was working with the LAPD at the time and gave a talk on chain of evidence," Angela responded.

"She knew I was from Maui, because my brothers gave her horseback riding lessons when she was in high school. We had nice talk after my lecture and reminisced about home." Keone added.

"Sounds pretty innocent. Too bad." Linda looked like she was about to say more when Max came back to the table to see what the ladies would have.

"Order anything you want on the menu," Keone said. "I'm buying."

Movement at the corner of his eye pulled his focus as a fit young woman jogged past, bounced up the stairs, and unlocked the offices of Resorts Unlimited.

While Linda and Angela ordered, Keone finished his cooler

and gave Max his credit card. "I'll pick that up when I've finished with my interviews upstairs, Max."

"Sure ting, Big Guy," Max replied

"Ladies, I'm afraid I have to scoot, but let's get together again soon, on purpose next time."

"Catch ya later, Keone." Angela stood up and hugged him around the waist. "And thanks for encouraging me to take that test." Her head only came up to the middle of his chest.

Keone weaved his way through the outside tables and climbed the stairs to Resorts Unlimited. He'd get around to Sam's boss and co-workers, but Keone always preferred to start his questioning with the person at the front desk. Receptionists always seemed to absorb more of what was going on than those stuffed away in private offices or cubicles and were generally anxious to talk.

Chapter Eight

After Gwen Tanaka removed his lunch tray, Sam reviewed his three recent interactions: Gwen, Bob Wayne, and Sergeant Boyd. Why were they all so obsessed with left and right? Why were they showing him all these weird, reversed images, the clock, the newspaper? Why were all those cars at the light stopped on the wrong side of the road?

"What the hell's going on here?" he whispered to the empty room.

He noticed a woman in scrubs sitting outside the room across the hall, reading a paperback book. *She's probably some kind of therapist waiting for her next appointment. I'd really like to see the cover of that book.*

The therapist's back blocked his view. Ringing the call button would bring his nurse but not cause the woman to turn, so he banged his head on the over-bed table. Before the nurse could run in and shut the door, the therapist turned to look at the commotion. The book in her hand had a familiar cover. Sam recognized it as a John Lescroart thriller. But the title was in mirror writing along with all the other words.

In that brief instant, before the nurse could close the door, he glanced into the room across the hall and saw the television was showing *The Price is Right*. The camera focused on a stage prop with increasing amounts of money. The amounts were all in mirror writing.

That was too much. They couldn't have carried the joke this far. Something was wrong with the rest of the hospital. Maybe more.

Nurse Tanaka hurried to the bed and pulled him back from the over-bed table. "What's going on, Mr. Loftus? Are you troubled?"

"I'm simply fabulous."

"But you were banging your head on the table."

"Was I?" Sam temporized. "Ow, yes, my forehead hurts. Do you think I just fell asleep, and my head banged the table?"

"No, I heard two distinct bangs. Then, when I came in, I saw you bang it a third time and your eyes were open. Don't you remember?"

"Damned if I don't." He saw Bob Wayne peer into his room door. "Maybe it's a reaction to one of those drugs you're giving me through this plastic tunnel in my arm. I do have a few allergies."

"Nurse Tanaka, I'd like you to stop all the piggy-back and oral meds until after his tests. And remove the table from the room between meals," Wayne ordered, then turned to Sam. "Do you mind?"

"Do whatever you need to keep me safe. I'm sure glad Gwen came in when she did. I could have knocked myself senseless."

The nurse's look seemed skeptical. Sam was glad the detective wasn't there. Boyd wouldn't have been fooled.

After Bob peered at him, poked, and prodded, he left the room. Gwen rolled out the overbed table.

When Gwen returned, she brought some tape. "I'll tape your call button next to your right hand. If you need anything at all, push it. No more head-banging."

Sam smiled and nodded—slowly. He guessed this little bit of acting would mean a few more tests but didn't care. Getting wheeled around more of the hospital would just provide more opportunities to glimpse the outside world.

Sam couldn't help noticing Gwen had taped the call button by his left hand. Something was clearly wrong here. And he was damn well going to find out what.

Chapter Nine

Inside the offices of Resorts Unlimited, Keone introduced himself to receptionist Kimberley Kanamalu, a lovely island girl of about twenty. Keone liked the term island girl. It recognized that she was from the islands but didn't try to sort out her ethnicity. Hawai'i was the melting pot of melting pots. Keone was mostly Hawaiian. His size and dark skin announced that to everyone. But he also had a dose of Portuguese and Scottish mixed in.

"What can you tell me about Sam Loftus, Ms. Kanamalu," Keone began.

"Call me Kimmey. Everybody does. Everybody loves Sammy, too. He's a sweetheart. He always wishes everybody good morning. Every day. And he brings in food to share from home. His wife loves to cook, and Sammy loves to share."

"Does he work late or come in early?"

"Not really. He's always ahead on his work. He works steady all day, but never seems stressed out. He's very, very organized. All the other guys respect him for that. I don't think I've ever heard Mr. Casey criticize Sam for anything."

"Does he ever praise him?" Keone asked.

"You know, I don't think I ever heard him praise Sam, either. Sam doesn't like compliments. He likes to stay out of the spotlight, yeah? On his ten-year anniversary with the firm, they planned to make a big deal about giving him this special pen, but Sam found out. He begged Mr. Casey to give it to him privately. I just think he's kinda shy, but very sweet."

"Does he have any close friends at work?"

"Well, he and Lee Marder talk a lot at lunch. I hear Sam and Mr. Walden, his brother-in-law, were best friends when Sam moved here. But they had some kinda beef right after Sam came. They still get together 'cause they're 'ohana, but they're not besties anymore."

Keone's own 'ohana, Hawaiian for family, was very large but they remained close. 'Ohana was important on Maui. "Tell me about David Walden."

"Mr. Walden's a lawyer. He has an office in this building, well he did until he decided to become his wife's agent, about six months ago. Since then, he's been winding down his practice. I think I saw him packing some stuff in his old office this morning."

"Where's Mr. Walden's office?"

"Right down the hall on the left. See, the door's still open." Kimmey pointed it out through the floor to ceiling window on the front of the Resorts Unlimited office.

Kimmey said the boss should be in by two p.m. Before heading down the hallway to *attorney* David Walden's former office, he told Kimmey he'd be back after two.

KEONE RAPPED ON THE DOORFRAME AND ENTERED AN office cluttered with boxes and filing cabinets. Protruding from the top of one of the larger, wooden containers, he saw a man's legs and running shorts pointed directly up in the air.

"Mr. Walden?"

"That's me," Walden answered without extricating himself. "Are you from the moving company?"

"No. I'm from the Maui Police Department."

He heard a resonant bang as Walden's head connected with the side of the crate. After climbing out and studying Keone's credentials, he said, "I'm sorry, Detective Sergeant Boyd. What can I do for you? If this is about Sam's accident, I wasn't there."

Already distancing himself. "I realize that, Mr. Walden. But, as Mr. Loftus's best friend and a family member, I assume you spent a great deal of time with him prior to the accident."

"Why is that relevant?"

This guy really is a lawyer. "Mr. Loftus was driving on the wrong side of the road. We'd like to know why."

Walden seemed to relax and ran his fingers through his mane of red hair. He winced when he touched the spot where he'd connected with the packing crate. "Of course you would. Sorry, you caught me off guard. I'd be happy to answer any questions you have. Sam and I have been friends since college."

Not best friends. "Tell me about Sam."

"One thing I can promise you, Sam never messed with drugs. Here." He swept a pile of folders onto the floor, clearing two chairs. "Let's sit down. This might take a while."

I never asked about drugs.

"I met Sam at IU when we were both freshmen. Neither of us knew anything about the Midwest. We both wanted to study away from home, and IU offered to pay the full deal. I grew up in the Bay Area and Sam was from Southern California."

"Where in the Bay Area?"

"Palo Alto."

"Did you have classes together?"

"A few, but I was a science geek before I saw the financial advantages of being pre-law. He was always interested in math and business. I knew enough to take a few business courses, for when I had my own practice. But Sam loves numbers. He took higher math classes for fun that had nothing to do with his major. He was intrigued with astronomy and astrophysics, which are loaded with math."

Always provides more than he's asked. Tries to redirect the interrogation. "Did you do things together outside of class?"

"We shared a dorm room and hit it off from the start. We were both terrified of drowning, so naturally we decided to go white water rafting. There was a wonderful place called the Upper Gauley River in West Virginia where a lot of the Indiana, Ohio, and Kentucky guys liked to go. We decided to go with them one early fall weekend...."

Off on another story. "Did anything special happen during these trips?"

"Well, we each had a few out-of-boat experiences, but nothing lethal."

"Lethal, really?"

"The first time we went, a guy from another raft fell out next to an undercut boulder."

"What happened?"

"He got sucked under. Whoosh. And thousands of gallons of water pinned him to the base of the boulder."

"Guess that's the only time you went rafting."

"No way. We were young, sailing through college, and sure it would never be us that got pulled under. We rafted every year through our undergraduate years and twice a year through graduate school. Hell, Sam still does it. But, on the island, ocean kayaking floats his boat."

"Do you ever go with him?"

"I did once, right after he and Janet moved here. Too boring for me. Not like the adrenaline rush from rafting."

That contradicted Sam's comment from last night. "Do you enjoy any sports on the island?"

"I took up golf over here."

Now there's an adrenaline rush.

"The courses over here are so beautiful and you meet so many great people. It can really help you calm down. Never could get my wife to try it though."

What does he need to calm down from? "About your wives, how did you meet them?"

"The good old Indiana State Fair. A treasure trove of pork butts and other fried things on sticks, smelly livestock, and a fun zone filled with lovely young coeds. We saw them go into the haunted house ride and waited at the exit to accidentally bump into them."

"When?"

"Summer before our last year of graduate school, Kelley Business School for Sam and IU Law School for me. Although we lived in Bloomington most of our time in college, we lived in Indianapolis that summer since we were both doing internships there. We shared graduate student housing at Hewey Pewey."

"Where?"

"Indiana University and Purdue University at Indianapolis, IUPUI."

He did it again. What a schmoozer. Enough. "Your wives?" Keone didn't hide his impatience.

"Sure. Sure. We spotted these two hotties and decided to flip a coin for them. People exited the haunted house from two different doors. We made a deal that when the girls emerged from the haunted house, the winner would get the first girl who came out on the right and the loser the other one. Sam won the toss, Janet came out first on the right and the rest, as they say, is history."

"Did your wife come out on the right, too?"

"I don't remember. Besides, it didn't matter. She came out second."

But if left is right? "You each ended up marrying a girl based on how she got off a carnival ride?"

"Yep. It was the best decision we ever made."

"Did you ever date other girls after that, or even the other sister?"

"No. It was love at first sight. Or loves at first sights, I guess."

"You've remained friends ever since?"

"Not just friends, we're related. We both took our honeymoons here on Maui. Sam and Janet got married in June and were back in time for Julie and my wedding in July. We're at each other's houses for all the major holidays."

"Tell me about your wife." He needed to find out if Sam had any reason to believe Julie Walden was, or could become, his.

"She was pre-med when we met, but minored in performance art. She had dreams of being a pediatrician but also loved to perform. When we got married, she was worried that two demanding professions might make things hard, so she focused on performing, especially in children's theatre."

"Probably a good decision." *They made the choice that was best for him.*

"Yes, as it turned out. She was so damn talented that she ended up with a theater group when we moved to Maui. She even started writing plays for children. Then she tried her hand at writing children's books."

"Wait. What was your wife's maiden name?"

"Madison."

"Julia Madison. She writes the *Hawai'i Anna* books, yeah?"

"She sure does. Ten books and three movies later, I'm closing my practice to work full-time as her agent."

"What do you know?" He said this to himself, but Dave heard him.

"Yeah, what do you know? Well, it's been great talking with you. If you have all you need, I'd like to get back to packing."

"Just a couple more questions."

"Sure."

"Did Mrs. Loftus ever seem jealous of her sister's success?"

"Are you kidding? They're closer than ever. Besides Janet's as successful a designer as Julie is a writer. I keep telling Sam to quit working. Neither of us needs to work anymore. But Sam..."

"Yes?"

"Sam's a worker bee. Always plays by the rules. Rules are important to him. Too important. I think it's the OCD."

He'd struck a nerve. Did Walden have trouble following the rules? Did Sam's need to play by the rules affect their friendship? "What about children? I understand neither of you ever had kids."

For the first time Walden paused. "Well, Julie and I thought about kids at first, but she has all the kids who read her books. She does readings in schools all the time. Occasionally, she...But, no, we're completely happy the way we are. A kid now would just get in the way."

Whose way? "What about the Loftus's?"

"They can't have kids, something to do with Janet's plumbing. Janet investigated adoption. It was going to take a long time and would have meant looking overseas. Sam likes things to be in alignment, you know. He just couldn't see himself with foreign kids, especially ones who didn't look like him. He's not a bigot or anything. He's just..."

"A little anal. So I keep hearing." *Wants me to focus on Sam, not him.*

"He's not mental or anything, just very precise. Hey, you'd rather have an anal accountant than a sloppy one, right? He's a good guy and a perfect match for Janet."

"I met Mrs. Loftus last night. She seemed quite shaken by his accident."

"She puts on a good front, but underneath she has emotions. She loves Sam. They're very comfortable together, you know. They don't have to talk a lot to communicate. Julie's more outgoing than Janet, but Janet is a Chatty Cathy compared to Sam."

Shyness wasn't consistent with Keone's impression of Sam. "Must be sad, closing your office. I ate at Lahaina Coolers today, and Max told me you were a good customer."

Dave tensed. "Max should be a little more circumspect talking with strangers."

A quick glimpse of good old Dave's underside? Despite his short stature, Keone saw in Dave a man who knew how to coil his body for attack.

"Oh hell. I bet you're not strangers. Everybody on this island seems to know each other or be related. Max is a good guy. I love those burritos of his."

Keone watched Walden's body uncoil. "I'm recovering from one right now."

They both made laughing sounds. But there was no laughter in Walden's eyes.

"Did you or Sam ever take clients there for lunch?"

"No. Sam spends all day at his desk crunching numbers. My clients prefer a little classier atmosphere."

A lie. "One last question. Whose idea was it to move to Maui?"

"We all fell in love with this place on our honeymoons, but Julie and I moved here first. I had a great job opportunity, and she could do her writing and performing here as well as anywhere else."

What job opportunity? He opened a private legal practice.

"When Sam's company opened a branch here and needed a CFO, he and Janet jumped at the opportunity. They moved over about two years after we did. They started in Lahaina, and we were in Kula. After a year they moved to Pukalani, which brought us closer together."

So close that they only get together on holidays. "Thank you, Mr. Walden. I'll need to talk with your wife at some point, but you've given me what I need for now."

"Do you think Sam will snap out of these...uh...delusions he's having? He's a good guy. I'd like to see him get back home and back to normal as soon as possible."

I never mentioned Sam's delusions. "You need to ask his doctor about that. Has he had delusions before?"

"Absolutely not. Sam doesn't even read fiction. He spends his free time reading history, science, and a lot of that political crap that passes for non-fiction these days."

"Thank you again, Mr. Walden. Good luck with your packing."

Walden inserted his short frame back into the crate, again losing contact with the floor. Keone saw himself out.

Walden left a bad taste in Keone's mouth. He'd seen too many like him before. All Walden let you see was a role he was playing. The part of a friendly and non-threatening schmoozer. But Keone's questions had scratched that surface to reveal something less palatable beneath. Keone decided to learn more about Sam's *best friend*.

Chapter Ten

Sam was fed up. After an afternoon of being poked, prodded, and visualized with everything from sound waves to X-rays to some kind of radioactive crap, Gwen finally rolled him back to his room. He *had* gotten to see more of the hospital. But seeing more walls covered with mirror writing signs wasn't reassuring. Especially when those same signs hadn't been reversed when he'd visited an old friend from work here six months ago.

He even got a few glimpses of the parking lot and the road that passed the hospital. License plates were reversed, and traffic passed by blissfully on the wrong side of the road.

Late in the afternoon Bob Wayne returned. Sam was propped up in bed writing in a personal journal he'd begun. His entries appeared completely normal to him. To anyone else he probably appeared to be writing swiftly and effortlessly in mirror writing. He looked up to see Julie follow Bob into the room.

Julie glanced at the journal and tensed for a moment, then she gave Sam a hug and a chaste kiss on the forehead. Before Sam could grab her and embrace her properly, she'd moved out of range and taken a seat.

She sat down carefully, as though afraid to make a sound.

"Oh, Sam. I'm so sorry to see you like this. How are they treating you here?"

"Sweetheart, why has it taken you so long to come? I've missed you so much. How are the kids?"

"Everyone is fine, Sam. We're all just so worried about you." Sam noticed she looked over at Bob as if for approval.

Bob smiled, then turned to Sam. "I can't let Julie stay too long right now. We have a lot more tests to run. We're going to figure out how to make you well, my friend."

Julie relaxed at Bob's confident words.

"I promised to let you see Julie and here she is. You see, I do keep my word. But now she needs to go." Bob placed a hand under Julie's elbow, helped her up, and guided her to the door.

"Wait a damn minute. This is my wife. The mother of my children. I need to talk with her privately. Can't you give us a few minutes alone? Julie, please, come back. I love you, sweetheart."

Julie glanced back briefly. Sam saw tears in her eyes. She bowed her head and shook it slowly from side to side before disappearing through the door.

"Sam, she's having a hard time with all of this. You need to give her some space. Besides, you need to focus on the tests and do your best to help us help you. A couple of specialists will be visiting you over the next day or two, please tell them everything you've told me and listen to what they have to tell you."

"What's going on? Have I gone crazy or has the world?"

"We're trying to figure that out." His cell phone rang before he could continue. "Sorry, I have to take this."

Chapter Eleven

Keone checked his watch as he pulled into District Four headquarters. Four p.m. The grey concrete buildings held police, fire, and other county agencies.

His conversation with Sam's boss had been long and singularly uninformative. Sam was a great worker, quiet but friendly, had no close friends at work, was liked by everyone, and had never done anything remotely unusual. Keone wondered if Sam's boss had ever met the man.

Several colleagues, who'd heard about his accident, gathered around him as Keone entered the station. Word travelled fast in the MPD. He just hoped it hadn't travelled to his boss, yet.

"Glad to see you vertical, Big Guy," Hank Opaka said.

"Thanks, man. Say, who's got the con today?" he asked.

"Walker," Hank replied and looked like he'd just licked a lemon. "He's in the LT's office."

Keone had heard about Sergeant Roger Walker. He'd heard Walker was much better at taking credit than giving it. Still, he needed info from the senior man on duty about Sam Loftus.

"I don't know the guy," Walker began, after telling Keone how glad they all were that he was okay and offering him a seat in the office.

Why was the sergeant using his boss's office? That wasn't standard procedure. "You've never met Sam Loftus? Never heard anything about him? Nada?"

"Honestly, I looked him up on the computer when I heard about the accident, because I couldn't believe I'd never heard of someone who spent so much time in my territory. His file is nearly empty. Never had a moving violation. Hell, he's never had a parking ticket. Guy must really keep to himself. Nobody here knows him."

Keone suspected anyone that answered a question with honestly. "You said nearly empty."

"Oh yeah, I found one report. He accused a customer at Lahaina Coolers of insulting his wife. The officer he called told him that wasn't strictly against the law, and he dropped it."

"What about David Walden?"

"The Great Waldo? What's he got to do with this?"

Walker answered so fast he might have been waiting for this question. "He's Loftus's brother-in-law. Loftus thinks Walden's wife is his wife."

"I don't blame him. She's a knockout and does a lot for the community, too. My two girls love her books."

Deflection. "I'm more interested in Walden. He's a lawyer, yeah?"

"Yeah. He has an office in that complex on Dickenson. At least he did. I hear he's moving. We never cross paths professionally. He doesn't touch criminal law or even litigation. Contract law and estate planning keep him busy and more than pay the bills. I know him mostly from the golf tournament he organizes each year for the MPD."

Keone knew about that tournament. It made a lot of money for department charities every year. "Why do you call him The Great Waldo?"

"He's an amateur magician—and a great putter. He knows all kinds of weird putting tricks. We started calling him The Great

Waldo, Magician of the Greens. It kinda stuck. When we first talked about having a charity tournament, he came up with the theme, 'Making Magic for Maui's Moms.' The money all goes to family assistance programs started and sponsored by the MPD."

"You said he organizes the tournament?"

"He does more than that. Waldo brings a bunch of his wealthy friends over every year from the mainland and other places. They contribute big bucks just to play in the tournament. Boost the local economy while they're here, too. We play right up the road on the Royal Course at Ka'anapali."

Wealthy friends deserve a closer look. "Does Walden have a rap sheet?"

Roger's smile faltered. "Look, he's a good friend to the department. He's had some minor infractions, but our guys always give him the benefit of the doubt."

"So, he has a sheet."

"I've told you more about him than his file will."

"Can I get a copy?" Keone could bring it up when I got back Wailuku but wanted to see Walker's reaction.

"Sure. No skin off my nose. I'll have somebody print it out for you. But listen, this guy does a lot of good for us. You don't want to screw it up, imagining connections that aren't there. Get my drift?"

"Got it. The whole thing's routine anyway. I'll probably close the case in a week."

He'd have to be careful. Roger Walker was hardly subtle. Walden had important friends inside and outside the department, and the good sergeant was clearly one of them.

Keone was already stretching the scope of a crash investigation. Funny how often he did that on cases. A detective's job was finding and following leads. There were rules. Good rules. But he always considered them more like guidelines. Unfortunately, his superiors considered them rules.

~

Keone enjoyed driving back from Lahaina along the winding cliffside road but would have enjoyed it more in the Morgan. Pulling into one of the many lookouts, where tourists tried to catch a glimpse of the last few humpbacks at the end of the season, he called to set up a meeting with Mrs. Janet Loftus. She answered on the second ring with, "Loftus residence."

"Hello, Mrs. Loftus. This is Sergeant Boyd. We met last night at the hospital."

"Oh, yes, Sergeant. I remember. How can I help you?"

"I'd like to ask you a few questions as part of my investigation into the crash. I need to schedule a time for us to get together."

"Actually, you couldn't have called at a better time. My sister Julie is on her way over right now. Being together always helps when we are facing difficult times. Why don't you come by in a couple of hours, and you can talk with both of us?"

He wondered how often they'd had to face difficult times. "I don't want to impose on your time together."

"Don't be silly. It'll save you a trip and get this over with sooner."

Keone paused. Professionally, he was unsatisfied with this arrangement. He preferred to interview witnesses separately to avoid even unintentional influence on each other's testimony. On the other hand, after meeting Walden, he was looking forward to interviewing the wife without the husband present. "Okay. I'll stop by at seven. You live in Pukalani, yeah?"

She gave him directions before ending the call. He didn't need them, but he'd discovered over the years that when people provided directions to a police officer, they felt less threatened.

He checked his watch as he pulled back on the highway, relieved he had time to stop by his condo. He wanted to clean up and change clothes. His mind tried to reconcile the Sam Loftus he'd met with the one the man's friends and coworkers described. Did that bump on his head give Sam a different personality, rewrite part of his memory, both?

He would put on his sharpest-looking uniform but was sure this had nothing to do with everyone referring to Sam's sister-in-law as a knockout.

I'm a professional.

Chapter Twelve

S am pushed the bland components of his dinner around on his plate, a sharp contrast to the bizarre experiences he was having. He'd decided to behave as normally as possible, though he wasn't quite sure what normal was anymore. He began by initiating friendly conversations with his nurses when they came in to take his vital signs or bring his food.

Mrs. Millicent (Millie) Brown, Gwen Tanaka's mid-afternoon replacement, came through the door to pick up his dinner tray. She had a lilt in her voice and an easy manner that made Sam enjoy her company. He could tell she enjoyed having someone listen to her stories. Time to trigger one.

"Are you done with your tray?" she asked.

"Done as I'll ever be. Your brogue puts a smile in everything you say, Millie. How did a nice Irish lass like you end up on Maui?"

"My husband was a retired commander in the U.S. Navy. He fell in love with the islands when he was stationed at Pearl Harbor," she replied.

"How long have you been here?"

"Five years, but my Charlie only got to enjoy the first one, before..."

"I'm so sorry. I didn't mean to trigger sad memories."

"You didn't, Mr. Loftus. Every day we had together was a joy. I just wish I hadn't turned down his last offer to go deep-sea fishing on our boat. I was just beat after a long shift and sent him off with a friend. Unfortunately, the friend didn't know how to deal with a cardiac arrest." Millie's eyes glistened, but she continued, "He'd never had a hint of heart problems before that."

"You know, you can't blame yourself for what happened."

"You're sweet to be concerned. But I don't blame myself so much as wish I could've had a few more hours with him doing what he loved."

"I can understand that." He tried not to lay it on too thick, but he wanted each staff member he encountered to know what a caring person he was. He needed them on his side when the decision whether to send him home was made. Sam was committed to becoming everyone at Maui Memorial Hospital's new best friend.

Millie squeezed his arm and left the room.

He was surprised when she reappeared a few minutes later. "Mr. Loftus, you have another visitor if you feel up to it. Dr. Wayne approved the visit."

"Who is it?"

"An older gentleman. I believe he's a mate of yours from work. A Mr. Marder."

"Oh, sure. Send him in. He was my passenger when I had the accident." Sam used the word accident as often as possible to make sure everyone who heard him knew the crash was no one's fault, especially his.

Lee came through the door, balancing a potted plant and an oversized card in his hands. "Hi Sammy, you gonna make it?"

"I'm feeling pretty good, considering. I've got a little bump on my head, from the airbag, I guess. But all my components are functioning normally. How about you?"

"Pretty much the same. They kept me overnight for observation. But I guess they didn't observe nothin' interestin', so they cut me loose."

"I'm glad you weren't hurt, Lee." His tone conveyed how much he truly meant this. Lee was a good friend, his best on the island next to Dave and, of course, Julie.

"I'm just fine. Say, did that cop come see you? The one we hit."

"Sure did. Yesterday and again this morning. He seems like a suspicious sort. Probably upset about his car. Can't blame him. It was a brand-new Morgan."

"What the hell's a Morgan?"

"A very exclusive British roadster. There's a minimum year-long wait just to start the process of acquiring one. They make each one to order and encourage the buyer to visit their factory during the build. Must have cost an arm and a leg."

"That can't be good."

"He kept himself under control. But I don't think I made a friend."

"Sammy. I'm worried about you. You were talkin' kinda strange before the crash."

This was exactly what Sam was waiting to hear. He motioned his friend closer to the bed. "Lee, could you tell me exactly what I said?"

"Sure. Right after we passed the turnoff down to the marina, you know by Buzz's Wharf, a shiver passed through your whole body and you said, 'Did you hear that pop?' When I said no, you said, 'It was like a huge soap bubble. My God, everything's changed. I'm on the wrong side of the road!' Then you swerved onto the wrong side." Lee paused. "When you saw all those cars lined up, you tried to swerve back, but we started to roll and then it was: *Urch, screech, ring the mop. Don't forget the soda pop.*"

Lee always seemed to have a catchy phrase stored away for every occasion. "The airbag must have knocked me out."

"Me, too," Lee said.

"Have you told anyone about this?"

Lee looked embarrassed. "Well, I might have told that cop. I'm not sure. I was pretty groggy."

"Don't worry about it. I'm just glad you're safe and out of this place." Sam was sure Lee had told the detective everything. Lee was almost as law abiding as he was. Sam had told Boyd a lot that morning, too, before formulating his strategy.

"You'll be out of here, too, real soon. I know it."

Sam looked at his friend, pondering what to say next. Dr. Wayne didn't seem to know the left-right stuff happened before the accident, but Lee just confirmed it. He'd see about the specialists when they questioned him. But, for now, he decided to keep these facts between him and Lee. He doubted the cop would share much with the doctors. After all, this was an ongoing investigation.

He pointed at the card and plant. "What have you got there?"

"Oh. I forgot. Here's a card. Everybody at work signed it except Fran, she's on the mainland. And I got these here *Bromy lads* for you, because I know you have 'em in your garden."

"They're perfect, Lee! I don't have this variety in my collection."

"What's so special about these things? They look kind of deformed to me."

"Bromeliads are exotic and unusual plants. They're grown commercially just above where Julie and I live in Pukalani." Sam noticed Lee winced when he said Julie, instead of Janet.

"Are they good for anything—other than looking weird, I mean?"

"There's one that tastes pretty good. It's called a pineapple."

"Well, I'll be damned."

During the pause that followed, Sam decided Lee could provide him some needed help.

"Lee. You've got to be careful what you say to people until you talk to a lawyer."

"I'll back you up a hundred percent."

"I know you will. You're a good friend. But let's keep the part about what I said and did before the crash between ourselves from now on, okay?"

"Sure."

"Lee, how's your energy level?"

"The iron in my veins has turned to lead in my ass, but I'm still kicking."

"Could you do a favor for me?"

"Sure, Sammy, anything."

"My lawyer, Tom Conrad, probably doesn't know what's happened. You should talk with him. I'll pay for the consultation. He can tell you what you should and shouldn't say to folks about the accident. Oh, and be sure to always call it the accident, okay?"

"Say no more. I know Tom. He does work for the site management company, but you don't need to pay for it."

"I want to, Lee. And I want you to do one more thing for me. I'd like you to give him a message."

"Okay. I'll call for an appointment on my way home and go by first thing after work tomorrow."

"That would be perfect. He's usually in the office until about seven each evening. And, Lee, don't tell anyone else that you're doing this for me, okay? Have you got some paper?"

"Here, use the envelope. I forgot to address it anyway."

Sam started to write, then realized the problem. If Tom were like everyone else in this world, he wouldn't be able to read his handwriting. "Lee, my hand's a little shaky, could you write if I dictate?"

"Sure, Sammy. Shoot."

When the message was done, Sam read it, surreptitiously using the mirror in the over-bed table. "Thanks, Lee. I'll never forget this."

"You just get better, quick."

"I will. Mahalo—for everything."

～

DIANE CARVELL ALWAYS ENJOYED EATING A LATE dinner with her husband at the kitchen table, while he ate his breakfast. An astronomer's wife adjusted.

Brad seemed exceptionally buoyant when he arrived home that morning. He must have had good results in the lab. Maybe some of his frustration at not getting assigned to that other project was wearing off.

He was still smiling this morning as he read the newspaper.

"Have you read about that accident in Ma'alaea yet? Some crazy wrong-way driver. He's lucky nobody was killed." She started cleaning up around the kitchen and watched him quietly read.

Suddenly Brad's eyes opened wide. He mumbled what sounded like *same place and time* and hurried downstairs.

She was used to Brad's cycles of excitement and calm. She knew it came with the territory when she married a scientist. But what had once been an endearing eccentricity had become more frequent and more pronounced since they'd moved here.

2. Visits and Calls

"The first thing in a visit is to say 'How d'ye do?' and shake hands! And here the two brothers gave each other a hug, and then they held out the two hands that were free, to shake hands with her."

— Lewis Carroll

Chapter Thirteen

Saturday, March 16, 7:00 p.m.

Keone pulled up in front of the Loftus home in Pukalani, behind a green Jeep Grand Cherokee. The neat, simple house, neither new nor terribly old, was built in the standard off-the-ground style of Maui homes. Most homes on the island incorporated natural, tropical-style foliage, but the Loftus home sported a unique play on a formal English garden. The plant species were native or early transplants, but they were arrayed in ways he'd never seen before—and he was born here. The multiple species of bromeliads scattered throughout reinforced the garden's eerie aura. Keone thought ET might have designed this garden before flying back to that place he kept phoning.

He guessed the green Jeep belonged to Julie Walden from the personalized plate, "H A MOM", a subtle reference to the title character of her children's books, Hawai'i Anna. *Why am I taking so long getting out of the car?*

Janet Loftus greeted him at the front door and ushered him

into a spotless, if somewhat spartan, living room where another woman sat stiffly in a ladder-backed chair. "This is my sister Julie."

Keone's first impression was that these sisters didn't share much in the way of a family resemblance. Blonde Janet was short and thin, with the grace of a model. Her sister was taller and rounder, with long, wavy red hair. Where Janet was attractive and professional, Julie Walden was cute and unpretentious, even when uncomfortable and waiting for an unwanted interrogation. To him, she seemed vulnerable in a way that Janet didn't.

"Mrs. Walden, I'm Keone Boyd from the Maui PD." He showed her his badge. "I'm very pleased you made time for me." *Damn. That's not what I meant to say.*

"It's no bother. I'll be happy to answer any questions you have for me. But I doubt I know anything that will help your investigation." Julie's voice was quieter and slightly lower-pitched than her sister's, but she didn't seem in any way subordinate.

"Sergeant, if it's all right with you, I'll prepare us some coffee and biscuits," Janet said. "You must have questions for Julie that I don't need to hear."

Janet Loftus jumped a notch in his esteem. "Thank you, Mrs. Loftus."

"Please, we're Jan and Julie. We know you're here to help."

Julie nodded, and he decided to play by their rules, for the moment.

When Jan left the room, Julie seemed to relax a bit. A signal that he could begin questioning.

"Julie, I want to get to the biggest question first."

"Good. I hate people who beat around the bush. You want to know why Sam says I'm his wife, right?"

"Yes."

"I don't have a clue. Until last night, Sam always seemed to see me as either an extension of Dave or Jan. He and I have very little in common. I write fiction for children, and he hates fiction. I love kids. He's uncomfortable around kids. He's very detail oriented, and I leave all that to Dave—who leaves it to other people on his payroll."

He resisted the urge to pull out his notepad. "How would you describe your interactions with your brother-in-law?"

"Friendly. Non-invasive. Sam's a good guy, but more Dave's friend than mine. He's a good brother-in-law and has always been a supportive partner for my sister."

"Has he ever acted oddly around you?"

"Not until today."

"You visited him? In the hospital?"

"Yes, Dr. Wayne thought it might help snap Sam out of his... illness." She held her hands out like she wasn't sure what she should call what was going on with him.

"Did it?"

"No. I was only there for a minute or two, but the man in that bed was nothing like the Sam Loftus I know."

"In what way?"

"When Dr. Wayne told him I had to leave, he blew up. Shouted that I was his wife and the mother of his children." Her voice cracked, and she closed her eyes, as if to block out the memory.

He needed to direct the interview down a less emotional path. "I'm sorry that happened. I take it Mr. Loftus is normally less offensive."

Julie seemed calmer when she opened her eyes. "He's normally very sweet. He's a little on the quiet side, but not with-drawn or repressed or anything like that. He's usually very thoughtful."

"I've heard he's a bit compulsive."

"Sam's very precise in what he says and does. That may be why he's such a good accountant. But he's a very friendly guy. His dry wit complements Dave's broader, bawdier sense of humor. I think that's one of the reasons they were once such good friends. They seemed to shine brighter in each other's presence."

"You said Sam Loftus was *once* your husband's good friend. I understand they had a falling out after the Loftus's moved to Maui."

"You do your homework, don't you? It was about six months after they moved here to Pukalani. Jan and I were so happy to be close by, so were Sam and Dave—at first. Dave had a business proposition, and they agreed to discuss it on a two-day, ocean-kayaking excursion. They took off as happy as clams. When they got back, Dave was moody. He kept calling Sam, *that straight-arrow* and *number cruncher*, under his breath. I tried to get him to tell me what was wrong, but he just said, 'Nothing. We're just different that's all. I guess were not in Indiana anymore, Toto.'"

Jan returned with the coffee service and some classy European cookies.

"Thank you, Mrs... uh, Janet... Jan. Let me ask you the question I just asked your sister. What caused your husbands to grow apart?"

"I guess Julie told you about that botched kayaking trip."

He nodded.

"Afterward, I asked Sam, 'What is it between you two? You've been best friends since college.' He thought for a moment and said, 'I guess we learned different lessons in college. Dave is still Julie's husband and your brother-in-law, and I'll respect that.'"

"Do you have any idea what happened during the trip?"

"Julie and I hoped it was some little thing. Like, maybe David only liked to kayak in river rapids. But it must have been deeper."

David, not Dave. "I think you're right."

"I just remembered something that might be of interest to you, Sergeant," Janet said.

He decided to choose rapport over formality. "Call me Keone."

"Keone." Jan smiled. "What a lovely name."

He said nothing, hoping Jan would get back to the point.

"Anyway, Dr. Wayne called this afternoon. He asked me when

Sam and David had their disagreement and if they'd patched things up. He seemed disappointed when I told him how long ago it was and that they never really reconciled. He mentioned something about not being consistent with short-term memory loss. But I think he was talking to himself."

"Before the crash, did your husband ever behave unusually?"

"No. That's just it. He never does anything out of the ordinary. He's stable as a rock. I think that's what attracted me to him in the first place."

"He still takes medicine, though, doesn't he?" Keone was fishing.

"Yeah. I can't imagine why he said that to Dr. Wayne last night about not taking any magic pills? He takes medicine for acid reflux. Oh, and that anti-depressant."

"He takes an anti-depressant?"

"Yes. Sam went through a bad patch a few years ago. I always thought it had something to do with his break from David, but he's been fine since then. I think he just takes the medication out of habit. They've never even changed the dose."

Keone sipped his coffee and peered at the two sisters over the rim of his cup. Although Julie seemed the most open of the two, he sensed she was hiding something. The fact that she wore long sleeves and long slacks despite the warm Maui weather, coupled with the heavier than necessary makeup around her eyes, raised a red flag.

"Julie, could you tell me a little about your husband? I met him today and understand he's closed his legal practice."

The tension was back in Julie's posture and in her face. He'd hit a nerve.

"Dave and I are making some changes due to the success of my writing. He's a lawyer and has been uncomfortable with some of the agreements I've signed regarding my work. I didn't ask him to close his practice. It was his idea and—"

"What does this have to do with Sam and the accident?" Jan asked.

This was why he liked to interview witnesses separately. "Probably nothing. We just try to get a full picture of the subject's environment, and I know you two couples spend time together."

"Yes, we do. Julie and I have always enjoyed each other's company. As sisters, we may be a little unusual in that regard, but we've always been close. Our marriages brought us even closer. I can't imagine being far apart from Julie and David. And I know Sam feels the same way. Or at least he always has."

"Look, do you know if Dr. Wayne or his colleagues are making any progress with Sam?" Julie asked. "Jan's so lonely here without him."

Jan's eyes were starting to tear-up, a warning to Keone that it was time to bring the interview to a close, for now. "I'm sure they're doing their best. Dr. Wayne has brought in some specialists. He seems confident that together they can help Sam."

"I'm sure you're right." Janet dabbed at the corner of her eyes with a lace handkerchief.

Keone finished his cookie, then rose to leave. "Thank you both for seeing me so quickly and for the refreshments." He drew two cards from his wallet and handed one to each sister. "If either of you think of anything else that might help us in our investigation, call me anytime." He shook hands with Julie before Jan walked him to the door.

As she opened the door, Jan leaned in and spoke softly to Keone. "Do you think he's going to have any criminal charges from the accident?"

"I can't discuss an ongoing investigation, but you should focus on your husband's recovery, right now. Everything else is much less important."

With that, he left the Loftus home and headed back to his condo. He wasn't comfortable drawing too many conclusions, yet. But he knew one thing from today's experiences. Julie Walden and her husband were having marital problems. He'd stake his badge on it. He also couldn't shake the feeling that understanding the causes of the break between Dave and Sam might be relevant to unraveling events. He needed to speak to Julie alone again at some point and not because he found her so vulnerable. She raised questions in his mind.

What is she hiding with her clothing and make-up? What does she know about Dave's other business?

Chapter Fourteen

Evening at Maui Memorial Hospital was a slow time on the wards. As Sam finished yet another replay of Julie's visit in his mind, a stranger in a white coat entered his room. He guessed the first of Bob's specialists had arrived.

"Mr. Loftus, I'm Dr. Field. Dr. Wayne asked me to evaluate certain symptoms you've been displaying since the automobile accident."

"Which symptoms?"

"I'm a neurologist. I want to discuss the results of some of your tests with you. Some of what I am going to tell you may be disturbing, but please hear me out before reacting. I believe that I have a pretty good idea what's causing at least some of your symptoms."

"Dr. Field, you're the first person I have seen in the past couple days who seems to be willing to level with me. I appreciate that. I'm open to anything you have to tell me."

"Thank you. Your family doctor is concerned about you and your family. He wished to avoid sharing idle speculation until we had a solid diagnosis. First, let me assure you that some of your symptoms—possibly all of them—are the direct result of your injury in the car crash. Physical injury to the brain can cause very unsettling symptoms that are often unique for each patient. But a couple of your most pronounced symptoms have been observed, if rarely, in other patients."

Sam sat up straight in his bed and gave the doctor his full attention. *He thinks the changes happened after the crash, too.*

"I cared for a patient a few years ago, who suddenly developed left-handedness and the ability to read and write in mirror writing. In his case, this was the result of encephalitis and some related surgical procedures."

Mirror writing and reading. Sam suppressed a smile. "Did you cure him?"

"After some directed therapy, he was able to return to a completely normal life."

"I see. Go on."

"Well, the second major problem is your belief that your sister-in-law is your wife and vice-versa."

He began to interrupt, but Dr. Field held up his hand. "Mr. Loftus, you have to hear this. I know it will be hard. But we all want you to regain your health, and this is the only way."

He held his tongue but clenched his fists under the sheet.

"There is another rare anomaly called Capgras, uh, disorder. I have a colleague who's had patients with Capgras. I've asked him to meet with you tomorrow afternoon. He can explain this aspect far better than I."

Sam said nothing.

"You see, Mr. Loftus. I believe the crash caused the left-right problem and I have experience treating such a defect. My colleague has experience treating Capgras. It will take time, but I firmly believe that together we can return you to your mental and emotional state before the accident."

Sam was floored. Field really didn't realize that the left-right thing happened before the accident. Maybe none of the doctors did. He hadn't mentioned passing through the film to anyone else, except the cop and Lee. He needed to find out what was really going on but couldn't do that lying in a hospital bed. Maybe their faulty assumptions could work in his favor.

"Doctor Field. I can't tell you how relieved I am that you've discovered an underlying physical cause for my condition. Does this mean that I might be able to go home and be treated on, what do you call it...?"

"An outpatient basis. Yes, that's a possibility. But I will need my colleague, Dr. Drayton, to examine you first about the other aspect of your illness. I'm sure together we can start you on a regime of medication, therapy, and exercise that will quickly bring you to a state where you can leave the hospital. We must make certain there are no hidden issues, but I think it very likely that, with significant progress, you could go home in a few weeks."

"Thank you, Doctor. By the way, what is Dr. Drayton's area of specialization?"

"Dr. Drayton is a psychiatrist."

"You think I'm crazy?" Sam clenched his fists again.

"Oh, no. We just need to be sure that the symptoms are completely physical. I'm confident he will be able to assure both you and your wife that there are no dangerous aspects to your condition. I know you want everyone to be comfortable when you return to your family."

"Of course you're right, to allay everyone's fears." Was what he said, but Sam's thoughts would have been less palatable to the good doctor. *I'll return to my family all right. To Julie and the kids. And nobody will suspect that I know this is all a load of crap.*

LINDSAY KALANI BRACED HERSELF. WHEN A CALL CAME in this late on a Saturday anyone might be on the other end of the line. "Maui Police Department, Criminal Investigation Division, Detective Kalani speaking, how may I help you."

"Hello, Detective." The voice on the other end of the line paused for a moment before continuing.

"My name is Dr. Martin Hasselbach. I oversee all scientific research at the Haleakala Observatories for the University of Hawaii Institute of Astronomy. I assume you've heard of me."

"Yes, Dr. Hasselbach. I've read about your work in the Maui News. How can I help you, tonight?"

"One of our scientists, a Dr. Bradley Carvell, has been measuring certain field variations here on Maui for us and has found an unusual coincidence between a surge in a particularly rare field and the time and physical location of a traffic accident."

"Could you tell me the specific time, date, and location?"

"Four-forty-nine p.m. on March fifteenth near Ma'alaea Harbor," the voice replied.

"A colleague of mine has been working on that case. Could I have him call you back to discuss this with you?"

"I hate to take his time. I know how busy you people are. If you could just answer one question for me, I can have Dr. Carvell take it from there. We would like the name and telephone number of the wrong way driver that caused the accident."

Now it was Lindsay's turn to pause. "Dr. Hasselbach, I would really like to help you. But this is an ongoing investigation. The information you requested is not available for release to the public."

Another, longer pause before the man on the other end of the line said, "I understand. I'll let Dr. Carvell know about this policy and direct him to follow up with the person in charge of the case directly."

"The person in charge of the case is Detective Sergeant Boyd. Let me give you his direct number."

After she provided Boyd's contact information--which she guessed he would never use, the voice said, "Thank you very much for your help, Detective. I'm afraid I must get back to my own research now. Aloha."

"Aloha." If that was Hasselbach, she'd eat her badge.

Chapter Fifteen

Sunday, March 17, 6:45 a.m.

Eyes closed, Sam debated going back to sleep rather than face another day of everything being ass-backwards. He knew there would be more tests and more doctors today and doubted he was any closer to being released.

He sensed something different in his room.

Was that someone breathing next to the bed? Keeping his eyes closed, Sam decided to focus on what his other senses might tell him. From the direction of the breathing, he deduced the person was either a child or an adult sitting in a chair. There was a fragrance, not totally pleasant. He decided it was deodorant fighting a losing battle with male sweat. Was one of the doctors observing him as he slept? That would be better than his non-wife, Janet, sitting there staring at him. He supposed he should open his eyes.

"Hi, *Sam I am*. I was wondering when you'd decide to open those peepers of yours."

He pulled himself upright, reassured by the sound of his old college nickname. Sitting by his bed with a huge grin on his face was his best friend. "Dave. Am I glad to see *you*! Everything's crazy in this place."

"It's a place for sick people. What do you expect?"

"I need a reality check. Maybe you can bring some sense to my world."

"That's why I'm here, old friend. You know you can tell me anything. I've been hearing some weird stuff about you since that accident. How are you feeling, by the way?"

"Physically, I feel just fine. Bob Wayne brought in a specialist who thinks I bumped my head and went whacko. And that detective..."

"Oh yeah. Detective Sergeant Boyd paid me a visit yesterday. He's kinda scary. I hope he didn't scare a bogus confession out of you."

"No way. But he is a good investigator. He can make innocent guys like you and me feel like we're guilty of something."

"And what could you be guilty of? Rounding a number? Or me? Cheating at golf? I think cops scare the innocent more than the guilty sometimes." Dave laughed.

"You got that right, Davey. Damn, I'm glad to see you. You know when I told Bob Wayne that you were my best friend since college, he acted like I was telling a fib."

"I think he's the one telling fibs. He told Julie you think she's your wife and that I'm married to Janet. I mean Janet's great for you, but... That Wayne's such a rube! I figured you were just playing with him. Are you worried about doing time for the crash?" Dave grinned again, but his eyes stayed focused on Sam.

His heart skipped a beat. Dave wouldn't joke about his love for Janet. *What should I say?*

Dave saved him the trouble by bursting into a deep belly-laugh. "Hell, Sam I am, if I thought you were making a move on my girl, I'd fill a syringe with air and shoot it into that IV tube in your arm. Air embolism. No trace. You'd just be dead."

Sam had to say something. "You know me too well. Yeah, I'm

just playing with them. Once they decide it's all in my mind, I'll be back home with Janet and free of any charges."

"I thought so. I knew my old pal wasn't looney. And I also knew you wouldn't go back on the bargain we made on that kayaking trip. My business is my business, right?" Dave's grin gradually faded as he idly tapped on the IV tube running into Sam's arm.

Although he had no idea what his friend was talking about, Sam figured he'd better play along. "No worries. As Sergeant Schultz used to say on those old *Hogan's Heroes* re-runs we watched in the dorm, 'I know nothing—Nothing!'" Sam forced himself to laugh.

Dave rose from the chair.

"I hope you believe that I never wanted to hurt you or Julie," Sam said. "That's why I'm so glad you came while none of the doctors or nurses were around. I need to make them think my mind is a little warped. My doctors believe I'll recover. And don't worry, I will." He punctuated the last statement with a broad wink.

Dave grabbed the front of Sam's gown with his fist and twisted it tightly around his neck. "You better be conning them and not me, old friend. But don't take too long to recover, okay?" Dave's voice became a raspy whisper as he spat out these words. Then Dave smiled, released his grip on Sam's gown, patted Sam's cheek and sat back down. "I didn't like that giant Hawaiian detective sniffing around my old office yesterday asking all kinds of questions."

"What kinds of questions?"

"Doesn't matter. I don't like anyone sniffing around in my business. You were an idiot to reject the sweet deal I offered you when you first got here. My real business has made me somebody in these islands. But you promised you'd never tell anyone about it."

"I keep my promises, Dave. You and I, we're like brothers. I'd never share any of your confidences with anyone, especially the cops."

"Like brothers? Where the hell do you think we are? Back home again in Indiana? We haven't been on the same page since that day on the kayak. I risked everything to let you in on the ground floor. This better just be part of your sick act."

"It is. I've gotta keep it up until they cure me. You never know who could come through that door." Sam could barely keep his hands from shaking. This man was nothing like his dear friend. He seemed hardened and mean. Dave was always a joker. He liked to kid, like calling him Sam I am. But this man wasn't joking. He was deadly serious.

"I'm impressed. I never considered you much of an actor, but those docs seem convinced."

"They think my brain got scrambled in the crash, Dave. I couldn't believe how easy it was to fool them. But I have to ask you about Rain and Mist?"

"What? You're asking about the weather now? What's wrong with you? Maybe your brain really is scrambled."

"All part of the act, Dave. You have to believe me."

"I don't have to do anything, except keep my eye on you. If you keep away from me and mine and keep your trap shut, you might manage to end up in one piece. But don't test me. Got it?"

"Yes."

Dave switched to a louder, more jovial voice. "That's great, Sam I am. You just do what the doctors and those pretty, little nurses tell you, and you'll be good as new. I'll see you soon, old friend."

With that, Dave slipped out the door and left Sam dazed and exhausted.

What in God's name is happening? The Dave he knew would have tried to find some way, any way, to help him. Even if he thought he was crazy, Dave would have humored him, not thrown Sam's condition back in his face. This Dave scared him. This Dave was dangerous.

Sam struggled to find some shred of reality in what he'd just experienced. But, before he could order his thoughts, Sergeant Boyd came through the door Dave had so recently closed.

THE MAN KEONE BOYD SAW IN THE HOSPITAL BED WAS not the confident, if confused, Sam Loftus he'd interviewed the day before. This man was nervous, unsure, and weary.

"Mr. Loftus. Do you remember me from yesterday?"

Sam pulled the sheet up to cover his hospital gown. "Sergeant Boyd. Yes, I remember you. But I'm not sure about much else."

"What do you mean?"

"Since we last spoke, I've been poked, prodded, and viewed in many ingenious ways. My visitors think I'm crazy and so do my eminent doctors. I've been told that left is right, my sister-in-law is my wife, my wife is married to my best friend, and, just now, my best friend paid me a surprise visit and told me to keep the hell away from his wife—my wife...." Sam threw his hands up, his eyes glistened with tears.

"Dave Walden was here?"

"You just missed him."

"That is a lot to handle in twenty-four hours," Keone said. "I've spent that time learning more about you, your friends, and your family."

Sam didn't comment.

"Do you want to know what I've found out?"

Sam looked away. "Not really. I don't think I could handle one more piece of information. Is Dr. Wayne aware that you're here?"

"Yes. He's allowed me another fifteen-minute visit. In strict compliance with the law in cases such as this."

"Cases such as this? Is this a case? What are you talking about? I thought I was in an accident."

"It's my job to confirm that. Something you said yesterday

caught my interest. You described the crash to me and clearly demonstrated that your confusion began before the accident—when that bubble enveloped you.”

“That what?” Sam replied, putting a confused look on his face.

He flipped open his notebook. “You said, and I quote, ‘I felt like I passed through a kind of film, like an invisible bubble, and heard a loud pop.’ Have you forgotten?”

“If I said something as loony as that, I see why they’re keeping me in here. I just felt dizzy and thought I was on the wrong side of the road. That’s all.”

Now he’s lying. “Has anyone coached you on what to say to the police since we last spoke?”

“No one here has said anything about the police, except Bob, when he told me I needed to talk with you yesterday. I’m sorry if I said anything weird. I was still pretty out of it.”

“Did your friend Dave mention that I’d been to see him?”

“I don’t think so. Once I explained it was my injuries that made me into a raving lunatic last night, he apologized. He became concerned for me. Asked about my injuries and things.”

Lying again. Keone noticed that Sam looked up and to the left when was lying. “He’s your best friend?”

“Friends since college. Married a pair of sisters, you know.”

“Yes, I know. You just think you married a different sister than he does. Sounds like that made him a little, I don’t know, testy.”

“Dave’s a great friend. Once he understood what was really happening, he focused on how he and Julie could help Janet and me.” Sam’s eyes went up and to the left. “The doctors tell me I’ll get everything straight again if I let them work on me. I really want to get out of here, so I’m going to do exactly as they say.”

“Time’s up, Sergeant.” It was Sam’s nurse, Gwen Tanaka.

“Thank you, Mr. Loftus, you’ve given me a lot to think about.”

Once outside Sam’s room, Keone waited for the nurse to emerge.

"Nurse Tanaka, has Mr. Loftus had any other visitors since I saw him last?"

"Dr. Wayne brought a woman yesterday, I think it was Sam's sister, or sister-in-law. Another older man visited in the evening after Dr. Field saw him. I think Millie said his name was Marder. Dr. Wayne authorized that visit as well."

"Who's Millie?"

"Nurse Millicent Brown. She works the evening shift."

"I see. What about his brother-in-law, Mr. Walden?"

"Dr. Wayne specifically prohibited any unsupervised visits from him or his wife."

"Is there any time he could have slipped in unnoticed?"

"Well, the nurses are all together in the conference room for change of shift report between 6:45 and 7:15. There are usually some therapists and food service folks around then. I could check."

"Would you please? Has Sam received any calls?"

"Dr. Wayne had the phone in his room removed before Mr. Loftus arrived."

"Thank you, Nurse Tanaka."

Keone didn't think Sam imagined Walden's visit. He also knew it had been anything but friendly. Walden had been too careful not to be observed.

Sam Loftus hadn't lawyered up. He'd been threatened. That visit from good old Dave had shaken him to his core. Sam and Dave might be playing the parts of best friends, but their wives told a different story. Walden was certainly lying, and Sam wasn't telling the whole truth anymore, either.

Keone Boyd was not a good person to lie to.

Chapter Sixteen

When Keone parked his cruiser at Maui Police Headquarters in Wailuku, he looked forward to spending the rest of the day and most of the evening in the tiny cubicle assigned to him. The normally tedious process of transferring the notes from each of his interviews into the appropriate case file documents on his computer was a welcome respite from the strangeness of the past few days.

From the first two days of his investigation, he had interview notes for Dr. Robert Wayne, Dave Walden, Julie Walden, Jan Loftus, Lee Marder, Sam's boss, and co-workers, and his two short interludes with Sam. Today, he would interview Dr. John Field, Julie's former agent and publisher, the president of the decorating firm Jan worked for, and her three active clients.

This morning, after Julie Walden provided Dave's client list by e-mail, he'd call a cross-section. He would also call the Ka'anapali Golf Course and obtain a list of the high rollers involved in the charity golf tournament.

Entering every piece of information into the computer, he went into the zone. A detective's job was filled with a series of pieces. Places, people, events, physical evidence, and oral evidence are usually obtained in a somewhat illogical order, based on witness availability, crime scene clearance, lab reports, and even the illogical order in which a detective becomes aware of events. He knew the start of this case wasn't the moment Sam Loftus totaled his new Morgan. Everything that happened was the direct or indirect result of something that happened prior to that moment.

Putting all his findings and speculations down in one continuous session always helped him identify potential causative elements and events. It was kind of an act of faith to do all this work with the expectation that a path for subsequent investigation would emerge. But he was seldom disappointed.

After more than an hour of reviewing, editing, entering data into the computer, and making some calls, he created his *cards*. Each of these large post-it notes contained key information about the case: people, places, interactions, physical evidence, even hunches. He used to use actual index cards and a corkboard wall, but his cubicle walls were now white boards to which he could stick the post-its. He showed potential connections by drawing lines with colored Dry Erase markers—much more efficient than the strips of yarn he used to use. Single lines represented individual connections between specific notes, such as the link between Dave Walden and Ka'anapali Golf Course.

Once he posted all the notes and mapped all the connections, he rarely had to return to the computer. As new information came in, he added it to the computer files, created new notes, and linked these to existing notes. Links occasionally needed to be erased, but that was rare. He was pretty good at this.

He picked up his notes and markers and was about to stick the Sam Loftus card in the center when Lieutenant Tony Alcala tapped on the entrance to his cubicle. "Got a minute, Big Guy?"

"Sure, boss. What are you doing here on a Sunday?"

"Me first. What the hell are you doing here. Didn't I hear something about a major car crash with one of my detectives pinned in a jumble of scrap metal that used to be a sports car?"

"I was lucky. The medics checked me out."

"And told you to go to the hospital and see a doctor."

"I went to the hospital right after the crash. And I saw a couple of doctors." Keone knew how to spin things.

"Was one of them Hiram Lloyd?"

"Yes. I did run into him there."

"But he didn't examine you, did he?"

"No. That was another doctor."

"Was he an ER doctor?"

"I don't think so." Keone plucked one of his post-its off the table. "Dr. Wayne was the guy. He was there to examine his own patient, a Mr. Sam Loftus. He spent some time with me after he finished. He didn't suggest any further treatment, so I returned to work. I'm sure I can get a note from him if you need one."

"No. I just wondered why Dr. Lloyd said none of his doctors had seen you."

He should have known that little prick, Lloyd, couldn't resist complaining to Tony.

Tony glanced at the cards on Keone's table. "What're you working on?"

"Well, I know we're short-handed. So, since I was uniquely familiar with the crash, I offered to collect some data for the accident investigation."

"That might be against department policy. You were a victim of the crash, for Christ's sake."

"You want me to turn it over to somebody else? I'm putting everything into my report."

"No. You're right about us being short-handed. Just wrap it up quickly."

"I'll be done in another day, two days tops. The cause of the crash is clearly related to the mental state of the wrong-way driver. I've already interviewed him, his work colleagues, two close friends, and his wife and sister-in-law."

"Why the sister-in-law?"

"Since the crash, Loftus believes she's his wife and that his wife's his sister-in-law. It's sort of confusing."

"Just close the case. Fast. I've got better things for you to work on."

"Sure thing, boss," he said to Alcala's rapidly departing back.

Keone heard a snort from the next cubicle, followed by the squeal of a chair being pushed away from a desk.

"Dodged another one, eh, Keone?" Frank Kulima's rotund form filled the entrance to Keone's space.

"What?"

"I lost count of how many department policies you violated in just the last twenty-four hours. I wish I knew how you get away with it."

"I consider them more like guidelines."

"Right."

"You're just pissed because I made sergeant before you."

"I'm not bothered in the least. I know you'll screw up. I've got my eyes on you." Frank pointed two fingers at his eyes and then at Keone.

"I don't like threats, Frank. I'm not in competition with you."

"No threat intended. I'm just a good detective doing his job. Enjoy your afternoon. I've got real detective work to do." Kulima made a sharp about face, almost toppling over from the rapid redistribution of blubber, and headed out.

Keone didn't have time for this shit. He needed to analyze his data while it was still fresh in his mind.

After another hour, his wall looked like a spider's web, with colorful lines linking key people, places, actions, and miscellaneous other information. He circled certain key links that needed to be further examined. He traced his fingers over three key connections, the ones between Julie and Dave Walden, Sam Loftus and Dave Walden, and Dave Walden and the high rollers. Of course, he would pursue the Julie-Sam connection and the Janet-Sam connection, but he sensed this wasn't where he would strike gold.

Hearing another tap on his cubicle entrance, Keone turned to see Lindsay Kalani's smiling face.

"Howzit, Big guy?"

"Getting better. Hey, I didn't know that you and Max from Lahaina Coolers were related," he replied.

"Uncle Max. He and my dad were hanai brothers. He helped raise me after my mama died. I love that old rascal."

"Me, too."

"But hey, I came here for a reason. Last night I got a call from some guy interested in your crash case."

"What guy?"

"Well, that's where it gets interesting. He called from the land-line of Dr. Martin Hasselbach up at the observatories on Haleakala. He identified himself as Hasselbach and said he had a scientist who wanted to interview the wrong way driver in your crash."

"What scientist?"

"A Dr. Bradley Carvell?"

"What did you tell him?"

"Said it was an open investigation, and I couldn't disclose any information."

"Good."

"I gave him your phone number in case he wanted to follow-up after the case was closed. But I don't think he will."

"Why?"

"After I explained about the open investigation, he got off the phone in a hurry. My guess? It wasn't Hasselbach."

He tapped his abdomen. "What else did your gut tell you?"

"Might have been the scientist that works for him using the boss's phone. Something didn't smell right." Lindsay's expression conveyed exactly that impression.

He could smell it, too. "I've learned to trust your instincts. If I don't get a call, I'll follow up with Hasselbach after the case is closed. Mahalo, Detective."

Chapter Seventeen

Sam had done his homework on Dr. Evan Drayton. According to both Gwen and Millie, Drayton was a fussy man. He liked to dress informally but would rush home and change if he spilled a drop of anything on his clothing. He loved neatness and order. In this, at least, they were alike. As an accountant, Sam liked to see everything add up. Unfortunately, his current situation didn't add up at all.

His first session with Drayton would take place this afternoon. The intervening hours had been filled with multiple batteries of oral and written tests, administered by various mental health technicians with complicated titles. The only allowance they made for his condition was the use of mirror-image copies of each of the written tests. He assumed they made similar copies of his answers so they could evaluate them.

When the meticulous Dr. Drayton at last made his entrance, Sam was ready. He found the interview entertaining. The good doctor tried to get him to open up about his experiences. He found it easy to answer all the queries without exposing his conviction that his mental state was not a disorder, but reality. He did, however, grill Drayton about the disorder Field had mentioned, Capgras.

"Capgras Delusion was first described by a French psychiatrist in 1923," Drayton began.

Oh, it's a delusion, is it? No wonder Field had trouble spitting that out.

"He called it *l'illusion des sosies*," Drayton continued, "the illusion of doubles. Several cases have been identified throughout the years. I had a patient with Capgras. I'll call her Barbara. She was thirty years old and believed that a stranger had replaced her husband. She refused to go home from the hospital with him. When sedated and taken to her home, she refused to sleep with her husband, locked herself in a separate bedroom, and pulled a gun on us when we suggested she be returned to the hospital."

"Did she have a head injury, like me?"

"No, she was psychotic, but the disorder has also been observed in patients with head injuries."

Drayton too thought everything was the result of the crash. Drayton and Field were stretching to find an acceptable diagnosis when there was none.

They were wrong. But, if keeping them satisfied would get him out of here, he would play along.

"Let's assume for a moment that you and Dr. Field are right. Who am I to say, as a layman?"

"A very enlightened approach, Mr. Loftus."

"Thank you. I can see how I could learn to un-transpose left and right through something like occupational therapy. I suppose I could even be trained to read what appears to me as mirror writing. But how could I ever learn to accept a different woman as my wife?"

"That's an honest and logical question. In the few cases of Capgras where I, or others, have been successful, it has been a long slow process of adaptation. It also requires complete commitment from the patient and his loved ones. But it can work."

"What can work?"

"CBT."

"I'm unfamiliar with that term."

"Sorry, Cognitive Behavior Therapy. It's most often used in cases of post-traumatic stress disorder, or PTSD. When a soldier returns from a particularly horrendous experience in combat, you can't just throw him back into civilian life. It requires a gradual re-adaptation to a formerly familiar environment."

"I heard about PTSD on *Sixty Minutes*. But how would it work for me?"

"I haven't finished detailing the entire protocol, but I can give you the basics. You would go through a series of steps to re-acquaint yourself with your former life. You would live in your house and sleep in your bedroom."

"Sleeping with someone I don't believe is my wife?"

Drayton smiled. "No. She would sleep in a separate bedroom. You would live together like housemates in the first phase as well as the second."

"What happens in the second phase?"

"Once you feel a sense of comfort and security in your own home, we would gradually add external activities. One of the first would be to return to work."

"I would really like that. I miss my job."

"Other external activities would follow. You could entertain or go out for dinner with your wife or to a friend's house."

"I would love to be able to spend time with our friends again." *Julie more than Dave.*

"You could see that as a reward for achieving intermediate goals. In the third phase you would take the next step in re-establishing your relationship with your wife as lover and partner. Up to this point you will have re-established your friendship, which is how you first operated in your original courtship. You only take the final step when you and Janet feel you're both ready."

"You can't imagine how frightened I am right now."

"I do understand, though. That's why we'll take it one step at a time."

"I'll try," he said. *The fool just told me how I need to play this.*

"The first and most important step is that you trust me and

agree to accept that you are ill and need help. If you can do this, Dr. Field and Dr. Wayne have agreed to place you under my care and abide by my decisions regarding your rehabilitation."

Sam's heart leapt in his chest. *Bingo.* This was the opening he'd been waiting for. *Easier to fool one of these morons than all three of them.* Besides, he didn't know how far he could trust Wayne, who seemed to blab everything to Dave.

What he said was, "Dr. Drayton, you have been totally honest with me, so I will be the same with you. I know I'm screwed up. The evidence points to the fault lying in my mind and not in the outside world. I'm frightened of the treatment plan you just described. Still, if there's a chance this could give me back my ordered life, I'd be a fool not to try. I'll have to take this at my own pace, though. Some of the things you suggest give me chills at this point. I am a very methodical individual. That's probably why I love mathematics. One proof leads to another in a logical progression until you are able to accept concepts that once seemed impossible."

"Mr. Loftus, I can see we are going to be able to work together to solve your problem. I'll begin by assigning you to a longer-term care component of the hospital while you receive physical and occupational therapy. When we send you home, you'll be able to read and write in a manner acceptable to society and left and right will have the same meanings for you that they do for the rest of us."

"Thank you, Doctor. God bless you." Sam didn't have to fake the tears that slid down his cheeks.

Chapter Eighteen

Keone's mind struggled with competing questions as he pulled up in front of the Walden home in Kula.

Why had Julie Walden called him at the station and begged him to rush to her house? He'd only met her once.

Why was he so worried about her safety? If this crazy case were a hurricane, she represented the eye of the storm.

He surveyed the Walden home as he parked his cruiser in front of the driveway—in case he needed to prevent someone from exiting. Dave and Julie's house was a Maui standard transformed into a luxury estate, as different from the Loftus home as he could imagine,

He guessed it had once exhibited the classic two stories common to hilly parts of Maui, with a wooden top floor overhanging an open carport attached to a cinderblock lower floor. But the upper floor had been reconstructed with steel piers and floor to ceiling windows that seemed to go all the way around the house. The style reminded him of homes he'd seen on Mt. Tantalus in Oʻahu. The ones actors rented while they worked on the longer-lived TV series filmed there.

The carport had been replaced with a completely enclosed four-car garage. Lush landscaping led up the side of the hill from the garages, with tall metal gates and fences enclosing everything from the sidewalk inward, including the driveway.

He walked to a gate to the right of the garages, where he found a button to press.

"Yes?"

"Mrs. Walden? It's Keone Boyd."

"Thank God. I'll buzz you in."

An annoying beep announced the gate was now unlocked. He entered through a formal Japanese garden with a gravel path that led up the hill to the back of the house. He crunched up the path, which turned left under a grape arbor between the back of the house and a free-standing building on the right. On the right, through an open door, he could see a game room that opened at the rear onto a pool and patio. The only occupant he could see was a large pool table, so he continued over a Japanese, arched bridge to the front door. The aromas of exotic flowers filled the air. On the bridge, he gazed down into a pond filled with the colorful movement of koi. *Is this a home or a resort hotel?*

He heard Julie stumble as she approached the front door. When it opened, he could see her hair was bathed in blood. Bruises marred her lovely face and exposed shoulders. Her posture and the dark stains on her clothing suggested he would find similar marks on her back and the back of her legs.

"My God, what happened?"

"Hit me." She collapsed into his arms.

"Who hit you?"

"Dave," she gasped. Her eyes rolled up and her knees buckled. He caught her as she collapsed.

Keone felt her full weight in his arms. Feeling shards of glass protruding from her legs, back, and shoulders, he adjusted his hold so he wouldn't push them further in before carrying her through a debris field that was once a sunken living room. Broken crockery, shards from a cracked mirror, and splintered furniture were scattered across the room. The remnants of a shattered glass-top coffee table crunched under his shoes as he made his way to the one couch that appeared free of broken glass.

He gently laid Julie on the couch on her side, checked to make sure she was breathing normally, and made a quick visual inspection for flowing wounds. She'd thrown a dishtowel over her head. The wound on the back of her scalp had saturated the towel but was now seeping not flowing. Still, he rearranged her position to allow her head to maintain pressure on the bleeder.

He called the incident in, ending with, "I've got one civilian down. Will need EMT's and a bus. Clearing the house now." Removing his Glock 45 from its holster, he searched room-by-room until he'd cleared the whole house. The last door he'd found was an entrance to a stairway at the end of one hall. He'd flipped on a light and saw the stairs led down to the garage, with Julie's jeep next to an empty space, probably for Dave's big caddie. Walden must have fled before he arrived.

Back in the living room, he lifted Julie's head off the dishtowel to see the bleeding had slowed, brushed a lock of hair from her eyes, and confirmed the emergency response team was en route.

Keone crouched on the floor beside Julie and felt for a pulse. What he found was weak and thready, but steady. He considered calling the crime scene investigation team but decided to wait.

Keeping pressure on the back of Julie's head, he began a visual circuit of the room. Molding near the front door-latch freshly cracked. *Dave hadn't closed it gently when he fled.* He must've parked his car on the street and not in the garage.

The parquet floor of the entrance alcove was polished to a gloss, but the only bloody imprints he saw were from Julie's bare feet. She and Dave, like all Maui residents, left their shoes and slippahs outside the door. He'd seen a pair of women's sandals beside the doormat when he arrived. He suspected the evidence team would find residue from Dave's bare feet on the parquet floor as well. Dave had avoided stepping in any of the blood. Julie hadn't had that option.

Front door and entry were on the far side of the living room from the couch where he knelt next to Julie. He began his assessment beginning at the entry and proceeded in a clockwise direction. Two hallways led off the entrance alcove at two and ten o'clock. They each led to bedrooms, Julie's to the left and Dave's to the right

A wall unit containing expensive curios was centered on the small wall across from where he sat. A longer wall to his right held a mirror suspended above a shorter narrower couch, at a right-angle to where Julie lay. The mirror, which once reflected the lovely view from the floor to ceiling windows, was now shattered. The greatest damage was a circular scar about the size of a person's head. The area of the couch directly beneath was saturated with blood. So was the area around the glass coffee table that was shattered in front of the couch. Dave probably slammed the back of her head against the mirror first and then threw her face first onto the glass coffee table. *What a sweetheart.* Now he understood why Sam was so frightened this morning.

He completed his circuit of the room, which was open to his left, with the windows continuing along a large dining area, open to an even larger kitchen.

The visual circuit of the room took less than a minute. He turned back to Julie with a clearer picture of what had happened. But Julie's breathing had become labored, her color ashen, and her pulse threadier. *She must be bleeding somewhere else.*

He carefully rolled her over to find blood pooling under her right thigh. He felt around to find a large shard of glass... He couldn't remove the shard from the wound, without a risk of slashing something vital on the way out. He needed to make a tourniquet.

Keeping her on the side away from the shard. He removed his belt, wrapped it above the wound, and pulled it tight. The tourniquet had slowed the flow of blood, but he kicked himself for not finding the wound sooner. Her lovely face was pale, too pale. *I'm losing her.*

He used his handcuffs to attach the end of the belt to the arm of the couch long enough for him to run to the dining room and grab some quilted placemats to absorb the blood from her thigh and other wounds. The area on the back of her head was now just oozing, as were two other wounds he'd discovered on her face and arms, but he fastened a placemat to each with zip-ties from his utility kit and went back to holding the belt as tightly as he could.

He struggled to think of something, anything more he could do until the EMT's arrived. *Where are those guys?*

A second later, a chorus of sirens answered his question. He buzzed the gate open, ran outside, and slid around the corner of the house, waving his arms and shouting. The EMTs had braced the gate open and were running up the walkway as a patrol unit and an ambulance pulled up behind their truck.

"Up here. Serious leg, head, and back bleeds. Unconscious. Pulse fading," Keone shouted, then rushed back to Julie's side. Her breathing was shallow and rapid, like she was panting, and her pulse was weaker than before.

The first EMT took over Keone's position, applied an oxygen mask, and started replacing lost fluids. He pointed to the wound in her thigh.

The other EMT, Keone's friend Eldon Miranda, said, "I see it. Looks like I've got some stitching to do."

Keone walked outside to call the crime scene team and direct the ambulance guys to the entrance. He'd reached the garages by the time he'd finished the call to CSI.

He stared at the garages and felt he was missing something. Then he saw it. The light he'd turned on shined out the edges of the two garage doors on the right but there was no light from the two on the left. *That's it. Four garage doors but only two spaces in the garage.*

He walked closer to the doors to discover the two on the left were fake, just plastered onto a solid block wall. Connecting what he was seeing to what he'd discovered on his quick sweep of the house, he realized these doors were directly beneath Dave's study, one of the few rooms with no floor to ceiling windows.

He walked over to the patrolman standing by the gate. "Hey, Kono, thanks for keeping the site secure. Once the crime scene guys get here, I'll take over and you can help your partner check out the neighborhood for witnesses, yeah?"

"Will do."

"Oh, and keep a look out for Dave Walden, too."

"The golf tournament guy? Is this his house?" Kono seemed impressed.

"Yeah. He beat the crap out of his wife."

"You want us to put out an APB?"

"Definitely. We need to catch this bastard."

"You got it, Sarge." Kono grabbed his radio.

When Keone re-entered the living room, Eldon gave him a cautious nod.

While they secured Julie on the stretcher, Keone gazed at her battered face and arms. That lovely face was bruised, cut, and way too pale.

He forced himself to look away from Julie's face and concentrate on helping the attendants wheel her down the winding path to the street level. Julie's eyes flickered open as they reached the door to the ambulance.

"Julie?"

She turned her head toward his voice and reached for his arm.

"I've never..."

He leaned over struggling to make out her whispered words.

"Never seen him like that. Thought I could break it to him gently...."

"Has he ever hit you before?"

"Yes. But open palm, before. This time... fists. Hurts so much, Keone...."

He watched her eyes defocus.

The ambulance door slammed closed, and they sped off,

leaving Keone and Kono watching Eldon and his partner pack up and depart the scene, too.

When Kono glanced at him, Keone said, "I can relieve you now. Go ahead and help your partner survey the neighborhood."

"We'll send a report to you as soon as we finish."

"Mahalo. I'll hang around until the evidence guys get here." *And maybe check out Dave's end of the house over that phony garage.*

Chapter Nineteen

Sam knew the psychiatrist and neurologist were completely wrong about him but didn't have an alternate explanation for what was happening to him. Either he was crazy, or the world was. Neither alternative was acceptable. He needed to get out of the hospital as soon as possible to start investigating things for himself and would do anything to make that happen—even play damaged.

When his afternoon/evening nurse, Millie, came in to remove his dinner tray, she carried a telephone in her right hand.

"You are to be permitted incoming calls now, my love." She reached around and plugged the device in behind the bedside table, before setting the standard phone with no keypad within reach.

"Well, it's better than nothing," he said. "I just hope somebody gets the urge to call."

Millie squeezed his shoulder. "They will. You've earned this. All the nurses and techs are calling you, *our model patient.*" Collecting the tray, she left him alone.

He'd just leaned back on his pillow when the telephone rang.

He lifted the receiver as though the action alone could free him from captivity. "Hello?"

"Hi, Sam, it's Tom Conrad. I'm glad to see my protests are starting to bear fruit."

"Hi, Tom. Good to hear your voice. They think I'm crazy and treat me like I'm in jail."

"As your lawyer, let me advise you that this is the best thing they could possibly think."

"This phone they gave me doesn't allow me to call out."

"I know. I'm the reason you got that phone. I'm working on getting you outgoing as well. Anyway, Lee gave me your note. You must do nothing to disabuse the doctors of their delusion that you're delusional. I'm pretty sure this is just the ticket to get you off the hook for any charges stemming from your traffic accident."

"But you understand that I'm not crazy, right?"

"Sssh. Don't say that too loud. I know you're not crazy. But I need you to play along until I can sort all this out. Promise me?"

Sam decided to let Tom continue to think it was his idea. Since he was suggesting exactly what Sam planned to do anyway, "Okay, for now. But once I get out of this place, we're gonna talk."

"Sure, sure. I'll try to get you sprung from there as soon as I can. Just be smart, Sam. Bye."

Chapter Twenty

Once Kono was gone, Keone retraced his steps toward the house, He was especially interested in the component that sat directly above the part of the garage that wasn't a garage

When he'd checked to make sure the entire house was empty, he'd only gotten a glimpse of Dave's end of the house. There was a bedroom and a separate study, which resided directly above the half of the garage that he couldn't reach from the garage access.

He had just reached the front door when the crime scene van pulled up. *Damn.*

Keone was out of time. The crime scene team met him at the gate.

"You guys made good time," Keone said. "Let me show you which one is the front entrance." He walked them up, pointed to the front door, and said, "There's blood and a lot of debris in the living room. I left the door open when I went in. The medics treated the victim on site and transported her to the hospital."

"Did they go into any other rooms?" A CSI, whose name tag said Jenkins, asked.

"I stayed with them the most of time. They stayed right by her side."

"Did you go into any other rooms?"

"I carried the victim to the living room and laid her on the couch that's in front of the picture window. I also did a quick sweep of the house to make sure the attacker had left. He had."

"And you didn't touch anything?"

"Only some placemats from the dining room, which I used to staunch the bleeding. I know enough not to disturb the scene."

"I'm sure you do, Detective Sergeant Boyd. But you know I've gotta ask."

"No problem. If you don't need anything else, I'll get out of your way so you can secure the scene."

Jenkins nodded. "We'll take it from here, Thank you so much for your help."

Keone started to leave, then turned back. "Jenkins, could you do me a favor?"

"Sure, Sarge."

"I know it's outside the immediate crime scene, but could you take a look in the area above the garages and let me know if anything looks...uh...odd to you."

"No problem. I'll touch base with you back at the station.

"Mahalo." A smile crossed his face as Keone walked down the path to his car. He knew the crime scene guys liked to play amateur detective and looked forward to Jenkins' report. He headed for the hospital, sorting through what had just happened in his mind.

Dave Walden beat up his wife. Julie said he'd done it before, but without fists. Could Julie be having an affair with Sam? What did Julie break to Dave gently? And what was in Dave's secret room?

He knew from experience that finding things that didn't add up was often the key to breaking a case wide open.

Officer Ed Jenkins loved his job. Each case was a puzzle which needed to be pieced together to make sense of the events that had transpired. He slipped on his booties and stepped through the entrance alcove into what was clearly the crime scene.

For the next four hours, he and his team examined every inch of the house, but aside from its odd layout all the relevant evidence was in the living room and dining room. The living room opened directly off the entrance, but the two hallways that led away from the entrance area caught his attention. When they'd finished with the crime scene, he offered to do the basics for the rooms down the right hallway. He knew from their initial sweep that this was the direction to the study that had so fascinated Sergeant Boyd.

Ed proceeded down the hallway which made a sharp right turn. Around the corner he found the entrance to the largest of the two master suites. A few feet beyond the entrance to the bedroom, the hall ended with a door. He opened the door and saw the flight of steps that led to the garages. He was anxious to get to the study but knew he should check out the garages, since the suspect's and victim's cars were not parked in the driveway or on the street.

The light switch at the top of the stairs was in the on position illuminating both the stairway and the garage below. He walked down into a two-car garage, where a green Jeep Cherokee was parked with the license plate "H A MOM".

Each side of the garage had its own door and opening apparatus. He opened the first and walked outside to the driveway. Looking back, he found four garage doors. *What the Hell?* He wondered where those other two doors led?

Looking closer, he could see the other two garage doors weren't doors at all. Now he understood what bothered Detective Sergeant Boyd. Time to head back upstairs.

He rushed through the husband's huge bedroom, not surprised to find this room as masculine in style as the other bedroom, at the far end of the other hall, was feminine.

Clearly the owners didn't share a bedroom. Ed wondered what else they didn't share.

The far end of the bedroom was all floor to ceiling windows, angled out over the driveway. Looking down, he saw two garage doors, one opened and one closed. The room attached on the right, a study, didn't have any windows at all.

The study exuded the vibe of the man of the house. He noticed double locks on the currently open door, the only entrance to the room. Toward the front of the house, a massive oak desk was centered against a solid wall. The walls were paneled with rich dark wood, probably Koa. The flooring was Koa too, although covered almost to the walls with a cheap rug. The bright rug and wooden floor contrasted sharply with the pale wall-to-wall carpeting in all the other rooms.

Why put in an expensive Koa wood floor, then cover it up with a cheap carpet? Ed Jenkin's wanted to know what was under that carpet.

Chapter Twenty-One

Monday, March 18, 8:00 a.m.

Keone Boyd was mad. He glared at his carport before struggling into the worn-out Toyota that he still owned. The Morgan people had no interest in it as a trade in —nobody did.

He turned the key and listened to the ignition crank while the engine on his old beater struggled to start. He didn't appreciate this reminder that his one-time passion was once again years away.

It would be weeks before he'd get that letter Linda mentioned from the Morgan Motor Company and months before he'd get anything from the insurance company. Even the deposit was out of reach until then. How long would it take to get a replacement, three more years?

With a cloud of blue exhaust, the engine finally turned over. When he reached the site of his crash—now mostly cleaned up, he turned left and headed toward Lahaina rather than right toward work. Along the Pali highway Keone envisioned his upcoming visit with an old friend, who ironically spent a lot of time in parking lots, though he'd never owned a car.

~

HIS ANGER OVER HIS LOST DREAM AND HIS CONCERN about Julie Walden's health should be helpful in his planned encounter with Scooter. He'd busted Scooter, whose real name was Manuel Morales, multiple times before he became a detective. They'd grown up together in Makawao. Scooter had always been one fine schmoozer and started dealing *pakalolo* in high school. After school he'd graduated from marijuana to hard drugs. Now he provided *batu* to the moderately well-to-do.

His revived interest in Scooter was the result of a chance encounter with a scrap of paper that bore the words Scooter, batu, and Kahana, scrawled in Dave Walden's handwriting in a storage unit in Kula.

Last night, at the hospital, Julie had regained consciousness after being treated for her wounds. Keone sat by her side watching a bag of blood slowly infuse into her arm. She pointed with a finger bearing a device that monitored her pulse. "I need my purse."

He brought the bag to her from the bedside table, and she removed a ring of keys.

"This one might be helpful, until you can get back in the house." She handed him the ring with one key sticking out. "Dave keeps a lot of his old junk in this unit, including old files from his business. If you can't get into the house for a while, this might be the next best thing."

Keone had stopped by the storage unit on his way home from the hospital. When he unlocked the door, he groaned. It would take a week to go through every piece of paper in the vast collection. He turned to leave but found a torn piece of paper stuck to the bottom of his shoe. *Scooter, Batu, Kahana*

Pakalolo could be obtained many places on Maui when the

weather cooperated. Fields were hidden everywhere in the wilder parts of the island. But batu required processing. Known on the mainland as ice or crystal meth, batu was currently the drug of choice in Hawai'i.

Marijuana could be obtained from people without vehicles or whose vehicles hadn't moved in years, but crystal meth dealers needed wheels. Motorcycles and scooters were popular for those in the business. A great advantage of batu, which meant rock or stone in *Tagalog*, was the small mass and volume of a typical sale.

Young tourists looking to score thought the resident hippie town of Pa'ia was the hotbed for drug sales, but Keone knew the smart sellers were in Lahaina and Kihei—Kihei due to the average age of the population and Lahaina due to the average income. Scooter hung out in Lahaina.

Although most tourists thought of Lahaina as the cute little village along Front Street, it was the largest consensus designated place (CDP) in West Maui. Lahaina included the entire coastal area from the tunnel on Route 30 below Olowalu all the way up to Napili in the north. This was Scooter's domain—or at least every parking lot, large or small, in the region was.

Keone's beater, a rusted Corolla, drew little or no attention as he checked every lot from Kahana north. After a fruitless hour, he extended his search past Napili into the posh environs of Kapalua and finally struck gold. Scooter was holding court in the lot behind the Kapalua General Store. Scooter's chosen ride for the day was a powder blue version of his name.

Keone drove past without slowing down, then swung back along a side road, sliding into the parking lot at just the proper angle to block Scooter's egress.

Scooter still hadn't spotted him when Keone placed a very large, very strong hand on the tiny man's shoulder. "You're slowing down, Scooter. You were much harder to catch in the old days."

Scooter stiffened. Then he must have recognized Keone's voice because he shifted into pure schmoozer mode. "Howzit, mistah defective. To what do I owe this unexpected visit? You didn't get demoted, did you?"

"No, Scoot man. I'm working on bigger stuff than your pitiful shit. But I would like to have a little talk."

"You know I'd love to talk story with you. But time is money in my business. I think I could fit you in next week, Wednesday?"

Keone squeezed hard enough to pinch a nerve.

"Or now. Now would be good Detective Sergeant Boyd, sir."

Still squeezing Scooter's shoulder, Keone guided him to the Corolla, stuffed him in the passenger seat and started driving. "Don't even think about opening that door."

They drove well past Kapalua on the narrow road that circled the north side of the island. Keone didn't say a word until they reached an unmarked path that led down to a hidden location.

Scooter knew this place and what MPD officers occasionally used it for. "We don't need to go down there, Keone. That shit's worse than waterboarding."

"I don't know what you're talking about, Scoot. There's a lovely view of the ocean from that blowhole. You know, very few tourists ever find their way here. We'll have it to ourselves."

"I know the drill. You hold my head facedown over the hole and I hear the roar of the water until it finally bursts out and gags me. Just ask your damn questions."

"Okay. It's simple, really. One name—Dave Walden?"

"Who?"

"Wrong answer." He grabbed Scooter's shoulder again with enormous force and started him down the hill.

"Please, Keone. You and me, we go school to-gedah. That guy's crazy. He kill me."

"And I won't?" Keone asked in his gentlest voice.

"All right. But I don't know much. He's a converter. He gets the powder from important friends on the mainland and cooks it himself."

"Where?"

"He doesn't tell me. I'm small potatoes. Two guys between him and me."

"I need names."

"Shit. You're killing me. If I roll on them, where do I get my stuff?"

"Elsewhere."

"Look. I'll give you the guy next to Walden, but not my direct supplier. You gotta give me that much."

"You know, I was really angry when I came out here. I've had a shitty week. But this lovely scenery must be getting to me. Okay, give me the middle guy. But he'd better check out or we might get to take another pleasant drive together."

"Riley. His name's Riley."

"You know I'm just guessing, but I bet Mr. Riley has a first name."

"Damn it. Okay, Eugene. He goes by Gene, but his real name's Yevgeny or some Slavic shit like that."

"Yevgeny Riley? Really?"

"Okay, Riley's not his real last name. His real last name is Russian or Ukrainian. It's something like Riastokov."

"Riastokov, got it. I won't ask you for the patronymic. You did okay, Scoot. I guess I'll let you walk down to the blowhole alone. Enjoy."

Keone returned to his car, spun a quick U-turn with the Corolla, and headed to Wailuku. In the rearview he saw Scooter's lips moving and feet stamping but didn't really care.

JULIE ACHED INSIDE. NO MATTER HOW THEY ADJUSTED her hospital bed, some portion of her body felt twisted. Her whole life felt twisted. Dave always had a temper but never put her in the hospital before. Had she just convinced herself face slaps and shoves into the wall weren't that bad?

Dave was secretive and often angry at things outside their

home life. But she'd never seen him in an uncontrollable rage before. *Did I ever really know who Dave was—inside?*

A light knock on her door ended her reflections. "Come in."

The first thing to appear around the doorframe was a plush doll version of her character, Hawai'i Anna. The doll's hands held a diminutive bouquet of orchids and baby's breath. She recognized the huge hand holding the doll.

"Do you bring flowers to all the women you rescue from their violent husbands?"

"No. But then I didn't really rescue you, did I? Your husband was gone when I arrived."

"I'm still grateful, Sergeant Boyd."

"Keone." Was this the first time she'd seen him smile?

"*Keone.* I used to know what that meant in Hawaiian."

"It means *sand* or *homeland*, which is pretty much the same for me since I was born on Maui."

"Have you found Dave?"

"No, but we're looking. What he did to you is a crime. You must have guessed that not everything Dave does is legal."

"I knew he had desires I couldn't—wouldn't—satisfy for him. He's had mistresses since we moved to Maui. But we got along. He could get abrupt at times, but most of the time he was charming. He used to make me laugh all the time."

"What about drugs?"

"He would never talk about it, but I knew he used drugs. He did even in Grad school, but then it was mostly pot. Hell, everybody tried pot. He won't tell me what he takes now, but I know he needs it."

"Julie, he doesn't just take drugs. Illegal drugs are his main business."

Julie's entire body began to shake. It took almost a minute before she could control herself enough to speak. "You probably think I should have known, but I didn't. He made friends with so many important people here on Maui and all over the place. He was especially nice to me when we went out. I felt like his prize possession."

"No one should feel like another person's possession. I know the hospital will give you the names of some groups and counsellors that deal with abused women. Please find one you trust and talk with them. I have a sister that volunteers for this one." He handed her a slip of paper. "They can really help."

"Was your sister abused?" Julie asked.

"No, thank God, but her dearest friend was. She didn't get help and... well it didn't end well. Please take what they offer?" Keone's tough cop exterior seemed to melt away as he said this.

"I will. I promise," she said. And meant it.

Chapter Twenty-Two

Tuesday, March 19, 2:00 p.m.

Sam's first two sessions with Dr. Drayton had gone so well he could feel his freedom coming closer. He knew he'd have to work hard at reading and writing and convince them all that he was beginning to accept their definitions of left and right. It was an interesting mental challenge to learn their way without losing track of the real left and right. He had to keep a lot of things straight to make this work but knew he could do it. He continued to maintain his journal in his normal handwriting but needed to keep it hidden in his new location—the Molokini ward. It hadn't taken him long to discover that this was the hospital's psych ward.

Right after lunch, his new nurse, a man named Nestor, helped him into his wheelchair and took him to the first session of a day filled with physical and occupational therapy.

The PT specialist checked Sam's range of motion, pronounced him fit to walk on his own, and began the task of teaching him to rename every movement. *Move your right wrist* became move your left wrist, turn right became turn left, and so forth. This was tedious but not very hard.

He'd spent time yesterday in Occupational Therapy learning to do what for him was mirror math, mirror reading, and mirror writing. He was surprised how difficult it was. He thought the math part would be a piece of cake. Especially since the computer programs were identical to those he'd used at work for years. Rows and columns were still rows and columns. Spreadsheets were still spreadsheets but inverting the order of numbers and columns annoyed him so much that he struggled. The specialist assured him that he would improve over the days to come.

Today they focused on reading backwards.

"You did a great job on the alphabet yesterday, Sam," his therapist said.

"But I sucked at reading words. I know. It was like pulling teeth, having to sound everything out backwards."

"Okay, today we're going to try something a little different, yeah? See this list of short words, they are some of the words most frequently used in English."

"I think some of those aren't even words." Sam shot back.

"Good eye, Sam. Some of them are just syllables. But they are the most frequently used syllables in English. They'll help you recognize inverted words and syllables instead of inverted letters."

After a great deal of repetition, he discovered the therapist was right. Translating words like me (which looked more like em) and but (which looked like tub), reminded him of a game he used to play where he would challenge college friends to read a word or sentence backwards. He'd gotten pretty good at this over the years and guessed he could handle this current challenge as well.

In keeping with the short word focus, the specialist, whose name was Otis Talmadge, told him to call him OT. "Easy to remember. Same abbreviation for my name and my job."

At the end of the session OT gave Sam a long rectangular box with flashcards.

"These are to help you memorize words in addition to

sounds. One thousand flashcards in each box, but I recommend you start with one hundred a day. Okay, Sam?"

"Sure OT. I like a challenge." He planned to learn five hundred mirror words a day. First, he'd write the proper versions of each word on the back, so that first night he might only get through one hundred.

Everything he saw in this new world—magazines, newspapers, even television shows—were an opportunity to practice.

He returned to his room at 6:00 p.m. to find dinner waiting. Although exhausted he began writing on the backs of his flash cards, first in regular cursive and then in mirror cursive. After struggling to write with his preferred left hand, he even tried using his right hand. Sam experimented with a few styles, but finally discovered his best mirror writing resulted from writing backhand with his left hand. Although he wrote more slowly than normal, his penmanship was easier to read.

~

WHEN HE'D FINISHED WITH THE FIRST HUNDRED CARDS, Sam rang the call bell.

"Done with your dinner, Mr. Loftus?"

"Yes, Lisa. I'm so glad I'm off that bland diet I had before. I could even taste the vegetables tonight."

"I'm happy for you. Is there anything else?"

"I'd like to take a little stroll around the ward. The PT specialist told me I'm cleared to walk on my own, but I wanted to make sure you got the word."

"I did when I came on shift. But you need to let me know before you leave each time. And please use the IV pole for balance the first few times, okay?"

"Sure. And I'll stay on this floor, like you showed me when you took me walking."

"That's critical, Sam. Let me know as soon as you get back to your room. And keep it under a half hour this first time, or I'll have to come looking for you."

"Your wish is my command, my lovely angel of mercy."

"Stop that. You know that stuff doesn't work on me."

But it does, Lisa. You're already calling me Sam. This ward's evening nurse was even easier to schmooze than Millie.

He made a complete circuit before taking a brief side trip to the ward's small waiting area. On a previous walk, he'd spied a particularly well-concealed space under the windowsill, behind the curtains, where he could keep his journal and the burner cell phone his lawyer smuggled to him that morning, via Lee Marder.

He waited for the area to empty, stashed the journal, and pushed the phone's quick dial.

Tom Conrad answered on the first ring. "I have good news, Sam. The affidavits from your doctors have been filed with the county court and Maui PD. My discussion with Chief Watanabe confirmed that, if everything's in order, no criminal charges will be issued. The case could be officially closed as early as tomorrow. And because of the neuro/psych angle, your name will not be released to the public."

"That's great. Now I just have to keep up my end of the bargain."

"I know what a pain it is to pretend they're winning. But, if you keep giving them what they want, you'll be out of there before you know it."

"You know, Tom, you might just be right."

3. Investigations

"All this time the Guard was looking at her, first through a telescope, then through a microscope, and then through an opera glass. At last he said, 'you're traveling the wrong way,' and shut up the window and went away."

— Lewis Carroll

Chapter Twenty-Three

Wednesday, March 20, 8:15 a.m.

Keone had just settled down at his desktop to continue his exploration into the nefarious secret life of David Walden when he heard a tap on his cubicle. It was Lindsay Kalani.

"Hi. Linds'. Whatcha got for me?"

"Morning. Two things. First, the LT wants to meet with you at eight-thirty in his office."

"Did he say why?"

"Naw, just passed me on my way in and told me to tell you. There's also a guy here to see you."

"Who?"

"Officer Jenkins from the crime scene team."

"Could you tell him to meet me here? I've got to throw some stuff together if I'm meeting with Tony,"

"Sure. Oh, now that the Loftus case is closed, do you want to check back with Dr. Hasselbach up at the observatory, or should I?"

"No, I'll give him a call and close it out. I'll let you know if you were right about who really made that call about the accident."

~

As soon as Jenkins entered Keone's cubicle, he handed him the crime scene report.

"Mahalo, but you didn't need to hand carry me the actual report. A copy would have been fine."

"I know, Sergeant, but I wanted to share what's not in the report—before I finish it." Jenkins leaned on one foot and then the other. *Why so nervous?*

"Sit down Jenkins." Keone motioned with his hand to the chair next to his desk, then flipped through the report.

Jenkins sat stiffly until Keone looked up. "I see your team found Walden's footprints in the entry. You also showed evidence that he'd left the scene in a hurry in his car, which was parked on the street. Both of those details could help us nail him." He closed the file. "So, what isn't in here?"

"I checked out Walden's study and found a trap door under the cheap rug. The door was metal and had a digital lock on it. I didn't have the tools or time to try to get in."

"Understood. I appreciate the info, but why not put it in the report?"

"There's more. Of course, I could be wrong, but I'm not. I smelled some familiar chemicals coming up from that hidden room. You know a lot of our cases involve drug operations."

"What did you smell?"

"The key components necessary to make crystal meth from unrefined."

"And you think, if you put that in the report, vice will take the case away from us."

"Yep."

"Look, thank you for the heads up, but I don't want you to stick your neck out." Keone handed the file back. "Finish it up.

I've been investigating Walden and know he has drug connections."

"Thanks, Sergeant. I appreciate that."

"What's your first name, Jenkins?"

"Ed, Sergeant."

He stood up offered his right hand. "Keone."

KEONE GLARED AT HIS WATCH. FIFTEEN MINUTES. Alcala must really be pissed off. He had never made him wait more than five minutes before.

Another ten minutes crept by before Alcala's assistant, Karen, ushered him into Alcala's office. She wasn't smiling.

Alcala didn't look up from the reports on his desk. "Take a seat, Sergeant."

Keone stewed another five minutes before Alcala looked up. He knew enough to keep his mouth shut until the lieutenant spoke.

"It is my understanding that the accident investigation is now closed. Is that correct?"

"Yes, sir. I got the notification."

"Can you think of any reason to keep the accident investigation open?"

"No, sir. Sam Loftus is not guilty of any crime associated with the crash."

"You led me to believe that your interactions with..." Alcala looked down at a sheet of paper before continuing, "...Mrs. Julia Walden, were related to that investigation. Is that correct?"

"Yes, sir, they were. But—"

Alcala cut him off. "No buts. Why were you visiting her yesterday?"

Had Kulima followed him to the hospital and ratted him out to Tony?

"She's a material witness in another investigation."

"What investigation would that be?"

"The investigation into the criminal activities of her husband, Mr. David Walden, who nearly beat his wife to death three days ago."

"Why am I unaware of this investigation?"

"Because it was a fortuitous offshoot of the crash investigation. Well fortuitous for us, if not for Walden. I believe Walden is up to his neck in illicit drug operations on this island with connections back to some major players on the mainland."

"Go on."

"I felt his wife might have some relevant information about that." Keone wasn't lying. He just wasn't telling the whole truth. He had developed a certain protectiveness toward Julie. But he could keep his personal and professional interests separate.

"You better have information to justify that statement, Sergeant. You're walking a fine line here. First, simple drug enforcement and domestic violence are outside our focus. Second, Dave Walden has a lot of friends in this department. Third, I've heard how attractive his wife is."

From whom? Kulima? Walker? Someone higher up? Keone hesitated, evaluating his emotions, before looking Tony in the eye. "The only one of those that worries me is the second." He set a folder on the lieutenant's desk with the data he'd accumulated about Dave Walden and his high-roller friends plus the results of his interview with Scooter. He would let Jenkins report speak for itself when it was final.

Alcala read the entire file as Keone sat motionless. The lieutenant said nothing, but his occasional nods gave Keone hope that the information he'd gathered was enough.

"All right You can nail this son of a bitch, but you need to work with the narcs inside the department as well as the DEA. Don't make a single move without their sign off." Alcala scribbled some names and numbers on a sheet of paper and handed it to him along with the file.

"Thank you, Tony."

"Keone, I've known you a long time and respect you as a detective. But you screw this up and I won't be able to protect you."

"I understand."

Alcala fixed his eyes on him. "Do you honestly believe the Walden woman has anything to do with the criminal activity?"

"No, sir."

"Then stay the hell away from her."

"Is there anything else, sir?"

"No. Beat it."

Chapter Twenty-Four

Thursday, March 21, 7:00 a.m.

Martin Hasselbach enticed Brad from the lab with the promise of discussing some new findings from the boson project with him. He felt much more comfortable confronting Brad in his office than in the lab. Still, Brad seemed suspicious.

Once they were seated in the office, Brad spoke before he could. "Is this about the Ma'alaea Harbor event? Radha and I always try to help each other on our projects. He helps me on mine, too."

"Brad, I not only know about that but encourage it, as long as both projects make progress." Martin paused.

"Dr. Hasselbach, I'm really trying on my project, too. I just may have over-extended myself a bit." Martin noticed Brad's hands trembled as he spoke.

"Please call me Martin, Brad. I'm speaking to you more as a friend than a supervisor right now."

"I... I've always felt you had my best interests at heart."

"When did you last get more than a few hours' sleep?"

"Oh, you know, my circadian rhythm is a bit... uh... wonky, sometimes." Brad smiled.

"When?"

"I'm not sure."

"My guess would be that your last adequate sleep was many weeks ago. Am I wrong?"

"No. I've been trying to do my work here at night and work on the Boson event during the day. None of the pieces are fitting together. I, I..." Brad seemed to be struggling to complete his sentences.

This was the opening Martin had hoped for. Keeping his voice calm and reassuring, he said, "It's too much for anyone. That's why I assigned you and Radha to separate projects. Each one is sufficiently challenging. No one could do both even in peak health. And Brad, I can see you're not well."

"Do you want me to take a leave of absence?"

"That's what I recommend." Now for the tricky part. "But I want you to agree to do a bit more."

"What can I do?"

"I received a telephone call a yesterday from a Detective Sergeant from Maui PD. He said a case that I had inquired about was now closed, and he could talk with me or my colleague Dr. Carvell about it."

"I'm sorry. I used your office and phone without permission. I just wanted to talk to the guy who caused the accident. I figured maybe the pulse had affected his driving in some way and caused the accident. But when they told me it was still an open investigation, I let it go."

"But you didn't let the event go, did you? Radha shared the analysis you did with me, and it's not up to your usual standards. There are assumptions and short-cuts throughout. I was about to discipline Radha but recognized your work in the analysis. When I discussed it with him, he admitted he didn't completely understand all of your interpretations."

"I was just so sure this was the proof I needed. You have to admit the event is unusual." Brad's eyes teared up.

"It is, but still possible to explain without invoking a tachyon field. I demonstrated this to Radha, and I would be happy to do the same for you. but first you need to do some things for me."

"I will. I know this project has become too personal for me. An independent review of the data is completely justified."

"I agree. We will carry out that review, while you take care of you. First, you will leave the laboratory for a period of two weeks, starting immediately. During that period, you will work on no project either here, or in your home lab—Yes, I know about that. Finally, I'd like you see an excellent psychiatrist, who was recently recommended to me, and follow his counseling. He and your wife Diane will confirm that you do this. Do you agree?"

"I do," Brad said. "Thank you for this second chance."

"You're welcome." He hardened his voice before adding, "But I don't do third chances."

Chapter Twenty-Five

Monday, March 25, 5:00 p.m.

The wait outside Alcala's office was brief this time, and Karen smiled as she said, "Go on in. He's waiting for you."

Alcala walked around his desk as Keone entered and shook his hand. "Great work on Riastokov. Finding him on the mainland and liaising with those cops in New York to bring him back here was excellent police work."

Scooters tip had paid off. He'd even got the middleman's real name right. Yevgeny Riastokov (aka Gene Riley) worked for the Russian mob out of New York. "It wasn't too hard to convince the NYPD guys, once they discovered they were bringing him to Maui."

"I hate it when you try to be modest. You'll take the compliment and like it. I'm still working to erase Frank's bullshit from your file, and this will help."

He knew enough to keep quiet.

"This testimony you got from Riastokov is golden. What are your next steps?"

"Now that we got Walden's direct contact to roll on him and describe the conversion lab in the house that crime scene guy warned us about, I want to get an evidence team and hazardous waste disposal team in there ASAP. "

"You'll have a warrant by tomorrow morning."

"Walden's wife is set to be released from the hospital tomorrow and could be in danger and not just because of the chemicals used in the conversion process."

"I know. A number of these operations have blown up."

"We need to keep her safe from her husband, too. The more I learn about him, the more I'm worried about her safety."

"Better get the wife to a safe place until our team secures and clears the house."

Keone nodded.

"And what about Walden? We've got that bastard dead to rights. Why haven't we found him? Do you think he left the islands?"

"I sincerely doubt it, but I'd like to float that possibility with his mainland partners. DEA's sending me detailed files on all of them."

"What's the point?"

"I don't want them searching where I'm searching."

"Okay, but you work closely with DEA at every step."

"Will do."

Alcala sat behind his desk for another moment before speaking. "Keone, I know I was hard on you about the Walden woman, but you know it was for your own good."

"I do. And I haven't seen her since I interviewed her at the hospital after the attack." *Technically true.* The other times he'd checked on her were by phone.

"I know. Pissed the shit out of Kulima, too." For the first time in a long time Tony smiled like in the old days.

"Thanks, Boss. I'm glad you've got my back."

"Get outta here and don't make me regret it."

Keone would have someone get the Walden woman out of the

hospital and to a safe place, as Tony suggested. He just wouldn't bother Tony with the details.

Chapter Twenty-Six

Tuesday, March 26, 9:00 a.m.

When Keone entered her hospital room, Julie was sitting in an upholstered armchair writing a note on the over bed table. She looked up and saw him. "Keone Boyd. I haven't seen you for a while. They say I can leave today. I've got so much to do. I need to pack and call Jan to pick me up. I've arranged a place to stay at that women's center you and the hospital recommended." Julie was speaking so fast, Keone struggled to get a word in.

"Whoa. Whoa. Hold on a second. Don't you think your sister has enough on her plate with Sam? Our department would be honored to provide you a lift to the shelter."

"What a kind offer. But I need clothes, cosmetics, an overnight bag..."

"All taken care of. My colleague, Detective Lindsay Kalani, worked it out with your sister. They've put everything together for you from your house. We'll pick your luggage up on your way to the shelter"

"I thought no one could go in our house," Julie said.

"Only selected police personnel, like Lindsay, on a specific mission. But she used her cellphone to allow your sister to pick things out for you without setting foot in the crime scene."

"I appreciate that. I hope your detective wasn't at risk."

Keone smiled. "She knows how to take precautions."

"What about that other danger for me when I finally do go home. You haven't found him yet, have you?" Julie looked hopeful.

"No. But I have some paperwork here that should help with that. The first is the formal assault charge against your husband. You need to sign it."

Julie didn't hesitate. Many abused women find this part the hardest. The counsellor she'd been seeing in the hospital must be making progress.

"I also have a request for a restraining order. An attorney friend of mine put it together."

This time Julie hesitated. "Will I have to appear in court?"

"Probably not. But you will have to give a deposition. You can do that at the shelter."

Julie gazed at the document for a few seconds before her face took on a determined look and she signed.

"Do you think he'll come back?"

"With the charges he's facing? We can arrest him the second he shows his face."

"But he still has a key?"

"We considered that. All your locks have been changed at department expense." A deal with an old friend got this done at a reasonable cost. Since Keone was a member of the department, his statement was technically true.

"What if he's hiding nearby?"

"We'll check out every room in the house and sweep the entire neighborhood before we let you return. I've already asked the officer who patrols your neighborhood to keep a special look out."

"Why are you so concerned about me?"

"First, you're part of my ongoing investigation. Second, your husband has a lot to answer for and not just what he did that night. Finally, Hawai'i Anna told me you were very important to her and made me promise to look after you."

She picked up the doll and looked into her button eyes. "Did you really? You seem to have better taste in men than me, Anna." She made the doll nod its head.

A nurse came in with Julie's release form. "I'll help you get dressed and ready to leave the hospital. I know you're still pretty stiff." Turning to Keone, the nurse said, "You may return in thirty minutes." It wasn't a request.

~

KEONE WANDERED OVER TO ANOTHER PART OF THE hospital to catch an elevator to the psychiatric rehab ward, where Sam Loftus now resided. He'd promised Tony to make this visit, and he kept his promises. Well, most of them.

Sam was sitting up in bed and reading a newspaper when he entered the room. "Aloha, Sergeant Boyd. How are you this lovely day?"

"I'm fine, Mr. Loftus. How are you?"

"A little better each day. I'm starting to enjoy reading the paper. Though it still takes forever to finish, OT says it's great exercise for my addled brain."

"OT?"

"My occupational therapy guy's name is Otis Talmadge. He goes by OT."

"How handy. I stopped by to let you know that the district attorney has agreed to file no criminal charges against you for the accident. You'll still have insurance responsibilities and such, but your record will remain clean."

"That's wonderful. I've heard from my insurance company and instructed them to pay all claims."

Keone didn't want to go there. Time to go. "Aloha, Mr. Loftus."

"Aloha and mahalo, Sergeant Boyd."

As he left, Keone knew his interest in Sam Loftus and his recovery would not end with this visit. He had no illusions that Sam was over Julie. He planned to keep both of her alleged husbands as far away from her as possible. Not to mention keeping away himself—after today. She would be safe in the shelter, and he was sick of Kulima's insinuation that he was taking advantage of a vulnerable woman. She was a witness and a victim, and he was doing his job, damn it. *Would that jerk have made the same baseless claims if she was ugly?*

Chapter Twenty-Seven

When Keone returned to Julie's room, she was dressed and getting into a wheelchair for her ride out of the hospital. He'd used the valet to park his cruiser and went down in the elevator with Julie and her nurse.

He could tell that she was still sore and tired. But he also knew she wanted to get out of the hospital more than anything. Part of this, she'd told him, was because she needed to write and found it difficult in the busy hospital. At the shelter, she would have her own room, with a kitchenette and without constant interruptions.

When he first visited her, right after the beating, she talked about creating a story with Hawai'i Anna being in the hospital for some minor surgery. He'd even arranged for her nurse to take her to the pediatric ward in a wheelchair so she could write character sketches based on some of the kids. Maybe now she could put those to use.

When the valet brought the car around, Keone lifted Julie from the wheelchair into the passenger seat, fastened her seatbelt, and slipped the valet a tip before making his way behind the steering wheel. Before he drove off, he saw movement by the hospital entrance. Frank Kulima was just inside the door, watching them.

He could learn to hate that son of a bitch. But he was surprised by the man's dedication. Was there more to this than jealousy? A new and disturbing thought dawned. Was someone paying Frank to keep an eye on him... or Julie?

As they drove away from the hospital, he glanced over to see that Julie was looking at him. "Once again, you're rescuing me from somewhere I don't want to be. I hope this gets to be a habit."

Keone smiled. *To hell with Frank Kulima.*

"I'm taking you by your house to show you it's okay, and for Lindsay to give you your gear."

"Thank you. I appreciate that. Are you any closer to finding Dave?"

"We're pretty sure he hasn't left the islands, but we're still looking. We also have several leads to track down. The DEA are sending me information about his contacts."

"What exactly is under my house? You need to tell me more than *it smells like chemicals.*"

"I interrogated a drug dealer yesterday. He told me Dave is running a crystal methamphetamine conversion lab. He'd been there once, in the cinderblock cube beneath your house." There was no need to mention Riastokov by name.

"But there's no way in."

"I'm afraid there is. We believe the entrance is hidden in the floor of Dave's study."

"Why don't I just let you fold back the carpet and take a look?"

"I appreciate that. But it has an electronic locking system, and if what I suspect is in that room, I need to have a tight chain of evidence and a Hazmat Team. I've obtained a search warrant, and an evidence-gathering team will search the entire house later today."

"I'm guessing somebody already looked under the rug."

"Yes, one of the crime scene folks, before they left your house on the night of your attack."

"Look, I believe what you're saying about Dave. I had no idea he made or even sold drugs. But I know he used them. As I told you before, all of us experimented with pot in college, but Dave went deeper after we married and moved here. It's one of the reasons our marriage wasn't working. Do you really believe our house isn't safe?"

He might be overstating the danger of the lab blowing up a little, but the danger Dave Walden on the loose represented was real. "After we've assured the safety of your home, Lindsay can bring you back from the shelter to retrieve more things. But I don't think you should live there until we have your husband in custody."

"Could you please stop reminding me that I'm married to criminal? Just call him Dave, okay?"

"All right."

"And why can't you bring me back? Too busy?" Julie was kidding, but he needed to address the real issue.

"Julie, I'm sure you wondered why I stayed away from you after my last visit to the hospital."

"I know you have a day job. But I'm guessing there's more to it from the look on your face."

"Another detective accused me of taking advantage of you and lobbied my lieutenant to take me off the case. The only way I could make sure we nailed Dave was to agree to stop seeing you."

"You really are a good cop, aren't you? No matter how hard you try to hide it. Well, I'll consider forgiving you when this mess is all over."

Julie stared out the window for the rest of the drive to her home in Kula. Keone had been a perfect gentleman in all his interactions with her. If she were completely honest with herself, she'd been a little disappointed. She really liked him and appreciated how much care he was taking with her, but always felt a barrier between them. Now she understood why. A policeman's reputation meant everything.

When they reached her house, Keone pulled behind another police cruiser, and a lovely Hawaiian woman got out and opened the trunk to display multiple pieces of Julie's designer luggage. She was glad a woman had packed her personal items.

Keone got out and opened the door for Julie. "I'm not going in, am I?"

"No, but you are changing cars. Lindsay will drive you to the shelter," Keone said.

"Aren't you being a little too paranoid about that Kulima guy's twisted imagination. I'm a full-grown woman."

Keone made a motion to Detective Kalani, who got back in her cruiser. "I would trust Lindsay with my life, that's why I'm trusting your safety to her. I also want to be here while my colleagues clear your basement. We'll see each other again, soon. But, for now, please let me do my job."

Julie realized she was making this harder for Keone. Police procedure had to come first for this man. "I'm sorry that I shot my mouth off. I trust you, Keone. And I like you."

KEONE WATCHED JULIE GET INTO THE OTHER CRUISER and Lindsay drive her to the shelter. *Why do I feel like I'll never see her again?*

A Hazmat team, an evidence team, and an EMT unit pulled up behind him. He knew they would be equipped with all the necessary safety gear and the tools necessary to gain entry to the secret room under the study. The EMT's were there in case anything went sideways.

Suddenly, Julie Walden's safety dominated Keone's thoughts. What if Kulima followed us here? What if he followed Lindsay now? Keone hadn't warned her to look out for a tail. He had to get himself together, or they could both be in danger.

Scanning the neighborhood, he spotted a third unmarked cruiser. Before Frank could pull out and follow Lindsay, Keone strode over and stood in front of the car.

He'd surprised the other detective, but Frank tried to cover for himself, rolling down his window and waving Keone over. "I heard about your operation here, and thought I'd stop by to see if you needed a hand."

"We've got it covered, Frank. Don't you have some *real detective* work to be doing?"

"Lots of it. Like I said, I just stopped by to—"

"I appreciate your offer, but I'm sure you could be of more value elsewhere. Like *I said*, we've got this covered." Keone had held him long enough to make sure Lindsay was well on her way to the shelter. Only Julie, Lindsay, and Tony knew where they were going.

Frank started his car and drove off, slowly.

Keone took this opportunity to head over to his teams. The first thing he noticed was officer Ed Jenkins putting on protective gear.

"Glad you're here to show them the way. I have keys to the gate and front door. Mind if I accompany you that far without putting on all the gear."

Jenkin's turned to the leader of the Hazmat team. "You okay with that, Jon."

"Sure. But stand a good ten feet back when I unlock the front door."

Keone unlocked the gate and gave the keys to the team leader. The entire Hazmat team, he, and Jenkins started up the walkway toward the front door. Not only did he stand ten feet away from the door when they turned the lock, but Ed Jenkins, in full gear stood directly in front of him. It was a good thing he did.

The explosion created a shock wave that tossed Jenkins and Keone into the air. Jenkins grabbed Keone and rolled, softening his return to earth. Once they thumped onto the ground, he rolled so he was on top, protecting Keone from the debris he knew would pummel them next. A piece of the front door struck Jenkins in the helmet and glass from the window penetrated Keone's suede jacket, piercing his left arm in three places.

Keone tried to help Jenkins back down the hill, but he broke free and went into the burning building to help the Hazmat guys get out. Keone wasn't optimistic about their safety but understood Jenkins's actions. Without protective gear, the only thing he could do was make certain no one else was injured by the blast.

Eldon Miranda and his partner were checking out the evidence team, who'd been waiting at the bottom of the hill for Hazmat to declare the building safe to enter.

"Sergeant, you're bleeding." The other EMT pointed at his arm.

"You again," Eldon Miranda said, staring at Keone.

"Look—" he started.

"I know you're not gonna run back to the hospital and get the care you need. But you've gotta let me remove the glass and stitch up those slices in your arm before I let you go. Your girlfriend and Detective Kalani were lucky they left before this happened."

"Somebody should go and check out Jenkins and the Hazmat guys. I can wait." Keone was worried about his new friend.

"You head on up Tommy, I'll be right behind you," Eldon said, then swiftly stabilized Keone.

A shout from Tommy sent them both running up the hill. Keone saw Jenkins and the two Hazmat guys laying in the bushes at what had recently been the side of the Walden house

Jenkins was talking to the EMTs, "I found them to one side of the entry alcove after the explosion and drug them as far away from the flames as I could."

"You probably saved their lives," Eldon said and began removing the equipment from one of the Hazmat guys, while his partner took care of the other.

Keone removed Jenkins's helmet, which sported a huge dent

from where the front door hit it. This lined up with a huge gash on Jenkins's forehead. Eldon tossed him a compress and Keone pressed it firmly against Jenkins's head before an ambulance team arrived on the scene to take over. Before Keone could leave, Jenkins whispered in his ear, "Suspicious timing, yeah?"

Seeing he could add no further value, Keone returned to his car and glanced back at the crater, engulfed in searing blue flames, that was once the front of Julie's house. Keone noticed that the area where the real and fake garages once stood was completely gone. Ed Jenkins was right about the timing.

He knew the fire trucks arriving at the inferno had their sirens on but could barely hear them over the ringing in his ears. As he drove away, Keone thought back to Eldon calling Julie his girl-friend. Kulima's poison was spreading. But he wondered how safe Julie would be at the shelter. Wouldn't that be the first place Walden would look for her? A new plan started to form in his mind. He called Lindsay over his cellphone.

Chapter Twenty-Eight

Wednesday, March 27, 8:00 a.m.

K eone's first thought when he woke the following morning, *This couch was not made for a six-foot-seven, two hundred-seventy-five-pound man to sleep on.*

The second: *What smells so good?*

He followed his nose into the kitchen to find a table filled with luscious fruits, pancakes, thick bacon, Portuguese sausage, and, of course, Spam.

Julie sat at the table sipping coffee and playing with her plate of fruit. His sister Mahealani sat across from her.

"How did you do this?" He was amazed.

"Don't get your hopes up, Big Guy. Tutu didn't pass on her cooking genes to me, but I can do a basic breakfast." Mahealani punched her brother in his side.

Keone glanced at the clock before taking a seat at the table. He'd slept until eight, very late for him. Not surprising. He didn't leave work until after midnight.

"Did Dave do this?" Julie asked with no preamble.

"Sure looks like it. The timing makes an accident unlikely, but we're still gathering evidence."

"How? I never saw him, and the house has been sealed since he hurt me."

"He must have had it wired for just such a contingency. MPD will spend today canvassing the area, but last night one of the officers canvassing the neighborhood found a man walking his dog, who thought he saw Dave sporting a short beard, dark glasses, and a hoodie within ten minutes of the explosion."

"Sorry about your evidence," Julie said.

"I didn't really need it. But I wanted to make sure that poison never got on the street. Dave took care of that. Remember, I told you I have a witness who's been in the lab."

"How's that evidence guy? The one you thought had a concussion," Mahealani asked, before clearing the table.

"Ed Jenkins? He spent the night in the hospital, but the docs think he should be good to go home tomorrow for one week of recovery. That guy saved my life."

"I'm sorry I caused all this trouble for everyone." Julie looked about to cry. "You should have just taken me straight to the shelter."

"You needed your clothes and... other things. The house was the easiest place to meet."

"I've spent twelve years with Dave controlling every aspect of my life. Always telling me what I should do and punishing me whenever I questioned him. I saw you as the kind of man I'd wished he was. Then, you confirmed it by thinking about me, rather than doing the safe thing. That's why I was there. That's why Dave tried to blow us all up."

"Is that what you think happened?"

"Yes. It's all my fault." She stared off into space.

Keone gently turned Julie's face towards his. "If Dave was interested in killing you, he did a pretty bad job of it, don't you think? You were safely inside the cruiser with Lindsay, miles away, before he triggered the blast."

"I hadn't thought of that. You think he would have blown the lab up whether I was there or not, right?" Julie's eyes were locked on his. An experience he enjoyed.

"He had to. Too much incriminating evidence."

"Why didn't he destroy it earlier?" Julie asked.

"He didn't know for sure that I was suspicious about the lab. He had a lot of valuable material inside but couldn't get to it until we unsealed the crime scene."

"Which you would have done if I moved back in, right?"

"Right. That's why he was keeping an eye on it and you."

"But how did he know when I'd be released?"

"He had somebody watching the hospital. And I think I know who." Keone flinched, which sent a spasm through his left arm and into his back.

"How's your arm?" Julie asked.

"The couch was fine."

"I meant those mean looking things." She pointed to the stitches Eldon had put in last night, which were oozing blood into his T-shirt.

"Must be okay. They don't hurt at all."

"Liar."

Mahealani, must have noticed the stitches, too. She sat down beside him with hydrogen peroxide, swabs, antiseptic, and a fresh dressing. She turned to Julie. "Growing up on the ranch my first aid skills are well honed. Why don't you take a long, hot bath, while I see to this?"

"Great idea. And Keone thanks for taking away some of my guilt. Does anyone need to use the bathroom before I monopolize it."

"You may not have noticed," he said, "but my place has two. The workout room has its own. It was originally a bedroom. I have everything I need in there."

After Julie headed into the bedroom and closed the door, Mahealani said, "Lose the T-shirt, Big Guy."

Keone followed instructions and returned to eating his breakfast.

When they heard the water run in the tub, Mahealani looked uncomfortable. "How long do you expect to keep her in your bachelor pad, *Sergeant*?"

He got the message. "No longer than today. But she needs to stay somewhere safe until we have Dave behind bars."

"Where do you have in mind?"

"I came up with an idea last night. It's part of the reason I had Lindsay ask you to follow her over here when she picked Julie back up from the shelter."

"I just thought you needed a chaperone," Mahealani taunted.

"You're kidding, but I actually did. It's police procedure to have a female present when providing overnight protection for a female victim or witness. Julie is both."

"I'm guessing you've decided the shelter, where I work, isn't safe enough, yeah?"

"It's the first place Walden would look. I want you to keep her up at the ranch."

"Where you can keep an eye on her?"

"Yes. I mean no. Where you and Tutu and our brothers can. And where you can make sure she gets the counselling she needs. Does that counsellor who saw Julie in the hospital make house calls?" Keone knew he was walking another dangerous line but couldn't think of a better way to keep Julie safe from both Dave and prying eyes and ears in the department.

"Well, yeah. She lives in Makawao. But what will you be doing?"

"Catching Walden. And staying as far away from the ranch as possible."

~

While Julie soaked in the tub, Keone called the station and formalized the protective custody assignment for Julie with Tony. He strategically avoided disclosing which safe house he had her in and which officers he'd assigned to keep an eye on the location. He cited the need for absolute secrecy, given Walden's previous close association with the department.

"I understand, Keone, but be very careful. Accusations like Kulima's have a way of spreading through the department," Tony said.

"I will."

"The APB on Dave was extended to all forms of transportation off or between each of the islands, beginning immediately after the explosion. The DEA in Oʻahu is sending you all the relevant files on Dave and his associates, but they haven't arrived yet. I heard you took part of the blast and picked up some shrapnel."

"A CSI named Jenkins protected me from most of it. I just got some glass fragments in one arm. Eldon Miranda removed them and stitched me up. I'm planning to come in, just overslept." Keone's voice reflected his embarrassment.

"Forget it. You're taking today off. That's an order." Tony ended the call before Keone could complain. Keone appreciated the time. He still had work to do here, and his arm really did sting.

Another cellphone rang, Julie's. He picked it up from the table and noticed the caller ID—*Janet*. She must have heard about the explosion.

Keone answered. There was a long pause, so he said. "It's okay Janet, Julie is safe."

"Thank God. I heard on the news... I was praying you'd kept her away from that place."

He hadn't exactly but didn't feel like sharing all his mistakes with her right now. "Julie was miles away when the lab exploded. Now we have her in a safe house. I'm afraid that I can't reveal where, but she will be allowed to call you in a day or two. We have to brief her on how to keep her location a secret."

"From David. I understand. I won't say anything to Sam about what happened either."

Keone was pleased to see evidence that Janet's smarts extended beyond decorating. "How's Sam doing?"

"You know he's surprising me. He's passed all his occupational therapy tests and is studying up a storm to get cleared to return to work. Best of all, Dr. Drayton says he's making good progress toward being sent home."

"I'm pleased for both of you." Keone wished he could shake his continuing suspicion of Sam's recovery. It just seemed too convenient.

"I'll make sure Julie calls you as soon as we can allow it."

"Fine. Keone, thank you for looking after my sister. You're a Godsend."

"We'll keep her safe. Aloha, and good luck with Sam."

"Okay, Godsend, please share a little more about how we're going to keep her safe." Mahealani had finished with the dishes.

"You could hear that? Okay first, I need you to take her shopping."

Chapter Twenty-Nine

Wednesday, March 27, 3:00 p.m.

Shopping with Mahealani in the Shops at Wailea that afternoon was more fun than awkward. Mahealani told her before they arrived that she planned to supplement Julie's wardrobe with attire appropriate for the ranch, and might pick some things up for herself, too.

They were checking out when Mahealani explained that Keone hadn't lived at the ranch since he went off to college. "Our eldest brother, Padraig, inherited the ranch from our parents when they died."

"I'm so sorry. I didn't know you'd lost your parents." Julie felt terrible, but Mahealani just continued talking.

"I was just a baby, but Keone was ten. He remembers them. I can't wait to see you dressed like a lady paniolo. Let's go."

Julie knew the Hawaiian name for cowboys but was thrown by how frequently and quickly Mahealani changed subjects. She could do it too. "Keone told me that you work at the women's center, but what else do you do with your time?"

"Oh, I take classes at UH Maui College and dance at the Old Lahaina Luau."

"You must be good. We always bring visitors to that *luau*." Julie loved it, too.

"We try to be more traditional and help people see what life was like on the islands. There is so much more to our culture than most tourists ever see." The young woman's face took on a more serious expression.

"Tell me about your family."

"I'd rather introduce you to them. Let's go," Lani loaded their shopping into the rear of her Range Rover, then handed Julie a pillow. "You might need this. Keone told me to take the back roads to the ranch."

BY THE TIME THEY REACHED THE RANCH, JULIE WAS not only glad for the pillow but even more for the Land Rover. Even her jeep—before Dave blew it up—would have gotten bogged down a few places on this route. But the amazing views were worth a little discomfort. This was a side of Maui that she had never seen.

"Here we are." Lani pulled through a gate with the name Boyd-Kalama Ranch carved into an arch of dark, veined wood.

"This is beautiful. How could Keone bear to leave all this to become a cop?"

"He still comes up for holidays and barbeques. We're having one of those this weekend."

"I hope he comes. He should have more questions, or answers, for me by then," she said.

"You really like my clunk of a brother, don't you?" Lani looked at her closely.

"From the moment I met him. Wow, that's your house?" she asked.

Like a lot of Hawaiian plantation-style houses, a large veranda surrounded the three-story, main house. Hawaiians called the veranda a *lanai*. Theirs held multiple rocking chairs, two of which were currently occupied. A man even larger than Keone sat in one and a very old woman in another.

After letting Julie out of the passenger side, Lani ran over to the older woman who stood to greet her. They pressed their foreheads together and laid their noses beside each other, before breathing in and out and giving each other a warm kiss on each cheek.

As she followed Lani to the lanai, the larger man walked over to greet Julie.

"Aloha. I'm Julie," she said with a smile.

"*E komo mai. 'O Padraig ko'u inoa.*" He returned her smile.

"You're the oldest Boyd brother, yeah?" she asked.

He nodded.

She noticed that, like his brother, Padraig was a man of few words, but his were mostly Hawaiian. Luckily her limited Hawaiian included those for *welcome* and *my name is*. "Thank you for putting me up here. Or should I say putting up with me here?"

He switched to fluent English. "We have plenty of bedrooms and plenty of work to do. How do you feel about that?"

"I grew up on a pig farm. I'm used to hard work." Julie refused to be intimidated.

This time his smile was large and as welcoming as his words.

The old woman said something to him in Hawaiian that Julie didn't understand.

"Tutu said I talk too much. Time for dinner." He opened the door and indicated Julie should go inside.

"Oh my God," she said, as she took in the feast laid out on the dining room table.

"We eat a lot," Lani said. "But you gotta be fast."

Chapter Thirty

Thursday, March 28, 7:30 a.m.

Keone was happy to be back in his own bed. After the women left to go shopping yesterday, he'd changed the sheets, done a load of washing, and stowed the cot he had made up for Mahealani. He was pleased with how well Julie took the decision to move her to the ranch. There was no way Walden would look for her there. And if Julie's husband happened to blunder onto the ranch, he'd make sure his brothers knew exactly what to do. He hoped for Walden's sake that he didn't test that.

Anxious to begin his workday, Keone washed, dressed, and slipped out of the condo grabbing a bunch of bananas on the way out for breakfast.

~

THE IN-BOX ON KEONE'S DESK CONTAINED CALL requests from some of the high rollers who had previously ignored him. He guessed reports of the explosion at Walden's house caught somebody's attention.

The remainder of his desk was covered with files on Dave and all his contacts from the DEA, FBI, and Interpol. Now he understood why it took so long. His contact at DEA, Agent Freeman, was doing a comprehensive job.

He was pleased to note, from the report sitting separately on his chair, that the evidence team had completed their work. They identified the site of the explosion as the cinderblock, secret room. That was no surprise. But how they managed to discover evidence that the explosion was intentionally triggered and not the result of unstable chemicals or improper storage conditions was beyond him. They suspected the explosion was triggered remotely from outside the house. They also suspected that the bomber had visual sighting on the house given the timing of the blast just prior to their planned entry.

Interviews with more neighbors provided the most important additional evidence in Keone's opinion. Three neighbors, from two different homes, identified Walden only a block away from the explosion with a small device that "looked like a garage door opener" in his hand, just moments before the explosion.

That son of a bitch could have killed me.

He first concentrated on Walden's file from the DEA. Keone discovered he'd been right all along. Walden had been close to prosecution multiple times but was as slippery as an eel. He couldn't wait to dive into the files on the men the DEA suspected were Dave's suppliers and bosses. He recognized some names from the list of high rollers he'd gotten from the Ka'anapali Golf Course.

The phone on Keone's desk rang. "Maui Police Department, Criminal Investigation Division, this is Detective Sergeant Boyd. How may I help you?"

"Morning, Sergeant. This is Agent Freeman with the DEA, O'ahu office. I just wanted to make sure you received the files I sent over."

"Morning, Agent Freeman. And mahalo. This stuff is great. I'm glad you waited and sent the FBI and Interpol files along with the stuff from your guys. David Walden has quite a history."

"We've nailed a number of his middlemen but could never make anything stick on Walden or prove a direct link to his bosses,"

"I just looked over the lab report from the Walden home. There is absolutely no doubt that he was running a meth conversion lab in his secret room. The physical evidence along with the testimony of one of his highest middlemen, Riastokov aka Riley, provides enough to send him up for a long time."

"I've seen Riastokov's testimony. Would you send me a copy of the lab report?"

"My LT is having them copy you on everything they send to me." He continued to review the files as he talked to Freeman. "From your reports and those from Interpol and the FBI, it's clear some of his good friends, who sponsored the police charity golf tournament, were the next level up in his organizational chart. They're all very anxious to talk with me—now. You don't suppose they might want to know where to find good old Dave, too, do you?"

The agent hesitated a moment before commenting. "Sergeant, this could be the chance we've been waiting for. Walden is hiding out from you, but he's even more afraid that his bosses will locate him. We would be extremely grateful for any information you have or might obtain about his whereabouts. If you talk to any of his bosses, be very careful."

"Agent Freeman, I would love to find this guy for you. We're currently scouring Maui and know he hasn't left the state. I think he might be hiding out on another island or in the wilderness areas of the West Maui Mountains. Give me a couple days to follow up on some leads. If I get anything hopeful, I'll call. You're in Honolulu, yeah?"

"Yes. I can be there in less than an hour, by chopper. I'll look forward to your call."

Based on his review of the files, Keone selected a high roller to call. A guy named Pavin, headquartered in New York City, had ties to all the others on his list. Before he could pick up the phone though, Lieutenant Alcala stopped by for an update. Keone wished he'd waited a half-hour more, but he wasn't about to complain.

"What have you got on the explosion, Keone?"

"I just read the full report from the evidence team and the lab. Here's a copy for you."

"Bottom line?"

"The explosion was set off remotely and we have Walden a block away with a remote in his hand."

"How many witnesses?"

"Three, from two different houses."

"Good. What else?"

Keone spread his arms to indicate all the files on his desk. "DEA, FBI, and Interpol files on Walden and his golf buddies. He's in this up to his neck and we've got him cold. I just talked to Agent Freeman at DEA. He'd like to be in on the collar."

"Make sure that happens. Did he suggest anything else?"

"No, but he agreed with my plan to reply to at least one of these calls from the bosses. I plan to send them on the wild goose chase we discussed earlier to keep them from finding Walden first."

"How many are you planning to call?"

"Just one. There's a guy named Victor Pavin with ties to both Walden and Riastokov. He's very high up in the New York chapter of the Russian mob. I think he's the guy to spread the word."

"Good work, Keone. I'm glad Mrs. Walden wasn't there when her house went up. Good idea sending her to a shelter."

"Just doing my job."

"Why didn't you tell me you would be taking her to Lindsay

from the hospital? I'm not Kulima. And that wasn't crossing any lines. I know you need to keep her safe from Walden, and she still might know something that could help us find him." Tony's stare was unflinching.

"With all of Walden's connections in the department, I picked Lindsay, because I knew I could trust her. When I saw Frank Kulima at the hospital, I suspected I was right to be worried. I thought you told him to stop following me."

"I did and will again, but don't change the subject."

"I don't think Walden blowing up the lab had anything to do with us making the transfer to Lindsay there. But I did think he might be staking out the place when she came home, hoping to get inside after we unsealed the scene. The explosion intervened. I hadn't counted on that."

Keone, you can't always predict what a guy like Walden might do. He's so scared now, he could do anything. The move to the safe house from the shelter was a good call."

"Thank you."

"Just make sure you stay as far away from Julia Walden as possible. If you have specific questions to ask her that might help us find her husband, make sure a female officer is present at the safe house."

"I will," Keone replied. His sister didn't qualify as a female officer, but he hadn't asked Julie about the case after Lindsay left.

Keone entered the area code and number for Big Apple Expeditors.

"Can I speak to Mr. Pavin, please? This is Sergeant Boyd from the Maui Police Department returning his call." The wait was short.

"Sergeant Boyd? This is Vic Pavin. Did I meet you when I was out there playing in your charity golf tournament?" Pavin was Mr. Congeniality so far.

"No. I'm afraid I don't play golf."

"Too bad. It's a great game and those courses on Maui are to die for."

Keone waited.

"Uh, I heard you tried to contact me the other day. I'm sorry I missed your call. Called back on Friday, but you must have been out."

"Yes. I was dealing with an emergency."

"Really. I hope no one was hurt."

"Not seriously, but a structure was destroyed."

"I'm sorry to hear that."

"The structure belonged to a friend of yours, I believe—David Walden."

Now it was Pavin's turn to pause.

"You do know Mr. Walden, don't you, the Volunteer Chairman of that charity tournament you mentioned?"

"Oh sure. He's a nice guy. Is he okay?"

"I don't know. He wasn't in his home at the time of the explosion, and now he seems to be hiding from us. Do you know any reason why Mr. Walden might do that?"

"Hide from the police? No. I thought he was a big supporter of law enforcement, like my colleagues and me. Do you have any idea where he might be?"

The question I was waiting for.

"Mr. Pavin, I was hoping you might know the answer to that. He doesn't happen to be in New York, does he?"

"Why would he be here?"

Answered a question with a question. He's been interrogated before.

"I was hoping you could tell me?"

"What is this? Am I under suspicion for something? Who do think you're talking to, anyway? Do you know who I am?"

"I do now."

"What's that supposed to mean? I'm a well-respected businessman."

"Oh, I'm sure you are. Don't take my questions the wrong way. I just thought he had clients there, such as yourself."

"I am not Walden's client. I just know him from the tournament."

"I see."

"Yeah, well, nice talking with you, Sergeant. Sorry I couldn't be more help."

"You've been a great help. Thank you for your time. Aloha."

The call accomplished exactly what he intended. Pavin would tell his colleagues the hick Maui PD hadn't found Walden and thought he might be on the mainland. They would run around in circles trying to find him there, providing Keone enough time to find him in the islands, without any interference. He sent an email to Agent Freeman with a transcript from the call.

Now, he had only one mystery to solve. *Where the hell was Dave Walden?*

Chapter Thirty-One

Friday, March 29, 12:00 p.m.

The sound of a familiar voice pulled Julie's attention away from the stove. "Are you enjoying yourself?"

"Absolutely, Detective Boyd," she replied. "You have a great family and Lani is a gem. I was hoping you'd show up at this little shindig,"

"I never miss a family barbeque. But finding you here in the kitchen gives me pause."

"Don't worry. I didn't cook. Mahealani is just having me stir a few things while she checks on your brothers and the status of the meat. Hi, Lindsay, what brings you here?" Julie just noticed Keone was not alone. *Do I have competition?*

"Our lieutenant's condition for Keone coming was that I be present whenever the Big Guy questions you. Sorry. I think everyone is overreacting to Frank's lurid mind." Lindsay's face reddened slightly.

"Oh, I don't know. This big kanaka has a few positive traits," Julie said with a grin.

"I'm standing right here," Keone said.

"Well don't be. Go out and check on the meat with your sister. Lindsay and I need to talk," Julie pulled the young detective to her side and made a shewing motion with her hands at Keone.

Once Keone left, Julie asked Lindsay, "How's the investigation going? Any closer to catching Dave?"

"It's Keone's case, you should really ask him." Lindsay looked uncomfortable.

"I don't need details. I just need to know if he still needs help. I've been racking my brain trying to think of anything I know about Dave that could help." Julie had even reviewed photos on her cellphone looking for anything that might provide a clue.

"The answer's yes. He has all the evidence he needs to convict your husband, three times over, but we just can't find him anywhere. Keone's frustrated with himself. He knows this island better than anyone. He's looked places other people couldn't even get to. But no Dave. He really could use your help. But he wants you to enjoy the barbeque first, so wait for him to ask, yeah?"

"I will," Julie said. "I'll stick to questions about his family until he brings Dave up." Julie knew how to listen.

Sitting on a tatami mat with Julie on one side and Lindsay on the other, Keone watched his brothers carry huge sides of beef on spit after spit past clapping barbeque guests.

When the applause died down, Julie leaned over to him. "I hear you went to college in California."

He wasn't overjoyed that his family was sharing personal information about him with Julie, but the ranch was still the safest place for her. "I studied in the Department of Criminology, Law, and Society in the School of Social Ecology at UC Irvine."

"How did the guys on the Maui PD deal with a college boy?"

"Well, I didn't come right back home. I graduated in 2002 and took a job with the Santa Ana Police Department. I speak

Portuguese and Spanish and that helped me with the Hispanic population. When I transferred to the LAPD in 2004, I took a Masters in CLS online from Irvine. That and my performance helped me become a detective in 2008."

"Wow. I've never heard you say so many words at one time," Lindsay said.

"She asked. Anyway, a job opened up on Maui a little while after my promotion, so I came back home. They don't accept lateral transfers from mainland police forces, so I had to spend my first year in the outside districts before they rotated me through Lahaina, Kihei, and eventually Wailuku. I became a detective sergeant last year, focused on major crimes in the Criminal Investigation Division."

Lani rushed over to them, pulled Lindsay to her feet, and led them over to the massive array of delicacies spread across multiple picnic tables. Complementing the various cuts of barbequed beef —including ribs, brisket, steaks, and five varieties of homemade sausages—were plates and bowls heaped with every imaginable Hawaiian seafood, vegetable, and salad dish, from grilled Maui onions, baked beans, and poi to *lomi lomi* salmon and six varieties of poke. "Lindsay, around here you snooze, you lose."

"I can verify that after just a couple days," Julie added.

Keone noticed Julie heaped almost as much food on her long wooden trough plate as he did. He appreciated a woman that appreciated eating good food.

Sitting cross-legged around their knee-high table, Julie tried to continue the conversation from earlier. "So, a new detective sergeant, trained on the mainland. How did that go over with your fellow officers?"

"I felt a little friction from a few old-timers, but a lot of the younger guys knew me, or somebody from my family, which made me easier to accept. I picked up some street smarts from Santa Ana and LA, which helped the older guys trust me."

"You are exceptionally easy to trust. I'm glad you sent me to the ranch. I needed this. The counselor and Mahealani have been great, and your brothers have let me do some chores around the place."

Music interrupted their conversation, so they focused on eating and watching every male and female member of the family take turns doing *hula*. Looking a little embarrassed, Keone joined in. When he motioned for Julie to join him, she didn't hesitate, bringing a big smile to Mahealani's and Lindsay's faces and applause and shouts from the rest of the family.

After everyone was completely stuffed and nearly exhausted, Julie helped clear the tables with the other women in the family. They all made her feel welcome and shared more gossip about Keone in the kitchen.

She learned Keone's parents both served in the Coast Guard Medical Service. Keone's father, Patrick Angus Boyd, was a doctor and his mother, Malia Hokulani Kalama, was a nurse. They both died in an accident of some kind when Keone was just ten. They were in the inactive reserve by that time and had inherited the ranch.

When she finished cleaning up, Julie wandered onto the lanai to find Tutu sitting in a rocking chair playing the ukulele. The song she played was gentle and soft like the breeze that ruffled her pure white hair. Julie quietly occupied a rocking chair next to Tutu and rocked to the tempo of her song.

Keone climbed the stairs and kissed his grandmother on the cheek. Julie had learned from Lani that Tutu's birth name was Leilani Ululani Kanahele. Julie knew *leilani* meant heavenly flower and Lani told her *ululani* meant divine inspiration. The names certainly suited this spiritual woman.

When Tutu finished her song, Keone smiled at her. Then Keone spoke in Hawaiian until Tutu rose, grabbed both of Julie's hands, and leaned toward her. She pressed her forehead against Julie's forehead, her nose against Julie's nose, and inhaled her fragrance. Julie did the same in return. Then Tutu leaned back and smiled. Without a word, she placed Julie's left hand in

Keone's and squeezed them together. "Aloha," was all she said, before disappearing into the house.

After a few moments, Keone let go of Julie's hand, picked up the ukulele the woman left behind, and sat in the chair she'd vacated. He didn't sing, but his fingers brought a song from the ukulele that went right to Julie's heart. "Tutu asked me to play this for you. She likes you."

"I love that sweet woman. Your grandmother gave me the *honi* just now. I know what it's called, but I don't know exactly what it means," she said.

Keone kept playing as he said, "The honi is a mana exchange, a sharing of essences. When you touch foreheads, you touch *alo* to *alo* or bone to bone. But it's more than that. I won't get too technical, but Hawaiians believe in a third eye, an intuitive center, and when you touch in this way you are reading each other's intentions. The breathing when your noses touch is a sharing too. A sharing of the *ha,* the breath of God. Honi is an honor. Tutu acknowledged her respect for the mana you carry."

Tears flowed down Julie's face.

~

By the time Keone finished his song, Julie had stopped crying and Lindsay had joined them on the lanai. He knew it was time to ask and answer questions about the case.

"Julie, I need your help. I'm certain Dave is not on Maui or O'ahu. Police in Kaua'i have also come up empty. There's absolutely no way Dave could have hidden himself on Ni'ihau. Only Hawaiians are allowed there and a *haole* like Dave would be spotted and ejected in less than twenty-four hours. That leaves Moloka'i, Lana'i, and the Big Island."

"I lived with the bastard for twelve years. I must know something, but I haven't come up with anything on my own. Maybe together we can do better. Ask away."

"Okay. Is there any place I wouldn't know about where he

might go? I've checked every piece of real estate he owns, every friend or employee he has, and every contact of his in the islands."

"You're sure he's in the islands?"

"Yes."

"And you've narrowed it down to Moloka'i, Lana'i, and the Big Island?"

"Yes."

"You can forget the Big Island. With his asthma he avoids that place like the plague. He can't tolerate *vog*."

The volcanic version of smog prevalent in the vicinity of Kilauea's continuing eruptions caused problems for anyone with respiratory issues. "What about Lana'i or Moloka'i?"

"There's something about Moloka'i. What is it? It was right after we moved here. I wish I could remember."

Now Lindsay spoke up. "Just relax. Close your eyes and take a deep breath."

Julie did as she was told.

"Did you visit there for some reason?" Lindsay asked.

"Yes. But not as tourists. He needed to check something out. Some property. That's it." Julie opened her eyes. "Dave said a client of his wanted to pay him with some undeveloped land on Moloka'i. We went and checked it out. Undeveloped was an understatement. It was just jungle. We had to drive for miles down dirt paths to get close enough to see it from the top of a cliff."

"Why didn't it show up on his real estate records?" Keone asked.

"He put it in his uncle's name for tax reasons. He said they might come over and hunt sometime. What a load of crap. His uncle could barely walk by then. The only building we could see was a tumbled-down shack. I doubt if it's still standing."

But what if it was?

The ferry left from Lahaina for Moloka'i at 7:15 a.m. tomorrow, and he'd be on it.

Chapter Thirty-Two

Saturday, March 30, 7:30 a.m.

Julie sat on the porch that surrounded the Boyd-Kalama main house and watched the bustle of activity around her. She could see running a ranch was a lot of work, even in paradise. But the people working there were doing what they wanted with their lives. Maybe it was time for her to do the same.

Keone's oldest brother climbed the steps and sat his massive frame down in the rocker next to hers. He didn't say anything. She suspected she'd need to speak first.

"Aloha, Padraig. You're in charge of the ranch, yeah?"

"Yeah." He untied the scarf around his neck and wiped the sweat from his face.

"How long?" She could use fewer words, too.

"From when Mama and Daddy died 'til I hit twenty-one, Uncle Kimo ran it for me. Taught me. Since then, me." Padraig looked at his muddy boots.

"He's the Uncle Kimo that Keone's going to see on Molokai, yeah?"

"Yeah."

"Think he can help?" Julie didn't want to finish the sentence with *find my husband.*

"Can? Yeah. Will? That's up to Keone." He looked up from his boots.

"Why?"

"Kimo hates authority, especially the feds. Wants to restore the legal government to these islands."

"Do you?" Julie knew she was on fragile ground here.

"Families fought for the U.S.A. in every war. Can't go back. But gotta remember." Padraig stood up. "Nice talkin with ya. Got some cattle to move."

Padraig walked to an ATV and gunned the engine. Julie realized she still had much to learn about the Boyd and Kalama families.

THE NICKNAME VOMIT COMET WAS BESTOWED BY numerous tourists upon the Ferryboat that ran between Lahaina Harbor, Maui, and Kaunakakai Harbor, Moloka'i. For Keone, the trip through the Kalohi Channel was a thrilling Hawaiian roller coaster ride. Known for strong winds and choppy seas, the ferry took this channel because it was smooth compared to the rougher Pailolo Channel, which lies between Maui and Moloka'i. *Pailolo* in Hawaiian means "crazy fisherman," referring to any fisherman who would be crazy enough to try to navigate that channel. The only time Keone suffered from seasickness was when one of his friends got their fishing boat too close to the Pailolo Channel.

Once ashore in Kaunakakai, he picked up the rental car he'd reserved and drove two hours to his favorite spot on the island, Uncle Kimo's. Hawaiians often refer to any older male as Uncle, but Kimo was Keone's actual uncle, his mother's brother. Kimo Kalama left Maui ten years ago because, he said, "It got *too.* Too many, too much, too fast, too loud, and too haole."

Climbing the front steps, Keone saw the lovely hand-carved plaque above Kimo's front door that expressed his philosophy succinctly. "*E Komo Mai o Moloka'i*. Now go the hell home." Uncle Kimo treated people of all backgrounds equally, so long as they stayed off his island. There were many like Kimo on Moloka'i. The dichotomy was that tourism brought necessary income to the island. Kimo accepted this only so much.

Keone wiped his shoes on Kimo's front doormat before removing them and peered through the tattered screen door. "Aloha. You deah, Uncle?"

"Keone? Why you no tell me you come?"

"Let's see. You got no phone, no mailbox, and hate visitors."

"Ah, you no visitor, you family. Get inside."

He needed Kimo's help with his search for Dave Walden, but he knew better than to ask. Things were done a certain way with his uncle.

"How you family on that haole island ovah deah?"

"Everyone is fine. We had a big luau yesterday and everybody came to the ranch."

After a half-hour drinking the paint-remover Kimo called coffee and catching up on family activities, Kimo asked the two questions that allowed Keone to request his help. "Why you here? How I help you?"

There was absolutely nothing that happened on Moloka'i that Kimo didn't know about. His work with a group dedicated to the restoration of the legal Hawaiian government and his status as *Ali'i* gave him a position of great importance on this island. From this point on, Keone would speak in Hawaiian in deference to Kimo Kalama's position in the family and on the island.

"Do you know about a haole hiding in the backcountry?"

"He's been here a few times before. Checking out a decrepit shack that he says belongs to his uncle. Name's Walden, yeah"

"Is he there now, Kimo"

"He was yesterday and so strung out on batu that I don't think he was going anywhere."

"Can you take me there?"

"I could show you where the shack is, but it's very hard to get to. First you need to tell me why you want to see him."

"Dave Walden is a con man and drug dealer, who's taking money from Hawaiians and sending it off-island. He beats his wife savagely and almost killed me."

"And?"

Keone couldn't fool his uncle. "And I care about her. I took her up to the ranch to keep her safe."

"Let's go. I'll show you where to find him."

"There is one other thing. I need to call in another guy to help me with the arrest."

"Other guy Hawaiian?"

"I doubt it. But he lives on O'ahu."

Kimo switched out of Hawaiian. "Hell. You call that damn place Hawaiian?"

Keone decided to say no more. He certainly wasn't going to mention that his 'friend' was a federal agent.

"I don't needa talk ta him, yeah?"

"No, just point us to the place where Dave's hiding out, then you can take off. We'll take it from there."

"Okay. Call dat S.O.B."

Keone stepped outside to call Agent Freeman while Uncle Kimo gathered up a few items and put them in his battered jeep.

The agent picked up after the second ring. "Freeman."

"Hello, this is Boyd, from Maui, about Dave Walden."

"Yes, Sergeant, what have you got?"

"I believe Walden is hiding out on an undeveloped plot of land on Moloka'i."

"I can be there in forty-five minutes."

"Great. It will take us a little longer. Let's meet at the Moloka'i Airport at 2:00 p.m. There's just one thing. What's your first name?"

"Tom."

"Mine's Keone. The local who is taking us to Walden needs to think you're just a friend of mine. You can't mention your affiliation."

"I'll have to identify myself to Walden when we take him."

"That's fine. Uncle Kimo will be long gone by then."

"You wouldn't be talking about Kimo Kalama, would you?"

"You haven't met, have you?"

"No. No. It's just that name comes up a lot here in the Federal Building in Honolulu. I bet you want me to avoid talking directly to him, right?"

"Right. I owe you one."

"I'll find a way to collect sometime."

Chapter Thirty-Three

Keone and Kimo took different vehicles to the little airport on Moloka'i. Tom Freeman's unmarked helicopter arrived just as they did. Keone went out to meet Tom and reinforced the need to maintain the façade that they were old friends. Tom played along perfectly, giving Keone a bear hug and keeping his arm around Keone's shoulder as they walked back to the cars.

Before they got into the rental, Keone waved an arm towards the beat up, mud-encrusted Nissan pick-up and said, "That's my uncle. He'll lead the way."

This was the only acknowledgement that Uncle Kimo was even there. Kimo stared straight ahead at the helicopter. Once he and Tom were in their seats and the engine was running, they saw Kimo tear out of the little parking lot, daring them to keep up.

"Can you tell me a little more about how you found Walden?" Freeman asked.

"His wife, Julie, remembered some property he bought in his maternal uncle's name. That's why it didn't show up in your searches or ours. She didn't know its location, except that it was on Moloka'i. My Uncle Kimo knows everything that goes on here but can only be reached in person. Until he confirmed that

Walden was here and that he knew where, I had nothing solid. That's when I called you."

"Got it. This is your collar for the abuse and arson, but I'll need to charge him with the conversion and distribution to justify our use of the helicopter to extract him."

"I understand. He's probably going to be pretty strung out. Kimo thinks he brought a lot of product with him. We might have to take him directly to Maui Memorial."

"Let's not get ahead of ourselves. Could he be armed?"

"We need to assume he is, but my instincts tell me he isn't. This guy's a schmoozer and beats up women. I bet we'll either have to wake him or scrape him off the walls of the shack to arrest him."

After an hour of spine-cracking travel bouncing down dirt tracks, Kimo pulled over and got out of his car. Keone stopped right behind and got out. Freeman trailed him by a good ten steps. He was developing a strong respect for the agent. This guy knew his stuff.

"Okay, Keone. Down deah." Kimo pointed down a steep cliff to a level area overgrown with every type of Hawaiian flora, dominated by three trees.

"Dat shack's between da two Kiawe and dat Monkeypod. You see?"

At first Keone didn't but, focusing his gaze, could just make out about one board width of the cabin through the trees.

Kimo reached into the bed of his truck and pulled out some climbing gear and two machetes in sheaths. "You gonna need deese."

"*Mahalo nui loa*, Uncle. I owe you."

"I know. Aloha." His farewell did not include Agent Freeman.

He was in his pick-up and out of sight before Freeman approached Keone.

"Thanks for humoring Kimo."

"No problem. Now where's this cabin."

"See the two kiawe at about ten o'clock?"

Freeman pulled binoculars from his backpack and looked through them now. "I would never have spotted that piece of the cabin with my naked eyes. You guys are good."

"We're Hawaiian."

"Do you think your uncle made me as DEA?"

"Maybe. The fact that you're a haole and probably in law enforcement was enough for him to ignore you. The fact he still brought us here just means he loves me more than he hates you."

"Nice." Freeman slipped the large backpack off his shoulders. "I've got rope and climbing gloves in my pack. We better get started. I'll call my pilot and give him the coordinates for that open area about three hundred yards from the cabin. No way we'll have reception down there." Freeman pointed down the sheer cliff-face.

Keone checked his watch. "I don't want to spook Walden. Our journey will take a hell of a lot longer than your pilot's. It's three p.m. now. Tell him to pick us up in two hours. If we're not there by then, we're screwed."

~

"Jan, I had to call you and see how it's going with Sam. Don't tell anyone, okay?"

"You can trust me, kid. You know that." Janet couldn't hide her joy at hearing her sister's voice. "I won't ask where you are, but Keone has kept me posted since the explosion. I know he's moved you at least once and that he thinks you are in very good hands."

"That is truer than you can imagine. He's off trying to catch Dave right now. If he does, things will change immediately." Julie's voice had a strength in it that was new.

"I'll pray for that. I've already contacted a lawyer friend to help you file for divorce. If that's what you want to do, that is."

"You know it is. But let's talk about you. How long until Sam comes home?"

"Dr. Drayton is talking about mid-April. Sam spends a lot of time in various therapy sessions, but I visit him during dinner. He can go to the cafeteria now, so we eat there. The conversation has been pleasant, if a little stiff. It's better than when he wouldn't let me visit, though."

"That's good, yeah?"

"Yeah. Dr. Drayton said to keep my expectations low at first. So far, Sam is putting in the effort and beginning to relax a little. He's excited about taking driving lessons."

"So soon?" Julie's surprise was evident.

"His Occupational Therapy guy, OT, did some driver's training with him and thinks he's ready for some laps around the parking lot."

"I'm sure you both miss work. I certainly missed writing when I was in the hospital. It's easier where I am now."

"Julie, I know this has been hard for you, too." Janet's throat tightened. She was running out of things to say.

"I'll think good thoughts, Jan. Can't wait until we can get together, in person, and talk all of this out over a nice Cabernet. Love you."

"Love you, too. Aloha."

A THIRTY-MINUTE DESCENT DOWN THE SHEER CLIFF face, punctuated at multiple points by razor-sharp, horizontal projections, left them far above the floor of the depression. Keone was an expert rock-climber and Freeman was handling himself pretty well until he unknowingly caught his line over one of the projections.

Before Keone could warn him to ease off, the edge wore through the rope and Freeman started to plummet. Keone braced himself for what was to come. He'd clipped an extra safety line onto Freeman's carabineer. When Freeman's descent halted with a jerk, Keone watched the agent look around for some explanation of his miraculous reprieve from death. When Freeman's eyes landed on Keone bracing against the cliff face with all his might, Keone saw him smile and shake his head.

"When did you hook that on?" Freeman yelled up to Keone.

"At the top."

"What if you'd fallen? Wouldn't that have taken me with you?"

"I didn't plan on falling."

Freeman scrambled back up to the ledge below Keone and then held the line taut so Keone could join him.

As they rested, Keone replaced Freeman's frayed rope line with a stronger, nylon span, like he'd used on the safety, and tested it.

"Okay, now that you've saved my ass, I think it's time we went from Agent Freeman and Sergeant Boyd to Tom and Keone, for real."

"Well, I was gonna wait until you saved my ass, but this works. Let's get going."

Keone let Tom lead the rest of the descent. They reached the bottom safely but tired. Keone handed Tom a plastic water bottle. The cabin was less than a mile away, but their path would be through dense tropical growth. He pulled his machete out of its sheath and began hacking the way forward.

"Tom, how do you suppose he got in here? He's no rock climber and Uncle Kimo told me there was no easier trail in."

"Chopper. I'm sure he has an on-island contact who could fly him in here and pick him up whenever things cooled down."

"You're probably right. That's probably the explanation for that cleared area we spotted. I doubt he used a licensed charter, though.

"Nah, but there are a lot of pakalolo farmers over here who need to get their goods to market. We call it the pakalolo *air force*." The DEA man sounded like he knew this from experience.

From this point, they continued through the brush deliberately but as quietly as possible.

Chapter Thirty-Four

Keone and Tom had hacked their way across three-quarters of the depression that held Dave Walden's cabin before they were able to sheath their machetes. They eased their way through low scrub until they were within one hundred yards of the cabin.

Keone held up a hand. "We should separate," he whispered.

"If you want to take the front, I'll take the back? I doubt there's a back door, but I'm sure I can find a window or something to enter through," Tom replied.

"Works for me. When you hear me kick in the front door, come in through the back."

Two, near-simultaneous crashes roused Walden to his knees. But he was in no condition to resist arrest.

Shaking violently in the corner, Dave slowly rolled his eyes towards Keone. "Boyd? Damn, you're good. I didn't think anybody could find me out here. Who's your friend?"

Tom showed him his badge.

"Shit. I'm screwed," Dave mumbled.

"Just be glad it's us and not Pavin and his friends," Keone replied.

"Please tell me you didn't talk to Pavin."

Keone hauled Dave to his feet, put on the cuffs, and shoved him over to Tom. "I sent him on a wild goose chase to give us time to find you. This gentleman will read you your rights and tell you a few of the things we're arresting you for. Personally, I'm arresting you for spousal abuse and arson."

"I wasn't trying to hurt Julie—"

"Stop. Not another word until he reads your rights."

Tom began, "I am Agent Thomas Freeman of the Drug Enforcement Agency of the United States of America, and I am arresting you for the illegal production and distribution of controlled substances. You have the right to remain silent...."

Keone left the fetid cabin with Tom trailing behind, half-carrying the fragile Walden. Keone checked his watch, *4:40 p.m.* "We'll have a little wait before—"

As if on cue, he was interrupted by the roar of a helicopter advancing towards them. He was glad they wouldn't have to wait for their ride.

"Get down. Now," Freeman pulled out his service automatic and fired several shots at the chopper.

Keone hit the ground, grabbed his own Glock, and rolled into firing position. Shells from an assault rifle were tearing up the ground around Freeman and Walden. But the shooter had ignored Keone, so far.

Taking careful aim, Keone put a few rounds into the helicopter's rear stabilizer. The pilot tried to pull up but couldn't clear the Kiawe trees. Keone hoped they were low enough and moving slowly enough to avoid an explosion.

They weren't.

Curling into a ball and covering his head for protection, Keone hoped the others had time to do the same.

The concussion from the explosion rocked him, but the shrapnel from the disintegrating helicopter flew over him, shredding the jungle foliage.

"Are you all right?" he yelled as he ran to Freeman's location.

"Walden's hit, but he'll live. I got my bell rung by a chunk of kiawe."

"That shout to get down saved my ass."

"Just trying to even the scales."

"Consider us square and probably good friends for life. But how could you tell that wasn't your chopper? When you yelled, I couldn't even see it."

"Neither could I. It was the sound. Then I caught a glimpse of that assault rifle poking out of the open door and figured they weren't here to make friends. That piece of crap," Tom said, indicating the rubble that was recently a chopper, "hadn't been serviced properly in months, if not years. We take excellent care of our helicopters. They're our most valuable assets for catching growers, processers, and dealers on the islands. I knew it wasn't our guy."

Keone helped Tom drag Walden over to where they'd stashed their packs before rushing the cabin. He pulled out the first aid kit and let Tom get on with bandaging Dave. While the other two were occupied, Keone approached the helicopter's remains. All he found of the passengers was one head in moderately good condition but no other identifiable body parts. He photographed the face and returned to find another helicopter heading toward them. The smile on Tom Freeman's face told him this one was friendly.

"Have you got a plastic bag in your pack?" he asked, holding up the remains by its wavy blond hair.

~

Julie Waldon pulled up to the entrance to Maui Memorial Hospital, behind the wheel of Keone's beater.

"What are you doing here?" Keone hadn't expected to see her so soon.

"Lindsay called the ranch and told us you'd caught Dave. Lani drove me to your condo. She knew where you hid your extra set of keys to this... uh... unique vehicle. By the way, who beat you up? Not Dave?" Julie asked, as Keone slumped into the passenger seat.

"No. He was pretty out of it by the time we found him. Most of this is courtesy of the island of Moloka'i, although a helicopter sent by Dave's former good friends in the Russian mob helped a bit."

"Tell me the whole story," she said.

"Well, we caught Dave hiding just where you suspected, but it was a hell of a hike in to catch him. He didn't put up any fight, being totally under the spell of the ice he'd brought. Then some unexpected visitors in a helicopter tried to put an end to him. A fantastic DEA agent named Tom Freeman saved Dave's life and mine, but not before they put a round in Dave's shoulder. He's going to be all right, though."

"What happened to the helicopter?"

"I sort of helped it land with a lucky shot, but we know what the shooter looked like." Keone avoided mentioning the severed head that he'd passed on to Lindsay Kalani at the hospital, along with Tom Freeman. "He's a well-known hit man from New York."

"You're not hurt?"

"No. I'm fine. They kept Tom overnight for observation. He has a concussion from a hunk of kiawe that hit him after the explosion. Detective Kalani will keep an eye on him. How was your day?"

"I've decided to divorce Dave. Don't be mad, but I called Jan today. I didn't tell her where I was, but I really needed to talk to her. She's talked to a lawyer friend of hers and he's willing to take the case."

Keone felt a complex array of emotions, none of which was anger at Julie. But this did change things.

When they reached the condo, Keone jumped in the shower, while Julie laid out goodies from Panda Express on the kitchen table. They ate in silence until Julie became uneasy.

"Okay. You're mad. I didn't follow your rules. I apologize. Just don't give me the silent treatment."

"What? Oh, no. I'm glad you're filing for divorce. You were never our prisoner, you know. You did the right thing talking to Jan."

"Then what is it?"

"I have no justification for keeping you here, with Dave in custody. If you would feel more comfortable in a condo of your own, I know a guy here in the complex who's looking to rent a unit just like this one."

"Tired of having me around, eh?"

"No. No. I just, well, with you filing for divorce, I thought you might be..."

"Ashamed of living with you? Look I've finished my counselling. I'm no longer the vulnerable little thing you found at my house that night. Does that mean you'll no longer care about me?"

"Oh I care, Julie. I like having you here. I like talking with you, being with you..." *I'm talking too much.*

Julie laughed and hugged him around his waist. When he resisted, she said, "You dumb ass. I'm falling in love with you, too."

"How did you know that I... because I wasn't sure that you...?"

"Just kiss me, you big, wonderful kanaka. We're not breaking any rules."

4. Adaptations

"'Contrariwise,' continued Tweedledee, 'if it was so, it might be; and if it were so, it would be; but as it isn't, it ain't. That's logic.'"

— Lewis Carroll

Chapter Thirty-Five

Tuesday, April 2, 2:00 p.m.

Dr. Martin Hasselbach waited outside Dr. Evan Drayton's office. He wondered if his decisive actions regarding Brad Carvell had made things better or worse.

The smile on Drayton's face as he welcomed Martin into his office provided him hope.

"Dr. Hasselbach, please have a seat. I am so glad you suggested me to Dr. Carvell when you did."

"Please call me Martin, Doctor. I truly hope you have good news for me."

"Okay Martin, I'm Evan. I want you to consider me a colleague on the journey to restore Brad to full recovery." Drayton's manner immediately made Martin more comfortable.

"Tell me, Evan, has Brad made progress over the ten days he's been seeing you? I would really like to see him back at work. Aside from this obsession of his, he's an excellent scientist." He meant this.

Drayton thought for a moment before responding. "Martin, let's start by agreeing to something, okay?"

Martin nodded.

"I won't pretend that I know anything about bosons and tachyons, and you let me make the clinical diagnoses."

"Agreed. Sorry."

"When you asked me to consider accepting Brad as a patient, you mentioned over-work and sleep deprivation as contributing to his unacceptable work product. You were right about both, and they certainly exacerbated his reactions," Drayton continued.

"I was concerned that I might have over-reacted?" Martin liked to cut to the chase.

"No, you suggested a colleague get the help he needed. The fact that he took your advice and came to me is a good sign. Another is that he also accepts that his work has become sub-par. I'm sure you understand that I can't discuss the specifics of my sessions with Brad. But he has agreed to let me share certain aspects that might assist you in your supervision of him during this recovery period." Drayton's face and manner became totally professional.

"I understand and totally respect doctor patient privilege."

"Dr. Carvell is fascinated by what he calls ..." Drayton glanced at his notes. "*The possibility of terrestrial manifestations of cosmic forces*. I don't know if there's hard science behind any of this, but I do know the emotional effects of being so close to what one wants to be doing and having to watch from the periphery." Drayton paused to let him absorb this.

"But intruding in another scientist's project is what got Brad into trouble. Are you suggesting I reward that behavior?" He was confused and a little angry at the psychiatrist's intimations.

"Martin, these are simply my observations. I know you had no ulterior motive in the assignments you gave your scientists. I also believe that you want what is best for them. Why not try putting both Dr..." Drayton looked at his notes again. "*Rathnachalam* and Brad on the terrestrial project. Have them work together and challenge each other's interpretations in a rigorous scientific way. You can keep a close eye on both. If they discover that Brad's interpretations are flawed, they can work together to discover what is really going on as colleagues, not competitors. Do you see where I'm going with this?"

Martin recognized that Drayton was offering him a chance to repair any unintended damage to Brad. He'd always seen himself as a mentor, developing scientists' skills without dampening their enthusiasm. "Maybe, I have been a bit oblivious to Brad's... uh... feelings. I never meant to keep him from a project of interest. Still, I must demand objectivity from those I supervise. Do you believe Brad is able to approach this project objectively if given the chance?" He also had a responsibility to the project.

"I know he wants to alter his behavior. Having him work on the project directly and openly and discuss his ideas, valid and invalid, with you and his colleague will help him do just that. As a scientist, he abhors mis-interpreting data, but he also knows every scientist can make errors, working in isolation." Drayton paused.

"Evan, I appreciate your analysis and willingness to pursue an experimental approach with the potential to achieve our goals." He had to admit that Drayton was making sense.

"I believe, if he can avoid being side-tracked, Dr. Carvell can and will provide what both you and he need. I recommend he continue his sessions with me as an out-patient after he returns to work. If I see any disruption in his recovery, we can reconvene and modify our strategy."

"Tell Brad he can report to work on Wednesday for his new assignment with the terrestrial analysis team. But let him know I will be watching the work extremely closely and will not hesitate to point out any deviation from accepted scientific rigor."

"Brad told me he would expect nothing less from you. Let's proceed with optimism and vigilance, okay?" Evan Drayton stuck out his hand and Martin shook it.

Chapter Thirty-Six

Wednesday, April 3, 7:00 a.m.

Jan leaned out the driver's window as Julie walked to her car across the parking lot of the condominium complex. "Are you ready, girl?"

"I hope so. I'd like to get back before Keone gets home from the station."

"No problem. Our appointment is at nine-thirty. You kinda like that Hawaiian of yours, don't you?"

"I'd do anything for him. But I need to do this without him. Do you understand?" she asked.

Janet nodded. "I see you taking charge of your life. And I'm proud of you for it."

"You're certain this lawyer is not affiliated with Dave or his friends in any way?"

"He does contract work for my design firm. George knows who David is but has never met him. And he's disgusted by how David supplements his legal income."

"Let's talk about something else."

"I'm bursting to tell you something, but I don't want to jinx it."

Julie was surprised to see her normally controlled sister so excited. "Is it about Sam?"

"Yes. I'm starting to see glimpses of the old Sam." Jan sounded like she did when they were teenagers, talking about their first crushes.

"Like what?"

"Little things. How he sits in his chair. How he kids about things."

"I'm happy for you, but don't get ahead of yourself."

"I won't. Keep your fingers crossed. I know I am. Say, you never told me how Keone found David."

"He followed up on a clue I gave him." Julie smiled broadly.

"You gave a clue to a detective?"

"I remembered that Dave owned some undeveloped land on Moloka'i that isn't recorded as belonging to him. Keone guessed he might be hiding out there, and he was."

"I hope they lock him up and throw away the key." David had never been high on Jan's list of friends and family.

Pulling into the parking lot by George Frick's office, Julie fought to keep her hands from trembling.

Jan patted her shoulder and said, "I'll be with you every second, Honey. You're doing the right thing."

Julie steeled herself, threw open the car door, and said, "Let's do this."

WHEN KEONE RETURNED FROM WORK, HE FOUND A handwritten note taped to his doorbell. "Come over to my new place for dinner. Don't worry, I didn't cook. – Julie."

After a quick shower and change of clothes, he walked to a door three units over from his and knocked twice.

Julie opened the door, gave him a kiss, and walked him into

the dining room of the condo she'd rented from his friend. "I had Janet take me to a lawyer today. He's helping me divorce Dave."

"Another example of you directing your own life. Like your decision to rent this condo. I bet the lawyer complimented you on that."

"He did. And he has no association with Dave, except hating him for providing the type of drug that his sister overdosed on last year." Julie sat at the table and began serving.

"Sounds like just the man for the job." Keone savored his first sip of what Julie called pottage San Germaine, although he would have just called it pea soup.

"I'm sure you've guessed from the quality of the meal that Janet made this feast for us to celebrate my first steps toward freedom." Julie grinned.

"Thank her for me. When will the lawyer have documents for Dave to sign?"

"His name is George Frick. I'm not asking for much, from the divorce. My finances are already separate from Dave's. I'm just requesting half of the proceeds from the sale of what's left of our house and having him stipulate that he has no claim to any of the proceeds from my books or the film contracts. George said he should have it ready by the first of next week." Julie sipped from her glass of a hearty French red wine. Another gift from Janet.

"Dave's own assets are probably tainted with his drug business proceeds, anyway. You're making a smart move. I'll be happy to get his signature for you when the documents are ready. He'd be a fool to contest any of this," he commented, turning his attention to their main course of steak au poivre and new potatoes.

"Will they let you do that? I mean the Feds?" Julie asked.

"Tom Freeman is my new best friend, since I gave him all the credit for Walden's capture. I'm sure he can get me in to see his prisoner. I am known to be a very persuasive person." Keone sliced off a large chunk of steak, smothered in that pungent creamy pepper sauce.

"They won't let you torture him."

"Please, don't let my size mislead you. I am well versed in the more subtle forms of persuasion. I assure you your ex will suffer no permanent damage." He said this without interrupting his enjoyment of the gourmet meal.

"Janet told me something today, about Sam," Julie said, enjoying her petite bites of the meal as much as Keone did his mouthfuls.

"What's up with the amazing Mr. Loftus?" he asked.

"If all goes well, he will go home with Janet in about two weeks. They've been getting along very well during his therapy and rehabilitation. She's looking forward to having him home, and he seems to be, too." Julie's face reflected her hopefulness for her sister.

"For Janet's sake, I hope Sam is serious about his desire to return to their normal life. But, even if he is, they have a tough road ahead. I hope she understands that."

"I think she does. She knows the danger of false hopes. Dr. Drayton told her that, at first, they'll just be housemates, with separate rooms and parallel lives. What develops from that could take months or years."

"I honestly hope they make it. I like both of them, despite what Sam did to my dream car." Keone chuckled to show Julie that he really didn't bear a grudge.

Chapter Thirty-Seven

Monday, April 8, 7:00 a.m.

When he reached the station, Keone found a voice message on his desk phone. "Keone, this is Tom Freeman. Give me a call when you get a chance. It's about Walden."

He didn't hesitate.

Neither did Tom, answering on the first ring. "Thanks for getting back to me, Keone."

"Your timing is excellent as always, Tom. I got the divorce papers from Julie's lawyer this weekend and wanted your opinion on the best moment to put them in front of Walden."

"Dave Walden is doing everything he can at present to receive his *golden ticket*," Tom said.

"His what?"

"Walden's new lawyer advised him to be as accommodating as possible and trade what he knows for a ticket into witness protection. We're close to a deal, but he knows just one screw-up on his part could ruin everything. He also knows what playing hard ball with us could mean for his longevity. The Russian mob is out for blood."

"So, you're saying I should talk to him soon. Today, Tomorrow, what?"

"I'd recommend tomorrow. We'll probably lock down the deal before the end of the week. When would you like to have access?" Tom asked.

"I'll fly to Oahu tomorrow morning and would be pleased to join him for lunch at your lovely Federal holding facility. Tell them that I'll bring the lunch." Keone smiled to himself.

"I'll meet you there to facilitate access, but you'll have him all to yourself."

"I may have someone with me. Let me run an idea past you..."

Keone assembled a call list of a few friends to help with his lunch for Dave Walden—to assure their discussion would be open and productive.

A knock on his cubicle postponed his calls.

"Lindsay, mahalo nui loa. I'm sorry I left you holding the bag at the hospital, literally."

"I found a nice safe spot in the morgue for that blond shooter's head. And keeping an eye on your friend Freeman overnight had an unexpected benefit. He took me to brunch Sunday morning, when they finally let him out of the hospital. I dropped him off at the airport after."

Was Lindsay blushing?

"Well, I appreciate your effort on the behalf of the department. We need to keep good relations with the Feds. How was he feeling?" Keone asked.

"His head still hurt, but the docs said it was a minor concussion. That's why they let him go."

"He sounded fine on the phone just now. Before we finished

our call, he asked me to thank you for your presence at the hospital. Is there anything else you'd like to share?" Keone grinned.

"Nothing that's any of your business, Big Guy." With that, she rapidly exited his cubicle.

Keone made his first call in preparation for tomorrow to a good friend in Lahaina.

Chapter Thirty-Eight

Tuesday, April 9, 12:30 p.m.

A loud buzzer announced Keone's entrance into the cell block that held David Walden. A second announced the opening of the cell door. David Walden was sitting on his bed and looked up at the sound. "Keone Boyd. Have they got you delivering lunches now?"

"I heard that they were keeping you separate from the general population for your safety, Dave. How's that working out for you?" Keone laid the tray on Walden's bed.

"So far, so good. My lawyer's working real hard to get me the best deal from the Feds. I don't mind a little isolation until that's done."

"Understood. I hear he's driving a hard bargain. Why don't you try the lunch? I think you'll like it." Keone's voice was calm and friendly.

"A burrito from Lahaina Coolers. How did you arrange for that? And plenty of Max's special hot sauce on the side. I owe you, Sergeant." Walden took a large bite and joy filled his face, along with a certain redness.

"I'm glad you said that because I have a couple of favors to ask you." Keone picked up the carafe of hot sauce and offered to pour.

"I'll be honest with you. I can handle the burrito, but the sauce is a little too much for me."

"It's a shame to waste it," Keone said.

"Well, okay. But just a little."

Keone carefully put a few drops on the burrito and watched Walden take a bite.

Dave quickly reached for the water bottle on his tray and sweat appeared on his forehead. "That's damn good sauce, but a few drops go a long way. What did you want to ask me?"

"Just one thing for Julie and one for me, okay?"

"If I can," Walden said in his best schmoozer voice.

"It's pretty easy. Just agree not to contest your divorce. With you in witness protection and all the charges we have against you, there's no point fighting it."

"I'm sure you understand that I'll have to see the distribution of assets first." Dave started to sound more like a lawyer.

"I just happen to have the document with me." He picked up the carafe again as he said this.

Dave looked the document over carefully and stared at the carafe in Keone's hand as it hovered over his crotch.

"Okay, okay. I won't contest it. You have my word." Dave wiped a couple drops of hot sauce off his pants with the napkin.

"I know what that's worth." Keone rose and tapped on the cell door, which opened again, allowing Tom Freeman to enter with a woman.

"Mr. Walden, I'm a notary and work for Judge Fernandez on Maui. He's officiating over your divorce settlement. Please sign here, here, and here."

Dave signed.

When the notary left with Tom, Keone set the carafe back down on the tray.

"I've given the Feds everything they want, and I've given Julie what she wants. Now, what do you want?" Dave's sneer seemed to deepen.

"To never see your face or hear your voice again on my island."

"No chance of that. The Feds assure me that my witness protection location will be in the middle of the mainland, as far as possible from both the east coast and here. I'll no longer exist."

He picked up the tray and left Walden alone in his cell.

As Keone came through the door of her condo, Julie reacted. "Well, I'll be damned. You're home early. Is there no crime left to fight?"

"No. I took care of all the bad guys, today. Including one you may know."

"What has my ex gotten himself into this time?"

"Nothing much. He's just been educated about a simple physical law called leverage. We discussed it over lunch in his cell in Oahu."

"Can he walk?"

"Oh, yes. I never touched him. He even avoided having to learn some facts about food placement that I offered to share."

"Ouch!"

"Dave has agreed to provide important evidence against his former good buds on the Eastern seaboard and elsewhere for a guarantee of witness protection. He also agreed not to contest the divorce. Judge Fernandez's notary got his signature on all the necessary forms." Keone produced copies of the signed forms from behind his back.

Julie snatched the documents from his hand. "You're good, Detective."

"Well, effective anyway. My friend Judge Fernandez has offered to fast track the paperwork. How would you like to be free from Dave by, say, Independence Day?"

Julie jumped up and threw her arms around Keone's neck. He felt her tears on his cheek.

Chapter Thirty-Nine

Monday, April 15, 4:00 p.m.

Janet Loftus prepared to take her husband home from the hospital, exactly one month after the accident that put him here. The rules were simple. She and Sam would occupy separate bedrooms. He would have no contact with Julie. He would not drive until he took and passed a defensive driving course and a state driving test. And he could return to work only after he met a set of criteria established by his employer and Dr. Drayton.

She entered the room with a suitcase. "Hi, Sam. It looks like we're finally getting you out of this place. I'm proud of how hard you've worked to make this possible."

"Janet, I couldn't have done it without your encouragement and patience with me."

She waved her hand at the compliment, but believed Sam meant it. A month ago, none of this seemed possible. "You go ahead and pack your things and I'll make sure Dr. Drayton has completed all the paperwork."

Drayton stood at the nurses' station, signing the necessary release forms. Tom Conrad was there, too, with a smaller stack of forms to sign for the court.

Drayton saw Jan and held up a finger as he signed the last form. "Janet, I have a couple more things to go over with you before you take Sam home."

"I know, I'm not to expect too much."

"Yes. But there's more. In our sessions I've told Sam what I'm going to tell you. Sam may look like the man who was your husband before the accident, but he isn't. He's dealt with several severe challenges and done well. Your support had a lot to do with that."

"I like to think so," Jan said with a slight smile.

"No, you really have made a difference. Sam has grown to like you and trust you, but that isn't the same as love."

"I know that."

"You know it in your head, but not in your heart. As I told Sam, when you go home together, I want you to imagine you are friends who have decided to share a house together. You have your own rooms, your own activities, and your own lives. Over time, you'll rediscover some common interests. You can help this by suggesting an activity you used to do together. A game you played together, a television program you watched, even reading in the same room can re-establish feelings. I'm not talking about memories exactly, just comfortable feelings."

"We used to love playing Scrabble and *Mah Jong* and always watched the evening news together. Is that the kind of thing you mean?"

"Perfect. Scrabble can also help Sam with his reading comprehension. After a month or so, you might consider a first date, something non-threatening like dinner or a movie. It took a while for you two to fall in love the first time. It won't be any different this time. Sam will have highs and lows, and so will you. But you need to be his rock, his firm foundation. You may want to scream sometimes but call me instead, okay? Any time, day or night."

"I will. Thanks for all you've done for Sam and for the advice. We'll make this work. However long it takes."

"I believe you have a real chance to succeed. I'll see Sam for an hour twice a week, at first. After he goes back to work, we'll try to cut back to once. My secretary will work it all out with you."

OT escorted Sam to the nurses' station. Noting Conrad and Drayton at the counter around the nurses' station, Sam waved. "I'm grateful to all of you, especially Dr. D. and the incomparable OT. Now, I hope you won't think it rude of me if I can't wait to get the hell out of this place."

Everyone chuckled at this. Jan leaned into Drayton's ear and whispered, "I like this Sam's sense of humor better than the old one's."

Drayton's expression was unreadable as he patted her shoulder. "Onward then, Loftuses. Enjoy your first night back in your home."

SAM SMILED AS THEY LEFT THE NURSES' STATION, BUT inside he fought with his emotions. Although ecstatic to be leaving the hospital after so long, he realized the home they were returning to would be unfamiliar to him. Janet would be looking for sparks of recognition. Could he fake them adequately?

As Janet drove them to Pukalani, he wondered if they would even live in the same house. The address on his, now voided, driver's license was the same as he remembered, but the house itself...

"Isn't it nice to see some familiar sights outside the hospital, Sam?"

"Well, the Queen K Shopping Center looks the same, but I wish everybody wouldn't insist on driving on the wrong damn side of the road."

"Now, Sam."

"Just kidding. Besides, I can handle it. I've driven in England, you know."

When they travelled past the airport on the Hana Highway, Sam had to admit everything did look familiar. He could even read the street signs now, without difficulty. They turned onto Haleakala Highway and entered Pukalani. He held his breath as they approached the house but exhaled when it looked just the same as it had when he left for work a month ago. His bromeliads were all right where they should be and the yard was green and lovely, if an inch longer than he used to keep it.

Entering the house, he didn't have to fake sparks of recognition. They were real. About half of the furnishings were familiar and in locations he remembered. The windows and doors were all where they were supposed to be.

I wonder.

While Janet took the suitcases to his bedroom, Sam decided to peek into the kids' rooms. He gasped. "Cindy, my little munchkin, where have you gone?"

Cindy's room was now Janet's workroom/office. In his mind he saw it as it was before. The bed with its fluffy pink comforter and lace-tipped pink canopy. The white dresser with her special treasures neatly lined up for display. Her rocking chair with that ridiculous blue bear she called Bluey filling the entire seat. He'd won it for her at the fair.

He stumbled across the hallway to Timmy's room. It was now an office, too, his office. He recognized the furniture and knick-knacks from his actual office in what was now the guest room, where Janet would be sleeping.

In his memories, instead of the neat desk and filing cabinets, toys were strewn across the floor. Legos predominated, but trucks and cars and a variety of rubber balls of various sizes were there too. Timmy's racecar bed had filled one wall and his simple wooden dresser the other. The top of his dresser, unlike Cindy's, was always invisible under a complex pile of rubbish.

"Timmy, I can't lose you, too."

"Sam?" He turned at the sound of Janet's voice, tears dripping from his eyes.

"It's okay." She handed him a box of tissues. "Go ahead and cry. I have. Our life has been turned inside out, literally. Why don't you go into our... your bedroom and lie down while I fix some dinner?" Janet said this with a gentleness in her voice that Sam needed and appreciated.

"Yes. I think I will."

He went straight to the bedroom, also fifty percent familiar, and flopped on the mattress. The feel of the Posturepedic was one hundred percent familiar. He hadn't realized how exhausting this would be. He fell asleep as soon as he closed his eyes.

Chapter Forty

Wednesday, April 17, 1:00 p.m.

Martin Hasselbach answered his office phone to find Evan Drayton on the other end of the line. "Hello Martin. How's Brad doing at work?"

"Evan. I'm glad you called. Brad Carvell is a new man. His work is tight and substantiated by data. He and Radha are benefiting from each other's perspective. I'm very pleased." He heard the relief in his own voice.

"Brad has seemed much more centered during our sessions as well. I'm guessing he's getting more sleep. Is he on a different schedule?" Drayton asked.

"Yes. They are working overlapping swing-shifts, so no one is stuck here all night. Brad is no longer the loner he was during his first months here. He and Radha are completing each other's sentences in meetings. This collaboration is working."

"Brad seems to be taking days off again and spending them with his wife, or so he tells me." Drayton noted.

"Yes, she called to thank me for his new work schedule and

mentioned the same thing. How often are you two meeting now?" Martin asked.

"We're down to twice a week. By next month, we'll down to one. I'm as pleased with his progress as you are. If anything changes, let me know, and I'll do the same. My next patient is here, so I better let you go. Aloha, Martin."

"Aloha, Evan, and mahalo."

~

"Howzit, Big guy?"

Keone was pleased to hear Angela Beyers' voice at his cubicle door. "What brings you this direction during the week, Ange. Has Hana fallen into the sea?"

"Not yet. I had to testify in a trial over here this morning, and I'm taking vacation tomorrow and Friday to create a long weekend. Lin has some remodeling for us to do around the house." Angela said. "We're thinking of inviting some friends over on Sunday to celebrate the new look. Are you free?"

"Can I bring a date?" he asked.

"Absolutely. Who's the lucky wahine?"

"Her name's Julie. I met her on my last case." Keone was so glad he didn't need to hide their relationship anymore.

"Julie Walden? Wasn't she the one that Kulima...?" Angela paused.

"He was full of shit. My LT shut his accusations down. Frank's been walking on eggs around here ever since." He knew Frank wasn't in his cubicle today, but he wouldn't have cared if he'd heard.

"He may be keeping a low profile here, but rumor is his complaint migrated upstairs."

"How far upstairs?" he asked.

Angela frowned. "I hate to be the one telling you this. It's only a rumor. But you might want to check with your boss. Just to make sure. Hope you can make it on Sunday. I'd better head to

Lahaina and put on my real work clothes before Linda checks up on me. Aloha."

"Aloha."

After she'd gone, Keone made an appointment with Tony for when he returned from visiting his kids on Oahu on Friday. The rumors Angela heard had a habit of being true.

Chapter Forty-One

Friday, April 19, 7:00 a.m.

For Keone, the last twenty days were the most wonderful of his life. The freedom to drop all his barriers around Julie was more than a relief—it was a rebirth. He always hated it in movies when a man or woman would say, "You complete me." But dating Julie made him realize he'd always been missing something in his life that Julie provided. It wasn't a dependency. He felt more independent than ever and knew she did, too.

"So, you ready to protect us Mauians from harm, mistah detective?" Julie teased.

"I will be, once I get my pants on."

"Carrying a concealed weapon, eh?"

"You know it. I'll try to get home at a reasonable time tonight."

"I've started writing again."

Keone was surprised at how good those words made him feel. "About time you started earning your keep around here."

Julie punched him, hard, in the gut. "Watch that trash talk, buster."

Keone lifted her off the ground, kissed her gently, and said, "I'm so proud of you."

"I'm the best damn thing that ever happened to you and don't you forget it."

As he closed the door, Keone realized he was glad to be out of the condo. It would help hide his nerves about the meeting that was scheduled for this afternoon with Tony Alcala, regarding a certain rumor.

~

It was almost four o'clock and Keone was waiting outside of Alcala's office, again. Tony had been distant for the past couple weeks but hadn't hassled him about anything either.

When Karen told him he could go in, her expression revealed nothing. Opening the door, he saw his boss was not alone. Chief Jack Watanabe was sitting in Tony's chair and Tony was sitting in one of the two chairs on the other side of his desk.

So, it wasn't just a rumor.

"Have a seat, Detective Sergeant Boyd," Watanabe commanded. "I need to ask you a few questions, and I want you to answer them honestly and completely. Do you understand?"

"Yes, sir."

"I know that you recently solved an important case and commend you on your investigation of David Walden. The information he is providing to federal authorities is extremely valuable." Watanabe did not smile.

"Thank you, sir."

"You're welcome, but that's not why we're here. We're here because some serious allegations of misconduct have been made against you by a fellow officer. Unlike your direct supervisor, I was not willing to dismiss them until I had personally reviewed the evidence. Nor was I willing to challenge the motives of the other officer without evidence. Do you know what I'm talking about, Detective Sergeant Boyd?"

"I believe I do, sir. You are referring to my relationship with Mr. Walden's ex-wife." Keone knew it was no time for half-truths.

"That is correct. Has that relationship ended?"

"No, sir. We are living three-doors down from each other in my condominium complex," Keone answered.

"Were you together before Mr. Walden was captured?" Watanabe showed no signs of letting up.

"I interviewed Mrs. Walden with her sister early in my investigation of the Loftus case. I also responded to a call from Mrs. Walden on the night her husband beat her. I visited Mrs. Walden three times in the hospital. The first was the night of her admission, the second was a follow-up visit to discuss her husband's activities, and the third was when she was released from the hospital. On the first occasion she provided me access to a storage unit with information helpful to my investigation. On the second occasion, I became convinced that she was aware of her husband's addiction but unaware of his role in the production and distribution of crystal meth. During the final visit, I drove her to her home in my cruiser where Detective Lindsay Kalani took custody of her and drove her to a shelter for abused women."

"That's all in your reports. Lieutenant Alcala and I agree your actions to this point were justified and within department policy. I am more interested in hearing about the nights you and Mrs. Walden spent in your condominium."

"To date, we have spent a total of three nights in my condominium. The first was the evening after her house exploded. I had Detective Lindsay Kalani bring her there from the shelter to keep her safe from her husband. I notified Lieutenant Alcala that I wasn't convinced of her safety at the shelter and that I would be moving her to a safe house."

"Did you inform the lieutenant that she was at your condo?" Watanabe asked.

"I did not. At that point I was quite concerned about connections Mr. Walden had within the department and decided to keep Mrs. Walden's location a secret from as many people as possible. Detective Kalani was always aware of Mrs. Walden's location and circumstances throughout the investigation of Mrs. Walden's husband."

"Did Lieutenant Kalani spend that night at your condominium, while Mrs. Walden was there?"

"No, I had her ask my adult sister, who works at the shelter, to follow her to my home and spend the night. My sister, Mahealani shared a bedroom with Mrs. Walden, sleeping on a cot. When I returned from the station at about 11 p.m., they were asleep in the bedroom with the door closed. I slept on the couch in my living room. The next day, my sister transferred Mrs. Walden to my brother's ranch in Makawao. I visited once to interview her about possible locations her husband might be hiding. That interview like all my interactions with Mrs. Walden were personally monitored by Detective Kalani. I don't need to remind you. that interview is what led us to the location where we captured Mr. Walden."

"You mentioned three occasions when Mrs. Walden spent the night with you in your condominium."

"The second time she spent the night was the evening after we captured her husband on Molokai. She picked me up from the hospital in my car and we shared dinner. On that occasion, she told me she was falling in love with me and had decided to divorce her husband. I suggested she rent another condominium in the complex, but she spent that night in mine. She did rent the other unit the next day."

"In all of the time that you spent with Mrs. Walden, before the capture of her husband, did you two have sexual relations?" Chief Watanabe asked.

"No. We didn't even kiss until the night I caught her husband. And I was so exhausted from my exertions on Molokai, capturing Walden, that I fell asleep after a few kisses, on my couch. Mrs.

Walden couldn't lug my massive frame into the bedroom, so she left me there and slept alone in my bed." He was almost embarrassed to admit this.

"Thank you, Detective Sergeant. Although not strictly consistent with department policy, what you've described is hardly serious misconduct. I'd consider the first a practical solution to an evolving situation and the second none of our business. I also understand that Mrs. Loftus received abuse counselling both in the hospital and at your brother's ranch before the second occasion. I take it the third occasion was after the second, and therefore irrelevant to the accusations, as well."

"Yes, sir," he replied.

"Do you have any questions for us?" Watanabe asked.

"Will there be a hearing on the accusations? Do I need an attorney?"

"There might have been, but events have been evolving on that front as well. Would you please update Sergeant Boyd, Lieutenant?"

"A key witness's testimony is now inadmissible," Tony said.

"What key witness?"

"Former Detective Sergeant Frank Kulima. It seems he had another employer in addition to the county of Maui—a Mr. David Walden. He was named along with Roger Walker from West Maui and a lieutenant from vice as being on the take. Walden even admitted to paying him to follow Julie around before and after the explosion at their home." Tony glanced at the chief.

"That lieutenant is the person who brought the accusations to me after Lieutenant Alcala refused. I played along to collect additional evidence before we arrested him along with Walker and Kulima."

"He was never following me?" Keone didn't try to hide his surprise.

"No, only Julie. But he is the one who tipped Walden about your accident."

"What about Dr. Wayne, the Loftus family doctor?" Keone always liked to see the t's crossed and the i's dotted at the end of a case.

"Walden was blackmailing him. He'll lose his license, but shouldn't have to serve any time," Tony explained.

"Where's Kulima now?" Keone was looking forward to encountering his old antagonist behind bars.

"Maui Memorial. When the officers arrived to arrest him, he tried to shoot himself in the head." Chief Watanabe relayed this fact.

"Is he seriously injured?"

"Not too bad. The dumbass missed and shot his right ear off," Tony replied.

Keone forced himself to keep a straight face. "So, what is my punishment?"

"You have to get your sorry ass back to work. And why don't you make things simpler for all of us and make an honest woman of Julie Walden." Chief Watanabe grinned at Tony.

"Now get out of here and get back to work," Tony growled. We're shorthanded, thanks to you."

WHEN HE ARRIVED AT JULIE'S CONDO, SHE HANDED HIM a huge, ice-cold schooner filled with Longboard lager. "You look like you had a hard day."

"I was interrogated by Tony and the chief about our relationship."

"Kulima never gave up? I was afraid of that," she said, then asked, "How bad?"

"I could have lost my job if they believed him. It turned out Kulima was working for your ex-husband and so was the lieutenant who blind-sided Tony and took the accusations to the chief. I get to remain on active duty in CID."

"You risked everything—for me."

Keone started to interrupt, but she held up her hand. "No, Keone, don't talk. It's my turn. I want you to know I understand what you might have lost by falling in love with me. Your career with MPD is a major part of who you are. I want to make the rest of our time together worthy of that risk."

By now they were sitting beside each other on her couch. Keone reached over and gently stroked her cheek. "It's already worth it."

She clasped her hands behind his neck and pulled his lips to hers. Emotions she'd only allowed to leak out before flowed through her, and she felt Keone give in to his own, as well.

When he lifted her off the couch in those massive arms, she felt them vibrate with energy. Once in her bed, she was amazed by the tenderness he conveyed in every touch, followed much later by a release that hinted at how much passion he'd been controlling.

She had never felt safer or more alive than now, in his arms.

Chapter Forty-Two

Tuesday, April 23, 8:00 a.m.

Sitting at the breakfast table, Sam realized he'd been living with Janet for over a week, and it had been nice. His days had been full between completing defensive driving lessons, his sessions with Dr. Drayton, and studying like mad to get recertified to do his old job. Strangely, the driving had progressed faster than anything. He guessed that's why Brits can learn to drive in the US and vice versa. Once he set his mind to it, he amazed his instructor. Today he'd see if he could pass the Hawai'i state driver's examination.

Janet seemed excited, too. She would drive him to Kahului for the test. He suspected she saw this as a first step on the road back to a normal life. Sam also knew she believed everything his doctors told her. He couldn't help feeling guilty for misleading this nice woman.

His island-style eggs Benedict, with seared *ahi* tuna in place of Canadian bacon, demonstrated Janet's skill as a cook. If she hadn't gone into decorating, she could have made it as a gourmet chef.

One reason for getting his license was to allow her to go back to work. He could tell she missed it. He couldn't wait to get back to work, either.

Watching her check the little book that she used for scheduling and addresses, reminded him of a series of little books he'd kept since college. Collectively they represented a detailed account of the thoughts and actions of Sam Loftus. He'd continued keeping that record in new journals all his life.

Is it possible my journals are here, in this house? The skeleton of the house hasn't changed. I always kept them—

"Is everything all right, Sam?"

"Just my weary brain gathering wool. Thank you for another wonderful meal."

"I have to make sure you have all the energy you need to pass that test today. I know you can do it."

"I look forward to being able to send you off to work, for a change." Sam had discovered that he really liked Janet, this Janet. Like the Janet in his world, she was more formal than Julie, with a polished surface that reminded him of a porcelain doll. But beneath that, he felt a real warmth that she reserved for very few people. And her husband was one of them. She loved her Sam deeply, which made him wish he could give her the happiness she deserved. But he had no memory of loving her, just liking her. Maybe finding his journals could help resolve matters.

Returning to his bedroom, once their bedroom, he closed and locked the door. He doubted Janet would ever come in unannounced, but he didn't want her to see him searching for his journals. Going to the left side of the bed, he moved the bedside table away from the wall and felt along the baseboard for a tiny tab of tin. His disappointment when it wasn't there was like a rock on his heart. He slid the table back and slumped on the bed.

Gazing up into the image in the mirror over the dresser, he had an idea. Moving to the right side of the bed, he slid the other bedside table out to find the little tin tab just where it should have been on the other side.

"Left is right, dumbass," he muttered to himself.

There behind the wainscoting were all his journals, beginning with the one from his freshman year in college. Although in mirror writing, which he could now read fluently, it even looked like his handwriting when he held it up to the mirror.

When he opened the first journal and began to read, he was overjoyed to recognize every word. His description of arriving in Bloomington and being assigned to the dorms was exactly as he remembered. The second and third paragraphs brought back especially pleasant memories.

When I reached my assigned room, the door was already open, and I came face-to-face with my roommate. He said his name was Dave and asked where I was from. When I told him Newport Beach, he said, "A fellow Californian, how wonderful. I'm from Palo Alto. We'll teach these damn Hoosiers how to enjoy college and still get better grades."

I liked him at once. He was a chemistry major and I math and business, but at this stage that was far less relevant than that he had cased the town and found the best place to get pizza. I threw down my gear and joined Dave on a walk down the hill, through the gates, and into the town of Bloomington, Indiana in search of Italian perfection.

Sam had tears in his eyes when he finished reading this section. He'd discovered a new focus for his attention—the study of Sam Loftus's life. He wondered if the journals would all match his memories or if they would diverge at a certain point, describing the life everyone here seemed to think he lived and not the one he remembered. He could just open the last journal and start reading, but he wasn't ready for that. He'd work his way up to it.

Janet knocked softly on the door. "Are you ready to leave, Sam? You said you wanted to be at DMV by 10:00 a.m."

Sam replaced the first journal, closed the door in the wainscoting, and replaced the bedside table before walking to the bedroom door. "Thanks for reminding me, Janet. I'm as ready as I'll ever be."

During the drive to the DMV, Sam asked Janet what she'd been working on when his return home took her away from her job.

"Well, Ms. Opal is redecorating some of the guest rooms at her ranch and wants a casual/elegant look. Try achieving that combination sometime."

"If memory serves, Ms. Opal is your code word for an immensely wealthy, former TV talk show host, who owns a good chunk of our island. Am I right?"

Janet smiled. "My lips are sealed."

From the day after he came home with Janet, they fell easily into this kind of comfortable banter. No matter how different the Dave he met here was, Janet was as warm and friendly as he remembered her.

Janet parked outside the DMV and walked in with Sam for his appointment. She put her arm through his, but it was an expression of friendship and Sam appreciated it. He hadn't realized how nervous he was at taking this damn test. He signed in and waited the usual Maui hour before his number was called. After passing the written exam, he went back to waiting until the driving examiner was ready for him.

Janet waited for a half hour while Sam disappeared to take the driving test. When Sam returned, she could tell from the look on his face he'd passed. They rushed together and hugged in honest celebration of Sam's accomplishment.

Sam suggested they share lunch at Koho's, a small local restaurant attached to the Queen Kaʻahumanu Center that had good food and even better prices. Sam had a plate lunch special of baked chicken smothered in their creamy white Koho sauce with rice and mac salad. Janet had the teriyaki version of the chicken with the same sides.

"Sam, this was a great idea. I love this place."

"Me, too." He knew she was thinking about times they'd been here together before but had refrained from mentioning it to avoid hurting Sam's feelings. For the hundredth time Sam noted what a thoughtful person Janet was.

She displayed that thoughtfulness in her very next sentence. "Sam, after we eat, why don't you drop me at home and drive on over to Dr. Drayton's office. I know he scheduled an extra session for after you took your driver's test."

His smile was broad once more. "Oh, you are one of a kind. I was hoping you'd suggest that. Something about driving gives a man a sense of restored freedom that's hard to match. I promise I'll be very careful of your car."

"It's our car, Sam," she said and quickly added, "Housemates often share cars."

"Yeah. Dave and I shared a beautiful old wreck in grad school."

"Did you think I could forget the snail? Who painted those swirls on the side of your old Vee-dub, anyway?"

"A very clingy art major Dave once dated. She really annoyed him, but he put up with her until she finished painting the car. Then he hooked her up with another budding lawyer that he didn't like very much. When they got married, Dave said the pairing saved two other people from horrible spouses."

"I'm sorry you two grew apart over here. I never really understood it until now, but I guess people change in different ways. I'm glad we continued with our family get togethers, I don't know what I would have done if I couldn't have stayed close with Julie."

Sam saw Janet regret mentioning her sister's name the second it left her mouth. He jumped in. "Maybe we'll start doing that again with Julie when I'm better. I don't think Dave's going to be available for a while, do you?"

She smiled at his joke.

That changed the mood, and he was glad.

After lunch they wandered around the mall a bit and picked

up a few things they needed to maintain their separate bedroom lifestyle. When they got home it was still too early for him to go directly to Drayton's office. The doctor had opened a spot for Sam at 3:00 p.m.

Janet again read his mind. "You go on. Explore the island a little before going to see Dr. Drayton. It'll do you good."

Sam liked this woman.

"How goes it, Sam?" Drayton always started the session with some version of this question.

"Still kicking." Sam's replies were also predictable.

"I'm glad you could come in on Tuesdays and Fridays. All our subsequent sessions will be at 4:00 p.m., okay? I thought that would be less of a problem once you return to work part-time."

"I appreciate that. I've got a lot to tell you about, today."

"Good. First, tell me about the house."

"It's a nice house and has some things in it that I remember. I do feel at home there for the most part."

Drayton jotted something down on a legal pad. "That's good. As for the items in the house that you remember, do you also remember buying them?"

"Yes. But my memories are of buying them with Julie."

"I see." Another note.

"I passed my driving test today. Janet let me drive myself over here solo."

"Remember what I've said about returning to normal activities. How did it feel?"

"Very good, Doc. Very good. I felt a sense of freedom."

Now came one of Drayton's patented conversation gaps. At the beginning Sam took them as challenges and never spoke until Drayton was forced to. This time though, Sam had something on his mind and wasn't going to play. "I found something else at home today. Something I remembered very clearly."

"Oh, what was that?"

"A collection of journals I've kept since college. I started reading the first one and remembered everything I'd written word-for-word."

"That's very interesting." Drayton seemed to stiffen briefly, before resuming his normal relaxed attitude.

Sam couldn't tell if he'd made a mistake telling Drayton about the journals but decided to push on. "I want to read through them in chronological order. I think they could help me get my memory back. My real memory." He knew how to play this game.

"I agree. Would you be willing to share them with me?"

Sam had to be careful here. "Sure. But, you know, I'd like to finish each book before I hand it over. I trust you, but I'd like to know if I got a little racy anywhere. I know you're a doctor and I won't censor anything. Do you know what I'm saying?"

"Certainly, Sam. I'll read them as you pass them on to me and never discuss anything in them with anyone but you."

"Thanks. I'm not ready to share these with Janet. I kept them private for a reason."

"Would you like to tell me why?"

"No. Well, not yet. I'm not sure what I'll find in them."

"I see what you mean. Let's talk about how your other studies are going...."

~

SAM PULLED UP IN FRONT OF THEIR HOME AND NOTICED again the excellent care Janet had given his bromeliad garden while he was in the hospital. She'd weeded, refreshed the mulch, and maintained his strict watering schedule. Whatever his feelings for her, he had no doubt this woman truly loved her husband. He opened the door to fragrant aromas coming from the kitchen. He guessed another mouth-watering dinner awaited.

After dinner they played Mah Jong, and Sam enjoyed the game. In his mind Janet taught it to him a few days ago, though

Janet's told him they'd been playing for years, both two-person and occasionally four-person with other couples.

"I really enjoy this game, but you're still beating the pants off me."

"You'll improve," Janet said and cleared the game table.

Watching Janet return the pieces to their case, Sam appreciated the grace in her movements. Her slender fingers seemed to float in the air as she reached for the tiles and silently replaced them in their case. Gentleness defined this woman. He found himself enjoying their time together.

"It's been a very exciting day for me. I think I'll turn in and read a while. Goodnight, Janet."

"Goodnight, Sam. Sleep tight."

Locking the bedroom door, he retrieved the first of his journals and continued reading. When his eyes closed a half-hour later, he was calmed by the fact that everything he'd read in the first three journals was familiar and unchanged from his memories. He'd assumed this would be the case but was reassured when it was. Journal number four was the one he dreaded reading the most. It should describe a certain state fair and meeting two lovely sisters.

Chapter Forty-Three

Friday, April 26, 9:00 a.m.

All week, Sam read his journals each night before falling asleep. But, with Janet back at work today, he planned to spend the entire morning and most of the afternoon reading.

Tuesday evening he'd reached the section about the Indiana State Fair and his fears were validated. From that point on the journal diverged from his memories. He could hear his own voice in the writing. In a mirror he could see it was even his own handwriting. It wasn't a forgery. But it described events he'd never experienced. Or had he? Were the doctors right, after all? Were his other memories a delusion? For the first time he considered the possibility and its consequences.

He realized that being Janet's husband had many advantages. He really liked this woman and she obviously adored him. They had a beautiful home and enjoyed their jobs. Was that so horrible? Julie didn't seem to care about him at all.

What about Cindy and Timmy? This thought represented an unbreachable barrier to acceptance.

He'd struggled to find other possible explanations for his experiences. Scoured the library, the web, and the media. A logical man, he had to find a logical way out of this living nightmare. Oh, yes, he had actual nightmares, too, every night. The worst last night. In it he woke up and remembered his life exactly the way everyone else did. He realized he had no children and went to work feeling everything was just fine. His screams on waking had brought Janet to the door to check on him.

"Just a dream," he'd said.

But what if last night was more than just a dream? What if his subconscious mind was trying to make sense of things? What if, some day during a session with Drayton, or dinner with Janet, or back at work, his mind just reassembled his memories into a pattern that fit his current life? Would that be a miraculous cure or a heartless punishment? He saw the danger but couldn't stop reading the journals.

He immersed himself in reading about a life he didn't remember, not even stopping for lunch. He jumped at the alarm he'd set as a reminder to leave for his session with Drayton. He grabbed the first four journals off his bed to take them with him and sealed the tenth journal, which he was still reading, back in the baseboard with the rest.

SAM ALWAYS FELT CALMER WHEN HE ENTERED DR. Drayton's private office. Everything seemed orderly and balanced. Drayton represented the same traits in his person, as he sat behind his desk waiting for Sam.

"Hiya, Doc." Sam decided to pre-empt the usual question about how he was doing.

"Hello, Sam. You seem to have something on your mind."

He'd recognized Drayton's skill of knowing when to let his patient take the lead.

"I brought the first four journals in for you to read."

"I appreciate your trust in me, Sam. I will not abuse it."

"I know you won't."

"Tell me about what you read."

Sam decided to be completely open with the psychiatrist, for the first time. "The first two books, about college, describe events precisely as I remember them and are recorded just as I remember recording them. The third book, about graduate school, is the same. The fourth book is the same until the last few pages."

Drayton jotted a note, something he seemed to do less frequently since Sam left the rehab facility. "Tell me about those last few pages."

"They describe our day at the Indiana State Fair. I still won the coin toss with Dave and still picked the girl on the right, but the girl on the right was Janet, not Julie."

"I see."

"The fifth journal describes our early courtship and all of the reasons I fell in love with Janet. I almost wished I'd been there."

"I believe someday you will remember being there. Go on."

"The sixth through ninth journals, which I've finished, describe our marriage and honeymoon and the close relationship we had with Dave and Julie before they moved to Maui. They also covered the next two years we lived in Indianapolis before we moved here."

"Was it similar to what you remembered?"

"Some of it was. The trip to Maui, the description of my work at the main office, my friends there, the times we spent with Julie and Dave, were very familiar. But the differences made them bizarre. I would say something that I remembered saying to Julie, but I was saying it to Janet. The friendships we developed outside of work were very different and with people I don't remember knowing. Before they left for Maui, Dave was different, too. He seemed to be high a lot and not on pot. This was completely wrong. Once he and Janet married, he never touched drugs again. He knew he'd lose her if he did, and he really loved her."

"But in the journals, he married Julie. Wasn't she more of a free spirit than Janet?"

"Not so much in my memories. In my memories we spent more years in Indianapolis, while she finished medical school. But, in the journals, she decided on performing rather than pediatrics and that environment can be...well...freeing, I guess."

"I told you in the hospital that you struck me as an educated and logical individual. Do you remember?"

"Yes, it was one of the reasons I liked you."

"You know that I believe that the memories you recall of Julie and your children are delusions."

"Yes." Sam tried to hide his disgust at the term.

"And I know you have trouble believing that. Something you may not know is that I believe intelligent, logical individuals have intelligent, logical delusions."

"Huh?"

"When a creative person has a delusion, it can be extremely unrealistic. But someone like you couldn't accept such a thing. Your delusions must make sense to you at some level. They must be internally consistent. It's one of the things that made me think of Capgras. People with Capgras are known for the internal consistency of their delusions."

"What makes you think my *delusional* memories are logical?"

"Your Left-Right Transposition explains the differences in your memories. You remember Julie coming out of the right door and Janet out of the left, but for you the right door is the left. We need to pursue this. Assume for one instant that you were unhappy with your life and felt that everything would have been better if you'd chosen the other girl. If left were right, you would have. Then everything you believe happened would have been perfectly consistent with logic."

"That sounds frighteningly plausible. But Janet said she and I were perfectly happy."

"Maybe she was and believed you were, too. But only you

knew if you were happy. And you have a way to find out what you knew."

"The journals."

"Yes. I encourage you to keep on reading."

"I will."

Chapter Forty-Four

Friday, May 3, 3:15 p.m.

It felt good to finish a day's work, leave the office, and walk down the stairway to his car. This initial week back represented the first time Sam had felt normal since the crash. Even the mirror numbers didn't bother him. He'd become truly indifferent to whether the columns were left to right or right to left. The reversed YTREWQ keyboard was normal to him now, as was the numerical keyboard. They even had a mnemonic for it in this world, *qwerty*.

He worked nine to three, Tuesday through Friday, which allowed him to make his appointments with Dr. Drayton on time. The sessions had become more and more interesting as he worked his way through his journals. Last night he'd finished reading the final set and found himself anxious to share some critical aspects with Drayton.

He now understood why he could no longer be friends with Dave Walden. He knew, too, how close he'd been to Janet right before the crash, and why she cared so much about him. He no longer feigned anything around her or Drayton. He saw Drayton as a friend and mentor.

He found his usual parking space occupied outside the medical clinic. *That'll teach me to come early.* The receptionist was happy to see him, and he enjoyed talking with her a little before each visit. "Hello, Maria. How is every little thing with you?"

"Pretty good, Mr. Loftus. And the doctor is in a pretty good mood, too. He just had a journal article accepted."

"He's saving the one he's writing about me for JAMA. I'm one of a kind."

"I think you're just a very nice man."

"Thank you, Maria. I really try to be."

Sam took a seat next to a young man in the waiting room. He knew he was early but was surprised the doctors 3 p.m. wasn't already in the office. "Aloha," Sam said to the young man.

"Aloha. I guess he's running a little late. He wanted to talk to my boss before me today. My boss is the one who recommended Dr. Drayton to me."

"What line of work are you in?"

"I'm an astrophysicist. I'm doing post-doctoral research up at the observatories on Haleakala."

"I've always been fascinated by astronomy and physics. I guess it's because I've always loved math. I'm an accountant. Sam Loftus." Sam stuck out his hand and the other man smiled and shook it.

"I'm Brad Carvell. I'd love to talk with you about my research sometime—if you'd be interested, that is."

"Would I? I devoured every episode of Cosmos, the original with Sagan and the new version with Neil DeGrasse Tyson." For the first time in a long time, he didn't think about his reason for being in Drayton's office.

"Dr. Drayton has really made a difference in my life. How about you?" Brad asked

"Absolutely. Evan's the best,"

As if on cue, Evan Drayton came out to usher Carvell into his office and leaned over to Sam. "Hello, my friend. I'm looking forward to our session today. Your E-mail mentioned you finished reading the last set of journals."

"I did. And they make all the difference."

"See you in a few minutes," Drayton said before he walked into his office behind Carvell. Sam could see another gentleman in the room before the door closed.

~

When it was Sam's turn, Drayton moved to the table where they were now spending sessions, so he could point out things in the journals as they talked.

"I've learned many things about myself and about my brother-in-law from these last few journals," Sam said.

"In one of the journals you gave me to read, you discovered he was involved in illegal activities when he tried to get you involved. That was during a kayaking trip, right?"

"That's right. I took him ocean kayaking. I thought we would enjoy tackling a new version of an activity we once shared. He went, but only to tell me what a jerk I was to play by the rules. He was strung out on some drug the whole trip. I had to dive in and save him three times, before I gave up and rowed us to shore. We were once as close as brothers, but now..."

"He was clearly a different person by this time."

"I understand that now. He made me swear to tell no one about the deal he offered me."

"Are you comfortable talking about it now?" Drayton asked.

Sam nodded. "It's all come out since he was arrested. He'd met a bunch of wealthy, high-level criminals vacationing here, and they invited him to a meeting in New York. He knew before he went that they were probably drug kingpins, but that only increased his interest."

"He was different from the Dave you remembered. Do you have any idea why he was not a user in your memories?"

"In my memories, he married Janet, who was totally grounded. She weaned him off pot and party drugs before they ever left Indiana. But here, in the real world, he discovered Maui was a great place to indulge all his baser interests."

He noticed Drayton smile at his use of the term *real world* to refer to the world described in his journals.

"What was the deal he offered you during the kayaking trip?"

"A full partnership in the most extensive ice distribution ring on Maui. He'd been working for the mainland bosses for a year when we arrived on Maui. He said he did something called conversion in a lab he'd rented and wanted to keep it going while he built a new lab somewhere more secure. He had another chemist, but he needed someone to manage the finances."

"You refused him."

"I lost my temper. Told him he was an idiot to get into something like this and that he needed to get out. He tried to punch me in the face, but his aim was off. I told him our friendship was over. He begged me not to tell anyone, especially Julie and Janet. I agreed to keep up an appearance of congeniality but told him that would be limited to major holidays—and it was."

"Thanks for filling in that gap for me. Let's move on to what you've just finished reading."

Sam paused before moving forward. "Evan, I started our relationship by lying to you and under-rating your talent as a psychiatrist."

"We're past all that now."

"Yes, but I want you to know how much I appreciate this second chance you've given me. I'm committed to using it wisely. I may not be able to remember loving Janet, but I do love her now. All of these journals have shown me how much I loved her before the accident and why, but these last two touched me more deeply than anything I'd read before." His voice faltered on the last two words.

"I see."

"Not really, but you will when you've read them. I want to

focus on something from the very last entry, the night before the crash."

"The last entry would have been on March fourteenth, right?"

"Yes. It was Janet and Julie's birthday and we got together at Dave and Julie's for dinner and presents. The evening dragged on for me, but the girls seemed happy with their presents. The catered dinner was fabulous. I suspected Dave was just showing off.

"Julie had a little more champagne than usual. She was only a little tipsy but started talking about Dave closing his practice to work full time as her agent. Dave tried to change the subject, but she kept on, saying Dave should just retire and play golf and leave managing her career to her longtime agent.

"Dave said it was time for bed and ushered Janet and me out of the house as quickly as possible. As we drove off, I glanced back and saw Dave yelling at Julie through the small window beside the door. As we turned the corner, I saw him draw his arm back to slap her

"Did you actually see him strike her?"

"No. That's why I didn't turn the car around or mention anything about it to Janet. I had a suspicion, but no proof."

"Is that where this stood, before the car crash?"

"Not quite. When we got home, I called a friend who still socialized with Dave and Julie. I laid it all out for him and asked what he knew. He hesitated, but eventually told me about my brother-in-law. He said that Dave was a player with multiple mistresses. The friend had seen Dave slap Julie across the mouth more than once. Dave always waited until they were outside or in their car. But the friend had seen him make contact."

"Did you tell Janet?"

"I decided to wait until the next evening." He opened the top journal to the last page. "I wanted to check the story with a few other people when I was at work, but I say in the journal:

I now know that Dave is hurting Julie. We need to help her get out of this situation. At dinner tomorrow, I'll tell Jan and get her to

take Julie to a lawyer friend we know. We must protect her. I must protect her.

"When I read that, I had an idea why my mind might have done this thing to me."

"To save Julie from an abusive relationship. Sam, I think you're on to something."

"Remember that earlier session when we talked about how the left-right transposition might account for why I thought Julie was my wife?"

"Yes, it made the coin toss connect you with Julie instead of Janet."

"But I think we're looking at this backwards. What if I really had amnesia, but retained the desire to save Julie from Dave?"

"And your mind changed one small fact to make it possible for you to save Julie without restoring your entire memory. If she were your wife, Dave couldn't hurt her anymore. He could never have hurt her at all."

"That's what I've been thinking. But what do I do now?"

"Exactly what you planned to do before the crash. Tell Janet."

"I will. Maybe that will give my memory a jolt and get me back on track."

"Maybe, but don't expect anything to happen too fast. I believe this is a critical step on the road to your complete recovery, but that road may still be a little longer than you'd like."

"I understand. But I can't wait to take Janet out to dinner tonight. We're having our first date night."

Chapter Forty-Five

Sam and Janet arrived at the Kula Lodge and were led to a table next to one of the floor-to-ceiling windows. From here they enjoyed a breathtaking view of the Valley Isle, from the bright lights of Kahului in the east to those of Kihei in the west. The darkness of the cane fields contrasted with the inverted bouquets of lights that narrowed as they stretched up the many canyons of the West Maui Mountains.

"Oh Sam, this view is just as beautiful as I remember it." He watched as Janet's eyes took in everything.

The restaurant was a feast for the eyes, as well. From the enclosed space where they sat, they saw tables spilling down the hillside on stone-tiled plateaus surrounded by luscious gardens. A huge cairn dominated the center of this lovely outdoor seating area. Although there were a variety of niches in the stone structure, one larger opening provided access to the wood-fired, pizza oven.

Over a steaming bowl of French onion soup—made with sweet Maui onions of course— they reminisced about how they met.

"I remember that day at the Indiana State Fair, when we first laid eyes on you two," he began.

"I know you thought you guys spotted us first,' Janet said, "but we'd caught multiple glimpses of you two cruising the midway before we got on that haunted house ride."

"Were we that obvious?"

"Oh, yes. When Julie and I exited the haunted house, we weren't surprised in the slightest to find you there. Remember how that moving wall made sure alternating guests exited on different sides of the ride? Julie came out first on one side and I came out on the other to find you waiting."

In his memories Sam waited outside the left door (his right) and met Julie. But he had read the journal and knew the other scenario so well he could recite it to Janet. "I believe you were wearing a yellow polka-dot sun dress."

"That's right. I'm surprised you remember what I was wearing."

"You looked so bright and fresh, as you do tonight." He was glad he'd read the journal to confirm that she'd worn the same dress as in his memories. This was the point where the journal and his memory diverged, but at least this piece was the same.

"You were wearing light grey slacks and a short-sleeve blue dress shirt—unlike your scruffy colleague in tank-top and shorts."

"I was always a little self-conscious of my scrawny legs, unlike Dave."

Their waiter placed two gourmet wood-fired pizzas on their table. The aromas made his mouth water, as Sam served one slice of each to Janet.

"I'm glad you remember we like to share. These last few weeks with you have been very nice for me, Sam. I hope they've been like that for you."

"They have, Jan. I hope you don't mind if I start calling you that. I know I used to."

"I don't mind."

"Every moment I've spent with you since I came home has brought me joy. We fit well together."

Jan smiled at him and took a bite of the pizza.

"Drayton and I had a valuable session today. I know I don't usually share things from our sessions, but tonight I want to, if it's all right with you."

"I'd like that." Jan looked up at him with hope in her eyes. "I have to admit to wondering what you two talk about."

"First, I need to give you a little background. The day after I came home from the hospital, I found something I'd hidden in the bedroom, my personal journals. I started keeping these when I entered college and never stopped. As you can imagine, these were written in mirror writing for me, but when I looked at them in a mirror, I recognized my own handwriting. Thanks to my rehab at the hospital, I didn't need a mirror to read them. I read one or two each day until I reached the present."

"Did they bring back memories?"

"The first few did, but they all provided important information. Everything in the journals until the moment we met at the fair was exactly as I'd remembered entering it."

"Then they diverged." The hope in her eyes faded and she produced a long sigh.

"Yes, but don't lose hope, Jan. As I read through the remaining journals, I discovered what Dr. Drayton and I think may be the cause of my delusions."

Jan's hands began to quiver. He had never admitted to having delusions until this moment.

"Up until today, Dr. Drayton was operating on the assumption that I had some suppressed desire for Julie and that was what caused the delusion."

"And you didn't?" Her tone suggested Jan had made the same assumption.

"According to the journals, I discovered that Dave was abusing Julie and wanted to protect her. But I had no romantic feelings for her. Before the crash, I had decided to ask you to confront Julie and see if you could convince her to leave Dave."

Jan's expression suggested some irony in what he was telling her, but he continued. "Drayton feels that the trauma of the accident pushed my mind down an alternative path to save Julie from pain. If I were her husband, she would be freed from Dave's abuse."

"That makes perfect sense. But why left and right?"

"Before you and Julie came out of the haunted house, Dave and I flipped a coin. I picked the right side to wait for my new girlfriend."

"And I came out on the right."

"You came out on the right for you, but Julie came out on the right for me, if left and right were switched."

"Whoa. Your mind came up with this whole mirror world thing just to create a logical reason why Julie was your wife?"

"That's what Drayton thinks. He's seen similar things before. I'm still not able to suppress those memories, but he feels my recognition of what is going on is a major step forward."

"It is. This changes everything."

"I think so, too. Neither he nor I can guarantee what will happen now, but he felt this might provide us with a glimmer of hope."

"It does, Sam. It does."

"By the way, Julie has to divorce Dave."

For the first time since Sam's accident, Jan broke into a hearty laugh.

He was caught off-guard, but Jan quickly explained.

Patting him on the shoulder she said, "Oh, my poor Sam. Let me catch you up on a little story that has been unfolding while you've been healing. Drayton wouldn't let me tell you about it before, but I'm sure it's okay now."

"Please do."

"Where to begin? Well, the afternoon after your accident Sergeant Boyd interviewed Julie and me at our house..."

~

Jan felt comfortable enough on the way home from the Kula Lodge, to ask one last question about Sam's session with Drayton.

"Sam, you've made me very happy tonight. You've always been a thoughtful man and the kindness you showed me tonight was very special. I understand you still have conflicting memories and promise not to push you. But I wondered if Dr. Drayton had any thoughts about your memory of the crash."

"It's fine, Jan. I don't mind talking about it. I've been concealing part of my memories from him, and from you. You see, I remember passing through a film, like a soap bubble, before I discovered we were on what I believed was the wrong side of the road and swerved into the wrong lane. I remember left being right before the accident."

"Before the accident. No wonder you doubted your doctors."

"Today I came clean with Evan. I told him what I just told you. Then he made a valid point, that I hadn't considered. These are still memories. If my memories of the distant past can be disrupted by the delusion, why couldn't those of the moments before the crash?"

She thought about this. "That makes sense."

"I'm not able to remember the way life really was, yet. But I am willing to accept the possibility, probability, that the other memories are part of a delusion. There really isn't any other logical explanation. And, as you know..."

"You're a very logical man. And a very special one."

When they walked up to their front door, Jan felt a familiar emotion.

"Thank you for a wonderful evening," she said, as she searched her purse for keys.

"Thank you, Miss Madison. Would you like to do this again sometime?"

"I would like that very much, Mr. Loftus."

Sam gently grasped her arm and turned her to face him. Their eyes locked for the first time since the accident. He seemed to hesitate then pulled her closer until their lips brushed. Suppressed emotion surged to the surface. They kissed, sharing their passion, locked in each other's arms. Finally, breathless, she ended the kiss. They gazed at each other with tentative smiles before she turned and entered the house.

Without a word, they went to their separate bedrooms and closed the doors. They had taken an important first step. But she understood a long difficult journey lay ahead.

For the first time since the accident, she dreamed of their days together before that calamity. For the first time, she allowed herself to believe those days would come again.

5. Another Looking Glass

"If you set to work to believe everything, you will tire out the believing-muscles of your mind, and then you'll be so weak you won't be able to believe the simplest true things."

— Lewis Carroll

Chapter Forty-Six

Monday, May 6, Morning

Timmy stared at the sand. He seemed to be working something out in his mind before proceeding with the construction of his sandcastle. Sam appreciated that about Tim. His son never rushed into things. Tim always had a plan in his mind and stuck to it. This reminded Sam of, well, Sam.

Cindy was off in the waves with her trusty boogie board in hand. She was a risk taker, who never hesitated to try anything. That's why he and Julie always kept a sharp eye on her.

Julie was riding alongside their daughter on her own board. Smiling as the surf splashed her eyes and the trade winds tossed her hair. She was an object of fascination to him. In her work as a pediatrician, she had to help parents deal with devastating tragedy. Her empathy was deep and honest. After all, she had two young children of her own. Her patients appreciated that.

Yet when she came home to them each evening, she brought none of this with her. She loved her work and her family but kept them separate. The kids knew she was a doctor who helped kids get well, but no work visits were ever allowed. She also refused to treat her own children. He was responsible for all bandaging and boo-boo kissing at home—a task he loved.

Cindy ran up from the shore break and threw her wet arms around her daddy's neck before planting a saltwater kiss on his cheek. Julie stopped to admire Timmy's sandcastle before joining Sam and Cindy. After toweling off, she smoothed out the blanket they were on and lay beside Sam on her stomach with Cindy beside her in the same orientation.

Soon Timmy ran up and grabbed his father's hand. "Come see my fortress of silly-tude, Daddy. It's super."

Sam stood with effort and followed his son down to see his newest creation. The smooth lines of the humped structure reminded him of a prehistoric mud hut, but he complimented Timmy on his craftsmanship. "It is a truly stable structure in harmony with its environment, yet has a somewhat dreamlike lightness. Good job, Tim."

"We're real, Daddy, not a dream. Cindy and Mommy and me. We're real. Don't let them make you forget us. We love you. We love you so, so much."

Now Cindy and Julie were standing by Timmy. "We're real. Don't forget us or we'll die."

As they cried these words, first Julie, then Cindy, then Timmy gradually started to lose their shapes. Were they being washed away by the tide?

～

Sam woke sobbing, tears streaming down his cheeks. He'd assumed once he understood his delusion, his subconscious mind would stop torturing him with dreams of the family he could never have.

He could accept the truth, why couldn't his wayward mind? His mind had been betraying him and torturing him ever since the accident. Hadn't he suffered enough? If he couldn't get past this, he really would go mad. He would have to take things more slowly. He would have to control his impatience to return to normal.

Normal was always important to Sam. He remembered when he was very young his father would make fun of his mother for her eccentric tastes. "Can't you just be normal?" he would say with a pretend scowl on his face. Sam's dad never had to say that to him. He loved normal. Normal was clean and neat and orderly. Normal was the way things should be.

The jingle of their home telephone interrupted his thoughts. Glancing at the clock on his bedside stand, he realized he'd slept in. Jan had already left for work without disturbing him. He scrambled to answer the phone. "Hello."

"Hello. Is this Sam Loftus?" a male voice said.

"Yes." Sam didn't recognize the voice.

"I'm hoping you remember the nerdy guy you met Friday at Dr. Drayton's office?"

"The astrophysicist. Yes, I remember. Brad, isn't it?"

"That's right Brad Carvell. I never trust my memory these days, so I wrote myself a note to call you and invite you up to the observatory to talk about my work."

"Wow. How did you find me?"

"I called your office first and a sweet girl named Kimmey gave me your phone number. I hear you're back at work three days a week."

"Just back. Last week was my first. I'm working Tuesday, Thursday, and Friday this week."

"I just called to see when you might be free for a personal tour of the observatory?"

"I would so love that."

"Is it possible to make it some day this week?"

"Actually, Wednesday would be great. I don't have anything planned. Would that work for you?"

"Perfect. Do you know how to get up here?"

"I know how to get to that first, big scary gate."

"I'll let them know you're coming. That's just the first gate, by the way. It's kind of hyper-secure up here. Just roll with it, okay? How about 2 p.m.?"

"Great. I'll let you know if I run into any problems." Sam hoped neither Jan nor Evan had objections. *This is just what I need to get my mind off... other things.*

"And, Sam, I'm going to show you things up here that will blow your mind. See you Wednesday."

After Brad hung up, Sam thought to himself, *First time I've ever been glad Kimmey's a flake.* No reasonable receptionist would give out an employee's phone number to a total stranger. Welcome to Maui.

Then Sam reflected on the last thing Brad had said, "...I'm going to show you things up here that will blow your mind..."

Hasn't my mind been blown enough?

JULIE JUST FINISHED RINSING HER SALAD BOWL FROM lunch when her cellphone rang.

"Hey, Julie, it's Jan."

"Hi, sweetie. I just finished rinsing some dishes, let me dry my hands, okay?"

"Sure. How's everything going? As if I didn't know."

"I can't lie to you, Jan. I've never been happier. Keone has really brought me through this. He's everything Dave isn't. Strong, quiet, caring, and naturally passionate. Nothing Keone does is ever for show. He's the real deal."

"I'm so happy for you. You deserve this."

"Thank you. You deserve to be happy too, Jan." She paused. "How are things with you and Sam?"

"Better. Much better. He's starting to believe the doctors at last. He and Dr. Drayton even have an idea why he thought you were his wife in his delusions. And, Julie, he kissed me last night after our date."

"That's amazing." She didn't want her sister to get too carried away.

"He's even returned to an old hobby, astronomy. He called me at work this morning and *asked my permission* for him to go on a tour of the observatories on Haleakala Wednesday with a friend who works there."

"I can see that would encourage you." Julie felt a twinge of concern. Were things moving just a little too fast.

"You can't imagine my relief. We discussed something on the phone that might help slam the door on his old delusions, and you and Keone can help."

Julie felt her defenses coming online. "What did you discuss?"

"Well, now that we know Sam never had any romantic feelings for you, he suggested I ask you and Keone over for dinner."

He suggested. "You told him about Keone and me?"

"Last night, after dinner. He was so happy for you. Drayton thinks a large part of his delusions were caused by his concerns about how Dave was treating you."

"How did he know?"

"After our birthday party, as we were driving away, he saw Dave raise his hand to slap you."

Julie remembered that evening and that slap, but still. "Do you really think it's a good idea to get together so soon? We wouldn't want to do anything to delay his recovery."

"I talked with Dr. Drayton before calling you. He thinks it's a wonderful idea. He's even coming to observe the interaction."

Damn. "When is this proposed get-together?"

"On our anniversary, next month. I wanted to give you plenty of warning and plenty of chance to back out if anything changes. Please say you'll consider it. It would mean everything to me, and Sam."

"Let me call Keone and see what he says. Your anniversary is June fifth, right? What time?"

"Seven. I'll keep my fingers crossed until you call back. Aloha, Honey."

Julie poured herself a cup of coffee, sat in a kitchen chair, and tried to digest what she'd just heard. She knew this was the next logical step in Sam's treatment plan and wanted to help Jan get her husband back. So, why did she feel like this was the worst idea ever?

She remembered the way Sam had looked at her in the hospital. She'd seen a passion and a pain in his eyes that frightened her to her core. Could a logical, alternative explanation take all that away?

Chapter Forty-Seven

Wednesday, May 8, 2:00 p.m.

The road up Haleakala volcano, despite all the switchbacks, was fun for Sam. He loved the crazy curves, amazing views, and the smell of grazing land and eucalyptus. Up here he felt free from stress, noise, and painful memories. He looked forward to a day when he could look back on his delusions as just that. He knew he was making progress and felt this visit to a new friend and old hobby could only help.

Turning off the main road that led to the visitor center for the National Park, he approached the first gate onto observatory property. An armed guard approached his window to confirm he had legitimate business at the observatory.

"I'm Samuel Loftus," he said, handing over his driver's license. "I'm here to visit Dr. Bradley Carvell."

The guard took Sam's license back to his shelter and disappeared for a few minutes. When the guard returned, he said, "You're cleared to proceed beyond this gate, Mr. Loftus. Dr.

Carvell will meet you at the next gate, where you will park your car. He will transfer you to the observatory in his vehicle."

Sam was glad to see Brad waiting at the next gate. A guard directed him to a small parking lot outside this second fence. When Sam walked back to the gate from his car, the guard again took his driver's license. As Sam passed through the gate with Brad, he did not offer to return it. Brad immediately grabbed Sam's hand and gave it a vigorous shake.

"Welcome, new friend. I can't wait to tell you about our recent discoveries, but there will be fewer questions if I give you a little tour first. We have quite a facility up here."

Sam glanced back toward the gate to find the guard had returned to his shelter.

"You'll get your license back when you leave. The security gets even stricter from here on in. Here, put this on."

Brad gave him a badge attached to a lanyard, which he slipped over his head.

"The lettering on the badge is time sensitive. In four hours, your name and visitor status will fade away to be replaced by the word 'void' in bright red. My name, as your host, will remain visible so they know who to blame for your unauthorized presence."

They passed through two more gates, both equipped with metal detectors, before arriving at the facility scattered across the very top of the crater's rim.

As they exited the vehicle, Brad winked and began an obviously canned lecture about the facility. "Haleakala Observatory is one of the most valuable sites in the world. Above the tropical inversion layer and blessed with clear skies in the night and evening hours, it is an excellent spot to observe the universe. The University of Hawai'i Institute for Astronomy manages this site, as it has for over forty years. Much of the work done here could not be conducted anywhere else on Earth. Scientists from NASA, the NSF, the Space Telescope Institute, the Pan-STARRS consortium, the Air Force, and many other prestigious institutions work here." His second wink came as he said the Air Force.

Sam saw multiple structures, many with the familiar spherical shape of observatories. Brad pointed out the Mees Observatory, the two Pan-STARRS (PS-1 and PS-2, prototypes for a larger telescope to be built on Mauna Kea on the Big Island), the LCO Faulkes Observatory, and the Zodiacal Light Observatory. Less conventional structures included the TLRS Laser Ranging System, the Maui Space Surveillance Site, the Advanced Electro-Optical System [AEOS], and the facility they were about to enter, which he referred to as home.

"There is a name for this facility. But if I told you, I'd have to shoot you."

"That secret, huh?"

"No. That stupid. It's the Southwestern Center for Regional Extreme Electro-Magnetic Wave Detection."

"S-C-R-E-E-W-D?"

"And guess how it's pronounced?"

He couldn't suppress laugh, then noticed Brad waited to open the door until he brought himself back under control.

Inside the door another round of security checks took place before they could enter the rather spacious, but bleak, cinderblock structure.

"We've entered on the top floor, which is at ground level. This is where all the offices reside, surrounding that huge square chasm in front of you. All of the equipment is down there, well below our line of site," Brad explained.

"Hello, Brad. Nice to see your friend arrived." A dignified, grey-haired gentleman approached.

"Sam Loftus, I'd like to introduce you to my boss, Dr. Martin Hasselbach. Dr. Hasselbach oversees all work here at the top of the world for the UH Institute of Astronomy."

"Pleasure to meet you, sir." Since the man didn't offer a hand to shake, Sam nodded his head towards him.

"The pleasure is ours. We have rather few non-scientist visitors here at the observatory. I hope you enjoyed your tour."

So that was the tour. Pointing at a bunch of domes and square buildings. He was a little disappointed, to say the least, especially since the building he was in had nothing that looked like a telescope. Still, he was here to learn about Brad's work, with all that complicated mathematics, so what the hell. "You have a very extensive facility. Brad told me this is the only place in the world where most of the work done here can be carried out."

Hasselbach smiled. Sam guessed it was because he'd quoted directly from the script Brad followed. "I'll let you two friends talk in your office, right, Brad?"

"Yes, sir. That's where we'll be."

Sam suspected Brad's words confirmed for Hasselbach that they would not venture beyond this non-classified space.

When they entered Brad's crowded work area, he closed and locked the door. "Sam, I apologize for rushing through the tour, but I have something much more interesting to share with you. My partner Radha and I have been studying a potential contact point between universes. And guess what, it's right here on Maui."

Sam was overwhelmed by the mass of information Brad presented to him. "Why have I never read about any of this, Brad?"

"Publications always lag a couple years behind discoveries, and the lay media lags years behind that."

Sam still had trouble getting his head around what Brad had just described. But if the fact that they were in Brad's office at a major research facility wasn't enough, his facile use of terms like Higg's boson, spontaneous symmetry breaking, tachyonic condensation, ripple cones, and string theory suggested Sam should at least listen to what the man had to say.

"Even scientists have difficulty understanding some of this stuff. When we met, I believe you mentioned watching that new *Cosmos* show when it was on, with Neil DeGrasse Tyson?"

"I loved it."

"Do you remember him talking about the multiverse?"

"Yes. He said there could be an infinite number of parallel universes displaced from each other in time. They would be invisible to each other."

"You'd make a good astrophysics student. What he described is a popular theory in physics that many people are studying, including me. It's why I'm here on Maui."

"Why Maui?"

"I learned about the presence of this facility through a colleague. It offered me the perfect tools to study a theory I have about contact points between parallel universes."

"Contact points."

"Yes. I won't inundate you with all the math, yet. But I think you'll find it fascinating. If these separate universes occasionally bumped into each other, just for a moment, it should be possible to measure it."

"Are you saying you've succeeded in measuring it?"

"Well, I thought I had. Multiple times. But so far, all our measurements have other possible explanations"

"What do you mean?

"I've been measuring these rare contacts for years. I discovered that the Hawaiian archipelago represents a uniquely active contact point, but my measurements were extremely inaccurate until I arrived here."

"At the eye of the storm."

"In a way, yes. The strongest single measurement to date was at 16:48:30 hours on March 15 of this year. It was located on the Honoapi'ilani highway near Ma'alaea Harbor. My supervisor, Dr. Hasselbach has found other possible interpretations of even that data, so I'm still looking. I got a bit obsessed about this particular reading which led to my visits to Dr. Drayton, but he's put me back on a more stable road. I even thought a traffic accident that happened at the same time might be related to my theories and contacted the police." Brad chuckled. "But I'm much better now."

He passed through the bubble at precisely the time and place Brad just mentioned. The accident Brad wanted to follow up on was his.

"How different from each other would these parallel universes be?"

"Theoretically the differences could be anything from unnoticeable to massive. The idea is that every possible decision could be made in any possible way. If I flip a coin, it could land either heads or tails, right?"

This sounded way too familiar. "Yes."

"In one of the major theories, if a coin lands heads in this universe, there is another parallel universe where it lands tails. That simple change results in a series of events which is different between the two universes."

"You mean like in one universe left could be left and in another right?"

"I suppose. Those words are just symbols for physical realities. Such symbols are arbitrary and could have developed differently in different universes. Many terms are based on established conventions. For example, up and down are based on action in a gravitational field. There's no up or down in space."

"Could someone from one universe adapt to such a dramatic difference?"

"Absolutely. I remember watching a movie in physics class in high school. It was from the late forties or early fifties. This scientist wears glasses that reverse up and down. At first, he's a mess. He can't catch a ball or read or anything. After a few months, he sees everything normally. They explained that the image the brain receives from the optic nerve is upside-down and the brain reverses it. When he took off the special glasses, he became completely uncoordinated again until his brain could flip everything back."

"But left/right inversion is different. A person with that just names things differently. Yes, the writing is backwards, but they can read writing that isn't backwards, too."

"You're right. I was just illustrating the adaptability of humans to change. What are North/South, East/West, Left/Right, and Up/Down? These are all conventions. The sun comes up in the same place, and the earth spins in the same direction in both the universe you described and ours. In that world Australia is still in the Southern Hemisphere, what we call 'East' they call 'East', what we call 'up' they call 'up'. In both worlds people write from different directions in English and Hebrew. Drive on the different sides of the road in America and the UK. Only the meaning of left and right are switched and everything that depends on this."

Everything that depends on this. Like whom a man decides to date.

"I don't know. I'm not sure. There might still be a flaw in your argument. You don't know everything I've experienced since the crash."

"What crash? I thought we were speaking theoretically." It was Brad's turn to look confused.

"Brad, I have a little information to share with you that you might find interesting. But you might want to sit down first."

Chapter Forty-Eight

Brad couldn't believe his good fortune. "This is amazing. I tried to find you a couple months ago, but they wouldn't tell me your name."

"They kept me locked up. Thought I was crazy. That's why I'm still visiting Dr. Drayton," Sam said.

"My treatment was successful. The day we met was my final visit with Dr. Drayton. I'm now officially on the project I was fascinated by." *And have access to all the equipment I need.*

"Could we both be crazy?" Sam asked.

"I don't believe in coincidences. Too bad you didn't keep a record of your experiences."

"I did. I keep a journal. I mean, I've always kept a journal, but I've continued to since the crash."

"Would you share it with me?"

"Sure. But you might find reading it challenging."

"Mirror writing. I have an imaging program that converts, it's helpful with some of my measurements. If you lend me your journal, I'll make a transposed copy and return the original to you."

A contemporaneous record. Brad couldn't believe his luck. So much better than interviews after the fact.

"I have the volumes since my crash in my car. I'll give them to you when you take me back."

"That'll work." He thought for a moment. "I'll just head home from there."

"Brad, I understand what you're telling me and why, but...I just reached a better place recently and I'm not sure I want to leave it."

"They've started to convince me, too. But look at this from my point of view. You're an integral component of the data that will prove or disprove my theory."

"I'm also very skeptical. I know I'll probably find a thousand holes in this once I've had a chance to think about it for a while."

"Good. I want you to. Hit me with everything you've got."

"Can we meet again?" Sam suggested.

"Sure. How about at my house? Here, I'll give you the address. You went right past it on your way up here. Can we meet...say...May fifteenth to continue our discussions? I'm usually free in the morning, after eight a.m."

"How about nine?"

"Perfect. I'll have your journal transposed and read before we meet. If I find any contradictions, I'll highlight them for you. And I expect you to read up on the multiverse and be ready with a battery of reasons why I'm full of it."

"Okay. Just remember, it's not personal."

Not for me, anyway, Brad thought.

Chapter Forty-Nine

Wednesday, May 15, 9:00 a.m.

As soon as Sam rang the doorbell Brad swung open the front door. *Was he waiting by the door?*

"Hello, Sam. Welcome to our humble abode." Brad turned to the woman hovering behind his left shoulder. "This is my wife, Diane."

Before Sam could give Diane a hug, Maui style, she bowed towards him. He bowed back. "I've met your husband very recently, but he's nurturing my love of astronomy and astrophysics. I even considered a career like his, but practicality won out. I'm an accountant."

"Sometimes I wish Brad was an accountant." Diane sounded serious. He was impressed by her soft voice and lovely face.

"I'm gonna to take Sam down to the lab and force him to drink a few Bloody Marys while we talk about good old cosmology," Brad said.

"Why not stay up here? Maybe I'd be interested in learning something, too."

"That's what I'm afraid of and precisely why we're going to the basement." Brad laughed at his joke.

Something seemed slightly off to Sam. He imagined the life of a research scientist's wife was no picnic, especially when the scientist was away all night, every night, but Diane seemed to be uncomfortable having her husband out of her sight. Or was he imagining things.

Brad's basement was crammed with scientific equipment. With this much here, Sam wondered how extensive his set-up was at the observatory.

"I was kidding about the Bloody Marys," Brad said, placing a cool mango iced tea in Sam's hand. "You'll need a clear head for this discussion."

"Your wife is lovely. Where did you meet?"

"As you could probably tell, Diane is Chinese. Not a Hawaiian of Chinese ancestry, either. She was born in China. We met in Hong Kong when I worked with her father."

"Is he an astrophysicist, too?"

"Yes, one of the finest in China." Brad seemed uneasy with this conversation.

"Has he visited you here on Maui?"

"No. We no longer collaborate."

Sam sensed he shouldn't push any further. Maybe Diane's father had been against the marriage. If so, it was none of his business.

They sat, sipping their tea, on a couch at the far end of the lab. Sam was only slightly surprised to see a white board, a required tool for all scientists, opposite the couch where a big screen HD TV might be in anyone else's basement.

Between the couch and the board was a large computer display table. On it was a detailed map of the Hawaiian archipelago. Numerous sites were noted with times and dates. Sam's eyes tracked over to the area near Ma'alaea Harbor on Maui to find the time and date of his encounter with the bubble duly noted. Looking around the rest of the lab, he saw the kinds of complex electronic equipment he expected. He also spotted a solvent cabinet, which seemed out of place in an electronics lab.

Taking a deep swig of tea, Sam asked, "Why a solvent cabinet? Do you do chemistry here?"

"No, but I do need to keep all of my electronics clean and conductive, a real problem with all the dust and wind up here." Brad walked over and opened the cabinet. "See, acetone, chloroform, ethanol, and ether. I only keep small, sealed vials for use in that fume hood in the corner."

He watched as Brad closed the cabinet, then turned to pick up some familiar journals from a lab bench. He also noted Brad forgot to re-engage the lock.

"I finished reading your journals covering the time since the crash. Here are the originals." Brad handed them to him like they were rare manuscripts.

"Well, did you discover any contradictions?" he said, as he slipped them into his backpack.

"None between your account and what I believe happened to you. But there are obvious contradictions between your experiences and the explanations the doctors have cobbled together." Brad sat back on the couch.

Sam stared at the scientist.

"You noted the most important one of these multiple times in your journal. For their explanations to be correct your left/right inversion had to be the result of the crash. But you crossed over before the crash when you went through that membrane." Brad said this with conviction.

But Sam knew one significant fact wasn't in the journals he shared with Brad. That information was in his current journal. "In a recent session with Dr. Drayton, he explained that, just as I have other memories from before the accident that are delusions, the memories from immediately before the accident could be delusions." Sam was sorry to burst his friends bubble, no pun intended.

"Very logical, but that explanation ignores one thing."

"What."

"If your passing through the bubble and discovering left was right was all a delusion caused by the accident, why did your friend Leroy Marder remember you commenting about it before the accident?"

Sam was speechless. How had he missed that? Was it because he wanted the nightmare to be over and was willing to accept faulty logic to accomplish that?

"I'm afraid you've crossed over, my friend. You're the first confirmed traveler between parallel universes." Brad's smile was contagious. Sam could tell this man, unlike his doctors, had no doubts about what happened to him.

He was still torn. He'd always hated fantasy and science fiction, and this seemed too close to both for comfort.

"Brad, if I believe you and that I'm not from this world, it would explain why I can't erase the vivid memories of my children. If they are waiting for me on the other side of that bubble, I need to find some way to go back home."

Carvell looked uncomfortable. He thought for a long time before answering. "Oh, Sam, I thought you knew. The energy spikes I recorded are way beyond anything our current technology could produce. It's not possible for me or anyone else to send you back."

Sam just sat there staring at the half-full tumbler of iced tea. He felt lost.

"But, Sam, although I can't recreate the effect, I believe I can do more than just measure it. I'm developing a predictive tool."

He looked up. "A predictive tool?"

"The Hawaiian archipelago is a hot spot for this phenomenon. I believe other spikes, like the one that brought you here, are inevitable. The tool I'm developing will allow me to predict where and when the next one will occur. By placing you at that precise spot at the proper moment, it's possible you could return home by the same kind of transposition event that brought you here."

Sam struggled with this but admitted it would be worth a try. "Okay. How soon will you be able to predict the next spike? Then how long will it take to forecast one with the proper characteristics to get me home?"

"I am confident I could develop a functional predictive tool in less than ten years. But I have no idea how frequent an event such as yours occurs. It could be years, decades, centuries. The peak that brought you here could be the largest in a series or the smallest or anywhere in between."

"Then I'm kind of back to square one." *Except now I'm not sure if I belong here.*

"I'm truly sorry, Sam. I will keep studying this phenomenon. If I discover anything new, anything at all, I'll call you."

"Thank you, Brad. It's better to know than to suppose. Say, could you spare a few books or articles about the mathematics underlying your theory? I think I should continue my education on the subject."

"Certainly, I'll just be a minute." Brad set his tea down and bounded up the stairs.

Sam did want to read more, but he also wanted Brad out of the lab for a few minutes.

Brad returned to the top of the stairs with his arms full and called down, "Let me carry these out to your car for you."

"Thanks." Sam joined him at the top of the stairs, with his journals in his hands. "Maybe studying these will help me avoid making a terrible mistake."

Once Brad had stashed the books and reprints in the backseat of Sam's car, the two friends embraced.

Sam drove away without another word, but with the seed of a plan germinating in his mind.

Chapter Fifty

Wednesday, June 5, 7:00 p.m.

Keone checked to make sure that Dr. Drayton had arrived before parking his car. Julie had shared the great progress Sam had made with Keone, as Jan had with her, but Keone planned to reserve judgment until he'd seen this new Sam for himself. Julie rapped "shave and a haircut" on the door instead of ringing the bell. After a few moments two short raps from the other side answered, "two bits."

Jan opened the door and said, "Knock, knock."

Julie smiled and said, "Who's there?"

"Sam and Janet."

"Sam and Janet who?"

"Sam and Janet Evening." Jan sang this to the tune of "Some Enchanted Evening" from *South Pacific.*

He guessed this was an old joke the sisters shared before the crash stole fun from their lives.

"Hi, Keone, thank you for coming. It means a lot to us."

He saw Jan was struggling to keep her eyes dry and gave her a bear hug. "Thank you for inviting us. I'm looking forward to meeting the new Sam."

"Actually, it's more like meeting the old Sam for the first time in a long while," Sam said as he joined them with a smile and two Longboards in his hand. Sam handed one to Keone as he took his coat and clinked a toast. Sam gave the other to Julie, who handed him her wrap, a colorful shawl made from multiple silk scarves.

"Here's to really getting to know each other." Keone meant this at multiple levels.

Drayton and Jan led the small talk over cocktails before dinner. Sam nodded in agreement with everything they said about his progress and smiled at all the appropriate times. He seemed extremely comfortable when Jan described his acceptance of his illness and desire to get back to the life he'd led before. Sam gave her a squeeze as she said this. She smiled and returned the squeeze before heading to the kitchen to put the final touches on dinner.

"We've fallen in love again," Sam said. "Jan is the nicest person I've ever known. Her patience has been awe-inspiring, after all the pain I've caused her."

"She loves you," Julie said.

"And I'm so grateful. It's time I apologized to you, Julie. I know how hard it was to see me the way I was in the hospital. I hope you understand that everything I said was the result of my delusion. I'm deeply sorry for the pain I caused and will try my best to make up for it in the future."

"You don't need to do this, Sam. Jan explained everything to us," Julie replied.

"Oh, but I do. This apology is an essential step on my way back to a normal life." Sam looked at Drayton, who smiled and nodded. Even Keone sensed the honesty in Sam's words.

Jan had set the table for dinner as they talked. "No more about the past. Let's have a great time tonight."

The dinner was fabulous and the conversation light and funny. The men retired to the living room for coffee as Julie helped Jan clear up.

"Why don't you tell us about your renewed interest in astronomy, Sam? Janet told me you've spent some free time with your friend at the observatory," Drayton said.

"Well, it's all part of the therapy really. You know, creating new memories to replace the delusions and reinforce the real ones," Sam replied.

"One of the observatories on Haleakala?" Keone asked, honestly interested. "How'd you get access? I've only been up there once when I was a kid. The security wasn't so tight then."

"A friend of mine gave me a tour, introduced me to his boss, and spent a lot of time bringing me up to date on things. He's a brilliant astrophysicist."

He noticed Drayton's smile faded a bit when Sam mentioned the scientist's occupation.

"That stuff's fascinating. I loved that *Cosmos* show that was on with Dr. Tyson. Did you see that, Dr, Drayton?" Keone asked.

"Call me Evan. I'm off duty. Yes. I saw most of it. Though I can't say I understood much."

"What's your friend's specialty?" Keone asked.

"Mostly electromagnetic energy fluxes in space. A lot of the work going on now is to explain new discoveries in that area and determine how they fit with the theory of conservation of mass and energy. I like it because it's all based on mathematics. You know, I'm basically a numbers guy. Before I focused on business, I read a lot in advanced math. A lot of that stuff is central to astrophysics."

Keone could see why both Jan and Dr. Drayton were pleased with Sam's new interest, but he wondered if there might be another connection. "Those theories can be pretty astonishing. I remember Dr. Tyson talking about something called the multiverse. Did you and your friend talk about that?"

Sam looked directly at Keone for the first time. "No. I mean, we haven't discussed that. Why do you ask?"

He's lying.

"Just curious. It sounded intriguing when Tyson talked about it, but I got lost after about two sentences." Keone laughed and Drayton and Sam joined in.

"Who does your friend work for at the observatories?"

"A guy named Hasselbach. He kind of runs the place." Sam answered.

Bingo. Sam's friend was Carvell, the guy that wanted information on Sam and used Hasselbach's name and phone to try to get it.

Drayton changed the subject. "Keone. I understand Mr. Walden has been transferred from the hospital to a holding facility on Oʻahu."

"Yes. He's been arraigned on multiple state and federal charges. I'm sorry about your friend, Sam."

"He's not my friend. He was once a long time ago, but what he did to Julie..."

"I know. If it's any comfort, he'll be out of circulation for a long time."

"You know, he tried to involve me in his crooked activities when we first got here. I should have gone to the police then. But we'd been so close for so long that I kept quiet."

"Keone, we've discovered that some of Mr. Walden's actions may have been the tripwire for all of Sam's delusions. It was his mind's way of trying to save Julie by making her his wife instead of Walden's," Drayton added.

"That kinda makes sense in a weird way. But don't you still have feelings for Julie, Sam?"

"I feel that she's a great sister-in-law, and I'm glad she's found a nice new... friend in you."

Keone saw a chance to test Sam. "We're more than friends, Sam."

"I'm so happy for you, both of you." Sam's smile never wavered, but his eyes flicked up and to the left.

Drayton smiled more broadly than he had all evening. Clearly, this was what he wanted to hear. It was what Keone wanted to hear, too. But, despite the honesty Sam tried so hard to display, he was lying.

"Does that mean you understand the children in your memories were delusions, too?"

Both Drayton and Sam tensed.

"Sam has made great progress, but this is a long process. We must take one step at a time. I wonder when the ladies will join us?" Drayton said, obviously uncomfortable with this topic.

"Evan, tonight is about honesty," Sam said. "On an intellectual level, I know that I imagined our children."

Keone detected another blatant lie.

"But Cindy and Timmy are still very real in my memories. I have accepted that my future is with Jan and have truly come to love her. We've discussed my feelings of loss surrounding the children. She's suggested we explore adoption, as we did once before."

Keone saw Sam weaving in truth with the lie.

"I'm tempted to consider this option. But Dr. Drayton has raised some concerns about us doing so before I've effectively dealt with my memories."

"I'm confident we can work through this. I look forward to supporting any efforts Sam and Janet make towards adopting—at the proper time," Drayton added.

Now the ladies did return and the conversation for the remainder of the evening was light and friendly.

As they left, Keone could tell Julie was convinced of Sam's transformation. He wouldn't disturb her with reality quite yet. He wanted to talk to some folks up on Haleakala first.

When they returned to Julie's condo, Keone had an important task to perform, which had nothing to do with the past or future issues between Sam and Janet Loftus, observatories on Haleakala, or the Maui Police Department. He walked Julie to the couch and had her sit down.

"I have an important question to ask, unrelated to tonight's activities."

"Shoot."

"How do you feel about a Fourth of July wedding?" He produced a small box from his pocket.

Julie's eyes went wider than he'd ever seen them as she slowly opened the box to display a four-carat diamond ring in a platinum band. "Did you rob a bank?"

"No. The insurance money arrived, and I thought, 'Who needs another Morgan Roadster?' I found something I love much more. So, Julie Madison..." He slowly descended to one knee. "Would you—"

Julie cut him off. "Of course I would, you big dumb kanaka. Get up here where I can kiss you."

Julie pulled Keone to his feet and covered his face with kisses. "Did you remember to save anything for the honeymoon?"

"How about a cruise of the Greek Islands?"

"You're on."

Chapter Fifty-One

Thursday, June 6, 9:00 a.m.

Sam held a lovely, flowered shawl in his hand. He'd retrieved it this morning from between the sofa cushions where he'd stashed it after removing it from Julie's shoulders last night. His performance went exactly as planned. Janet and Drayton still believed what they wanted to believe, and Julie was convinced as well. That damn cop was still suspicious, but that wouldn't matter after today.

Sam opened his new cell phone and tapped in a number he'd copied from Janet's. "Hello, Julie? This is Sam."

There was a long pause before Julie replied, "Hello, Sam. Thank you for the wonderful evening. I look forward to having you and Jan here sometime." Her voice sounded strained.

"We enjoyed it, too. That's why I'm calling. Are you missing a blue and yellow flowered scarf shawl thingy?"

"Oh, yes. I wondered where that was. I must have forgotten to collect it when we left." Julie's voice sounded more relaxed.

"No problem. That's what Jan thought." Sam turned his face

from the phone. "You were right, sweetie, it's hers. What? Okay, I'll ask."

"Is that Jan?"

"Yes, she's yelling at me from the shower. She says I should ask if we can bring it by when I drive her to work. One of our cars is acting up."

"That's really not necessary. I can get it anytime."

Sam knew Keone would be at work by now and suspected Julie wasn't anxious to face them on her own. "Just a sec." He turned from the phone and shouted, "She says we don't need to bother—Oh. Okay."

"Jan says it's no bother. I'll drive by and she'll run in with it. Do me a favor, Julie. Say yes. You know how she gets."

Another long pause. "Okay. I'll be here for the next couple of hours."

"Thank you, dear sis-in-law. We'll be by in about thirty minutes. Aloha."

"Aloha."

He set the phone on the table, proud of himself. Proud that he'd convinced Janet to leave early for work. Proud that he'd remembered the nickname he used to call Julie according to his journal. And proud he was able to imitate a two-person conversation, when he was totally alone.

He grabbed a towel, the chloroform he'd lifted from Brad's lab, and a large blanket as he headed for the car.

Keone drove his cruiser up Haleakala to speak with Dr. Bradley Carvell.

When Martin Hasselbach met him at the second gate instead of Brad Carvell, Keone didn't try to hide his confusion. "Dr. Hasselbach, I appreciate you making time to talk with me. But I asked for Dr. Carvell at the gate."

"Please come up to my office with me, Sergeant Boyd. I think I can enlighten you about Brad Carvell."

Hasselbach drove them to the laboratory in silence and used a digital keycard to get them inside the building that held Hasselbach's office, which was good sized but modestly decorated. Most of the walls were taken up with white boards filled with indecipherable formulae. They sat at a small, round desk covered with journals, many opened to specific pages. Hasselbach shoved them to the side so he could sit next to Keone with a yellow tablet between them.

Keone spoke first. "Dr, Hasselbach, I'm here because of the interaction between Dr. Carvell and a man named Samuel Loftus."

"I'm aware of their connection. Brad brought Mr. Loftus up here once for a tour of the facility."

"And where is Dr. Carvell?"

"He works evenings. I assume he is at home, asleep," Hasselbach replied.

"I see. Do you remember me calling you a few weeks ago in response to a call from your office?"

"Yes, Sergeant, I do. As I told you then, I never made a call to your department requesting information about an automobile accident, but I did look into the situation."

"Can you tell me what you discovered?"

"Most of our work here is classified. But I think it's important that I explain what I found out, how it relates to Dr. Carvell, and why it might be a good idea to keep Mr. Loftus away from him."

This wasn't unfolding the way he expected, but he was willing to roll with it. "Mr. Loftus is currently recovering from delusions associated with that car crash. Given his vulnerable state, anything you could tell me about Carvell would be helpful. And please call me Keone."

"Keone, I don't know how much you know about astrophysics, but there are thousands of theories involved in our research. A theory is validated by demonstrating that it is predictive of actual events. Such a theory remains useful until someone proves experimentally that it is flawed. Dr. Carvell was very interested in one particular theory and carried out experiments to see if he could measure evidence to support this theory."

He didn't appreciate the lecture, but decided to humor Hasselbach, for a while at least. "You mean like someone calculating that a comet will reappear at a certain time based on the physics, then testing to see if it shows up when they predicted it would?"

"Yes, exactly. You used a very appropriate scientific term, testing. A scientist must be open to his hypothesis being either right or wrong. This is essential for effective scientific investigation. Some of the greatest scientific discoveries were the result of proving a promising theory wrong. Dr. Carvell carried out wonderful work at another institution before he arrived here. That work involved testing hypotheses with strenuous data analysis and independent validation to assure the absence of bias. He disproved almost as many hypotheses as he validated. That's why I hired him."

"But something changed?"

"Yes. He had some evidence from his earlier work that the Hawaiian Archipelago was especially prolific in a certain type of energy flux and wanted to test that hypothesis with measurements closer to the site of these fluxes."

"And his earlier data was scientifically valid?"

"Yes. It had been peer-reviewed and accepted for publication in major journals."

"Doesn't sound like a problem."

"It wasn't—at first. But after he'd been here a few weeks, he started seeing fluxes everywhere, even in another scientist's project. When I reviewed his data, I found it to be neither comprehensive nor reproducible. He was seeing connections that weren't there."

"What did you do?"

"At first, I tried to get him to focus on his own project and had him measure a larger spectrum of wavelengths, which he did. But he kept sticking his nose into the other project and making wild extrapolations. In short, he was obsessed and no longer functioning as a dispassionate observer."

"I'm sorry to hear that. What did you do about it?" Keone asked.

"I counselled Dr. Carvell. And he agreed to undergo therapy with a very accomplished psychiatrist."

"Would that psychiatrist happen to be Dr. Evan Drayton?"

"Why, yes. How did you know that?"

"Because Sam Loftus is being treated by the same psychiatrist, and I suspect that's where the two of them met."

"How unfortunate."

"Unfortunate?" His patience was wearing thin.

"Dr Carvell recently returned to work and subsequently completed his therapy. Since returning, his work has been comprehensive and exemplary. That is, until the visit from Mr. Loftus."

"What happened after that?"

"Within a few days, his productivity started to wane. He seemed to be preoccupied with something outside the laboratory. I thought for a time it might be related to his marriage. His wife had been impacted by his previous obsessive behavior, as well. That was why I approved his request to take tonight off to deal with family issues." Martin hesitated.

"Could you give me his address and telephone number?"

Hasselbach wrote on the yellow pad and tore off a sheet. "He and his wife, Diane, live between here and Kula at this address."

"Did Carvell's research have anything to do with transposition of objects between parallel universes?"

Hasselbach was clearly taken aback. "How do you know about such things?"

"From two sources, the Cosmos program with Dr. Tyson and a conversation last night with Sam Loftus."

"I see. I can tell you that while the study of energy fluxes is of interest to this laboratory, we are not exploring parallel universes. However, speculation in this area could be extremely detrimental to someone suffering from delusions."

"Sam Loftus believes left is right and that his wife is his sister-in-law. If Carvell provided him a specious alternative explanation for his situation, he could have set his therapy back months."

"I can neither confirm nor deny that this was the theory that Carvell was trying to prove." Hasselbach said. "But I agree that you should speak directly with him as soon as possible."

"I may need to call you if my suspicions are confirmed. I believe Sam's psychiatrist may need to get some clarification from you, as well. But I will never ask you to violate your secrecy agreement with the observatory or its sponsors."

"That's acceptable." He took the sheet back from Keone and added his cell phone number. "Call me anytime."

A guard returned Keone to the second gate and his car. En route, he'd formulated an interrogation strategy for Brad Carvell. He hoped the wife would be the one to answer the door. He had a few questions for her that would be best asked in the absence of her husband.

He also decided to call Julie's cell phone to give her a heads up. After four rings, he heard, "This is Julie Madison, please leave a message at the tone."

His gut tightened and the hairs on the back of his neck stood up. What message should he leave. "Stay away from Sam." Seemed a bit too scary. All he had was a theory so far. He decided on, "Call me as soon as you get this."

Chapter Fifty-Two

Julie woke with a headache so severe she was afraid to open her eyes. She struggled to retrieve her most recent memories.

I answered the door, and someone pushed a smelly cloth over my face. Someone knocked me out. Who would...? Sam.

Slowly opening her eyes, she found the room in shadows. She was lying on her back on a lumpy bed, a sheet above and beneath her as well as a scratchy blanket. The linen smelled fresh but there was a musty odor beneath, probably from the mattress. She checked to make sure she was fully clothed, then reached out and banged her hand on a coarse surface. She ran her fingers along the wall and jerked her hand back after she picked up a couple of splinters.

The wall was made of rough wooden slats. *A cabin.*

She remembered Jan talking about a cabin that Sam's grandfather built past Hana. Everyone tended to forget that Sam's mother was born in Hawai'i. But Jan told Julie that Sam was always fascinated as a child with his mother's stories about growing up here.

Julie tried to rise from the bed but failed, defeated by a pounding in her head and an overwhelming wave of nausea.

"You need to take it easy, sweetheart. Chloroform is a terrible anesthetic. Its only advantage is that it's easy to get."

Sam's voice.

She'd guessed right. But why was he doing this? He said he and Jan had fallen back in love. He said he was trying to erase the other memories. "Why, Sam?"

"Because I can never return home and I miss my family." Sam's voice was calm, almost tender.

"Sam, I am not your wife."

"No. You're not. Not in this universe. I accept that. Janet and I have grown very close."

Janet, not Jan.

"I like having her as my wife. I had almost accepted Dr. Drayton's explanation of my condition, but then I found a flaw in his logic and learned from a brilliant scientist what really happened to me. Let me share it with you so you'll understand what I'm trying to do and why."

Julie realized that Sam's insanity had progressed a long way from what he displayed in the hospital. He was probably capable of anything. Her best chance to get out of here alive was to agree to listen. "Okay, Sam. What really happened?"

"I was driving home from work with my friend Lee Marder. Right after we passed the marina entrance at Ma'alaea, I passed through a transparent gateway between universes, and everything changed for me...."

IF THE CARVELL HOME WERE ANY CLOSER TO THE observatory, it would be in Haleakala National Park. Their view was breathtaking. Keone parked on the street in front of the house and walked up a gravel path to the front door. He was pleased when Diane Carvell, a small, slim brunette with Asian features, answered the door.

"Aloha. How can I help you, Officer?"

Most of the time Keone preferred plain clothes, but he'd worn his uniform to help him gain access at the observatory and had no time to change. "Aloha. I'm Keone Boyd with the Maui PD. I wondered if I might ask you a few questions about a man who may have visited your home."

"Should I get my husband? He is in his laboratory." She said this with an extra syllable, like the British do—*la-bor-a-tor-y*

"I'd like to talk with both of you, but it's best to do so separately, okay?" Keone didn't want to frighten the woman. Her sunken, red eyes suggested she might already be under some emotional strain.

"Where are my manners? Please, come in. Would you like something to drink? I have iced tea, POG, and water."

"POG would be fine." As she went to the kitchen to pour a glass of the Passion Fruit, Orange, and Guava concoction popular with tourists and even locals, He did a brief visual inspection of the living room. The decor was Chinese in style and very neat. There was a lovely contrast between different woods that gave the furniture a calming effect.

Mrs. Carvell placed two glasses on absorbent coasters bearing a bright floral pattern.

"Thank you." Keone took a large sip and made a point of sighing with pleasure. "This is wonderful. Tell me, has your husband had a visitor recently named Sam Loftus?"

"Oh, yes. Sam is a friend of Brad's who likes math and astronomy. Brad has been bringing him up to date on modern astrophysics."

"Are you a scientist, too?"

"No. My passion is art. We met when Brad was on a post-doctoral fellowship in Hong Kong. He worked with my father."

Diane Carvell has a lovely smile.

"Dr. Hasselbach said your name is Diane. I'm guessing Diane is not the name you were born with."

"You are right. My name in China is *Daiyu*. It means black

jade. My father called me his precious gem. He always supported my dream of becoming an artist."

"You must enjoy Maui. So many fine artists have made the island their home."

"Oh, yes. My mentor is one of them. She displays my work in her Makawao gallery beside her own. I am very happy here."

"Is your husband happy, too?"

"He wasn't—at first." An echo of what Hasselbach had told him. "Recently, he took on a new project and a more reasonable schedule. It made him very happy, for a while."

"Is your husband taking tonight off from work?"

Concern filled her eyes. "He said it was a holiday. I have trouble remembering all of the Hawaiian holidays."

"We have quite a few." *Just none today.* "I've spoken with Dr. Hasselbach about your husband's... extreme devotion to a particular theory."

She nodded. "Contact between parallel worlds. He believes he has measured the residue of these events here in the Hawaiian Islands. He believes most of his colleagues are... closed-minded—including my father. They no longer speak to one another. Do you think Brad might be ill, again?" One tear crept down her cheek.

Keone felt compassion for this nice, quiet woman. He handed her a handkerchief and gave her a moment to collect herself. "I'd like to talk with your husband now."

"Let me show you to the laboratory."

A conventional basement door bearing no locks led to the laboratory. Keone thought of the contrast between this and Dave Walden's hidden lab.

At the bottom of the stairs, Diane called out, "Brad. You have a visitor."

There was no response. Keone moved past Mrs. Carvell and into the laboratory. The walls were filled with electronic equipment and a huge computer display table filled the center of the room. It displayed a topographical map of the Hawaiian

Archipelago with specific locations highlighted with dry erase markings. The largest of these was in Ma'alaea, near the point where he first bumped into Sam Loftus, literally. "Could your husband be upstairs, Mrs. Carvell?"

"I do not think so, but I will look."

Keone didn't think so either. In his scan of the lab, he found a landline phone with an answering machine that displayed a recent message.

Mrs. Carvell returned. "He is not upstairs, and his car is gone. But I did not hear him leave."

When he approached the house, Keone noticed the sharp incline from the street to the garage.

Probably coasted to the road before starting the engine.

"When did you last see him?"

"We ate an early lunch together, upstairs, about eleven o'clock."

That was hours ago.

"Mrs. Carvell, is this telephone on a separate line from your home phone?"

"Yes. He uses it for contacting the observatory and other scientists."

"There's one message on the answering machine. It came in at quarter after eleven, probably when your husband was upstairs. I would like you to listen to the message. It could help me locate your husband so I can talk with him. Would you do that for me?"

"He would not want me to. He is very private."

"I can get a warrant, but that will take time. I know you are worried for your husband. So am I. Time lost now might be critical to helping him."

She still hesitated.

"I think the call might be from Mr. Loftus. I also think he may be in serious trouble."

She pushed Play on the answering machine. They heard Sam Loftus's voice, "Hello, Brad, I have her at the cabin. I want you to explain to her about how I crossed over into this world. I'll give you directions. Leave as soon as you get this. That curious detective she's living with will probably discover she's gone soon. Anyway, you take the Hana Road through Hana and past the 'Ohe'o Gulch, then...."

Keone was scribbling the directions down as fast as he could. It didn't take a detective's instincts to know the "she" Sam mentioned was Julie. That's why she hadn't returned his call.

He bid a quick goodbye to Mrs. Carvell and ran to his car. Knowing Julie was in the wilderness past Hana with one insane man and another on the way was beyond a nightmare.

Chapter Fifty-Three

Julie listened to Sam's wild tale of living in a world that was a mirror image of hers. It was clear to her that he truly believed everything he said.

"I almost accepted Drayton's explanation of my delusions after reading my old journals. I think the bond that I've developed with Janet made me more susceptible. I really do care for her. I didn't fake that." Sam paused.

Julie could see he was still conflicted about which explanation to believe. "What made you change your mind, Sam, about which explanation to believe, I mean." She continued to keep her voice calm and reassuring.

Sam went into detail about his accidental meeting with Brad Carvell in Drayton's waiting room, his visit to the observatory, their discovery of the common event that bound them, and Brad's discovery of the flaw in Drayton's explanation. She felt sorry for him. He had come so close, only to have Carvell infect him with his own delusions.

What disturbed her most was the way Sam changed when he talked about the impossibility of getting back to his—their—children, Cindy and Timmy. He nearly came apart when he described the hopelessness he felt. Now he described the plan he had to solve his problem.

"Janet and I have discussed adoption. She's fine with the idea."

"I agree, Sam. That sounds like the perfect solution."

"Not quite, but it could be. You see, my children represent aspects of my DNA and their mother's. I can't return to their mother, but you represent the next best thing."

"Sam, I don't—"

"Please. You must let me finish." He raised his voice for the first time and Julie simply nodded and tried to maintain her composure.

"I don't expect you to love me. I don't expect you to leave Keone. I just want you to do me a favor. You could even close your eyes and imagine you're with Keone. Janet and I would raise them as our own. I'm sure this can work for everyone."

So that's it. He wanted her to help him recreate their non-existent children. Right here on this moldy, lumpy mattress?

Sam continued talking, but it was almost as though he was talking to himself. "I'm not asking for a deep emotional commitment, just a few minutes of your time."

"Uh, Sam, I believe the process of bearing children takes a bit longer than that. You know, like nine months of my life—twice."

"Of course, you're right. It is a lot to ask of you, Julie. But remember, you'd be doing it for Janet, too."

"You honestly believe Jan would want you to do this?"

"Oh, no. She must never know. I'll work everything out through my lawyer so she will never be able to find out who the mother is. I'll pay for you and Keone to travel around the world during your pregnancies. I'll even take a large insurance policy out on you and make sure you have the finest doctors."

The flaws in Sam's plan were too numerous to count, but she knew Sam was beyond reasoning with. She had to think of a way to put off the inevitable until she could formulate some way to escape.

"My memories of Cindy and Timmy are as real as you and I sitting in this cabin right now." Sam looked off into space as he continued. "Cindy, the older one, bosses me around terribly. She's the one who broke me of my borderline OCD by showing me how silly I was behaving. She taught me to enjoy fantasy and playing games. Timmy is the comedian of the household. He can make expressions with that rubber face of his that make you laugh until your sides hurt. They both have lovely singing voices. I can remember them singing *There's a Hole in the Bottom of the Sea*, all the verses.

"There's a hole in the bottom of the sea, there's a hole in...."

Sam went into a fugue state as he softly sang the words of the song. It was over five minutes before he spoke again. He shook his head, as if to clear his thoughts.

"Well, that's my story. Do you understand now why I reject the delusion theory? I'm not angry with Dr. Drayton, you know. The real explanation was just beyond his understanding. I hope it's not beyond yours."

Julie needed to keep Sam talking. "It is a lot to take in all at once, Sam. I'm sure Dr...."

"Carvell?"

"Yes, Dr. Carvell. I'm sure he explained it very clearly to you, but it's a little harder to accept second-hand."

"I thought you might feel that way, Julie. That's why I invited Dr. Carvell to meet us here and explain it to you directly. He should be here in about an hour."

"That was very thoughtful of you. Maybe we could have a cup of coffee or tea and a bite to eat, while we wait."

"Certainly. You like Earl Grey with milk and one level spoonful of sugar, right?"

"That must be the same in both worlds." Julie smiled, though inside she was a jumble of fears and hopes. The clock displayed 3:30 p.m. Even if Keone got home at his usual time, found her missing, and somehow discovered where Sam had taken her, he would still be hours from Hana. Sam seemed calmer now. But she had to keep his mind occupied until Carvell came or he might decide to get busy re-creating their imaginary children.

"Sam, you told us last night what you discovered about the Dave in this world from reading your journals. Was that true?"

"Yes. But there were a lot of gaps between our disagreement on the kayaking trip and when I discovered he was hurting you." Sam brought the tea and some cookies on a wooden tray.

"Would you like me to fill in the gaps for you? I can even fill in the gap when we were on Maui and you and Jan were still in Indy."

"I'd be very grateful." Sam sipped his tea and gave Julie his full attention.

"As you know, Dave and I were married in Indianapolis and left immediately after the reception for our honeymoon on Maui...."

~

Keone had driven as fast as he could from Haleakala towards the Hana Highway in Kahului. But most of the rest of the drive to Hana would be along narrow winding roads with one-lane bridges. It would take hours. And when he got there, he'd be following scribbled directions from the answering machine.

He pounded his fist on the steering wheel while waiting for a large truck to finish its wide turn onto the highway, Keone suddenly realized how stupid he was being. He should call Janet.

Janet was married to Sam all those years. She would know if he had a place near Hana.

He dialed Janet's cell, which she answered on the first ring. "Sam, where are you?"

"It's Keone, Jan. I'm on my way to find Sam right now. We have a report that he is in Hana. Do you know of anywhere he might go there?" Keone intentionally didn't mention that Sam had kidnapped Julie. She didn't need to know that right now.

"There is one place I know about. His grandfather built a small cabin past Hana. He took me there once, but I have no idea of how to get there. Let me see if he has a street address in his address book. Just a minute."

He heard Janet walk into another room. Maybe this call wasn't such a great idea.

Chapter Fifty-Four

To Julie, Brad Carvell sounded like a college professor giving a lecture. "You see, Mrs. Walden, Sam had no delusions. He arrived here suddenly from a parallel universe, where things were as he remembered them. The power flux that I showed you matched precisely the time and location of that displacement. Unfortunately, with available technology, we're not able to return Sam to his point of origin. It's only natural for Sam, under the circumstances, to seek an alternative method to rejoin his children."

She thought Carvell was as loopy as Sam but knew Sam wouldn't try anything in front of him. "Dr. Carvell, thank you so much for clarifying what Sam tried to explain to me earlier. I have a few questions if you don't mind."

"Not at all. Ask anything."

"As a scientist, I'm sure you studied fields other than astronomy and physics."

"Yes. I took courses in biology and chemistry, as well as math, physics, the history of science, English composition, and philosophy. I'm fluent in French, Spanish, German, Italian, and Russian and can read Latin and Greek."

Am I supposed to be impressed? "During your courses in biology, did you study genetics?"

"Yes. I took classical and molecular genetics courses."

"If Sam and I produced an offspring now, in this universe, what's the probability that such a child would be identical or even resemble the child Sam sired with the other Julie in the other universe?"

"The odds of creating an identical child would be many millions to one. However, any child you produced together would very likely have some similarity to a potential sibling in the other universe. Just as a second child you conceived would have some similarities to the first."

"Can you guarantee we would produce a boy and a girl?"

"Of course not. But I can guarantee each would be either a boy or a girl."

Thank you, Doctor Obvious.

"I understand you're working on technology that might enable you and Sam to predict the time and place of another *bump* between two universes."

"That's right. But the development of the technology could be a decade or more away and then we'd still have to predict a rare event."

"I understand the problems. But, even if you had the technology and you predicted an event accurately, can you be sure Sam would return to his starting point? Couldn't he just be transported to another parallel universe?"

"Sam never asked me that question."

"Here's another question I'm sure Sam never asked. What if your wife was the person Sam loved in the other universe? Do you think she would go along with his plan to recreate his children? Would you?"

Brad looked like he'd received an electric shock.

Sam broke into the conversation. "We are not here to discuss fantasies." He rose from his chair, placed himself between them, and grabbed Brad by the shoulder. "Thank you, Brad. You've been of great help. I'll walk you to your car."

Sam hustled Carvell out the door before Julie could protest. But she knew she'd made her point.

Carvell was obsessed with his interpretation of coincidental events, but she saw the look on his face when she made things personal.

Julie glanced at Sam's clock. Keone could be there in a few hours.

Did she have a few hours? Did Keone have any idea where she was?

Don't go there. Keone would come. She had to be ready when he did.

Julie felt like she was walking on thin ice. She had to make Sam see the major flaw in his plan without pushing too hard. His hold on reality was becoming more fragile by the minute.

Sam returned and sat beside Julie on the musty bed. "Now you understand exactly what happened to me and the science behind it."

Sam on the bed beside her creeped Julie out, but she had to retain her composure. "Dear, dear, Sam. I can't imagine what you've been going through. I want to talk openly with you about everything, but I'm afraid I need to use the restroom first. Do you have some tissue?" Knowing Sam's interest in hygiene and neatness, Julie knew this would give her some breathing space.

"Certainly. It's in the outhouse. I'll walk you out there. I need to stretch my legs, too."

Julie couldn't believe that Sam was still trying to act as though they were just good friends discussing a very reasonable plan of action. He'd meticulously avoided words such as kidnap and prisoner and rape, but Julie knew exactly what was going on. Once in the outhouse, she refused to sit on the disgusting splintered plank that bore an ancient circular hole. Luckily, decades of disuse had made the stench inside endurable for a short period. She would use that time to develop a plan. If it failed, she'd have no choice but to run.

~

KEONE COULDN'T USE THE RADIO IN HIS SQUAD CAR TO contact Hana, too many people might hear. He'd need to call Angela Beyers on her cell. It seemed to take forever to reach a location where he had a good enough cell signal, could find a place to pull off the road, and could stop long enough to call.

"Hey, Keone. Don't tell me, you need my help again?"

"This may sound funny, but I need some directions and maybe your best ATV."

"It's getting dark here. Are you lolo?"

"No. I'm on a case."

"What kind of case?"

"An abduction and probable kidnapping."

"Does it have anything to do with a guy named Carvell?"

"Yes, but how could you know that? I haven't told anybody." *This case had as many twists and turns as this damn road.*

"You're on your way over here? This late? You really are crazy. Okay, stop, turn around and head back to the airport in Kahului. I'll call ahead and arrange for a chopper. But on your way there, listen to me. I have a story to tell you about a crazy guy who just came into our station talking about another crazy guy who kidnapped a girl and might be planning to rape her. Sound interesting?"

Keone's heart pounded. He switched on his lights and siren. "I'm turning around."

Chapter Fifty-Five

Sam became increasingly restless once they returned from the outhouse. Julie tried to have a normal conversation with him, but he kept turning the discussion to his imaginary kids. Julie decided to confront Sam with facts. She was tired of this rodeo and wanted to leave.

"Sam, I want to tell you exactly what I am thinking right now, okay? Then you can decide what you want to do next."

"All right, but you know what we need to do. It won't take long. I can use more chloroform if that would help."

"No. That won't be necessary. I am curious about one thing you haven't talked about. Dave. My husband was once your friend in this universe. Did his life turn out as badly in yours?" She felt this question would accomplish two things: keep Sam talking and lull him into a false sense of control.

"Dave is a wonderful person in my universe."

"Did he use drugs?"

"He experimented with pot at IU, but most people did. He only tried uppers once, in Grad School, not long before we met you two at the fair. After he started dating Janet, he didn't dare. They moved to Maui before us because you had to finish Medical

School. It was five years before we moved here, but Dave and I picked up right where we'd left off.

"Dave worked hard at his practice and was well respected. His focus was property law and estate planning. He made friends with a lot of the well-to-do but did a lot of pro bono work, too. When Jan's income made work unnecessary, he handed the high-income clients to his many protégés but continued to do pro bono work. He started a scholarship program to help young Maui College students afford law school on O'ahu. He even taught courses to prepare them and established the first four-year Political Science program at UH MC."

"How about Jan and me?"

"You were even closer than you are here. We did everything together. We took cruises to the Caribbean and the Greek Isles, before the kids got old enough to want to come along."

Julie sensed danger and steered the conversation away from the kids. "You said I was a doctor in your universe?"

～

SERGEANT ANGELA BEYERS DROVE HER IMPOSING FOUR-wheel ATV down the muddy, unpaved track that Brad Carvell pointed out to her. The cabin wasn't too far away.

A call came in on her radio. It was Keone in the chopper.

"Howzit, Keone?"

"Where are you?"

"Cheer up, Big Guy. I got you covered. I'm in a primo ATV less than a mile from the cabin following the able directions of Dr. Carvell, besides I've been there before. I've checked that cabin for vagrants a bunch of times. Not many places in Hana I don't know about. Oh, and I called your boss and convinced him to authorize that chopper. Bettah late than nevah, yeah?"

"I love you, Princess. You da one."

"You would have wasted precious time trying to find the cabin without me. And played hell making any kind of time on this mud flat in your clunky police cruiser—if you'd even gotten to Hana in time.

"When you're right, you're right. The pilot is homing in on the coordinates you gave us and says we should be there in fifteen minutes."

"Great, I should be there in less than five."

"Angela, there's a personal aspect to this case."

"I wondered when you were going to level with me." She'd already made the connection to Kulima's accusations.

"The girl being held in the cabin, Julie...I'm in love with her."

"And the guy holding her is married to her sister, right?"

"That's right."

"I'm guessing you want to go into that cabin alone, so your future brother-in-law doesn't accidentally get kind of shot up. Am I right?"

"Yeah. But I won't hesitate to take him down if I have to."

"I know you won't, Keone. But I'm gonna have your back."

"Sure. Just kinda have it from out of sight, okay?"

"If I can. I can see the cabin now. We can talk more later." Ange signed off.

She parked the ATV about a hundred yards from where Carvell said the cabin would be. After handcuffing Carvell in the backseat, she locked all the doors, removed a sharpshooter rifle from the trunk, and quietly approached the cabin with the rifle in her hands and her service revolver on her hip.

She worked her way around the cabin to a point where she could see the door most clearly and prepared a sniper's nest with a clear shot at the door and the cleared dirt space in front of it. Carvell had told her there was only one way in or out of the cabin and she'd just confirmed that with her walk around it.

Now she just had to wait for Keone, unless Loftus or the girl did something stupid in the next ten minutes.

～

"I remember when Dave brought little Rain to you with a tummy ache. He was a basket case, and you calmed them both down. Have I told you about Rain and Mist? Timmy and Cindy loved to play with those two lovely girls." Sam was going there again.

No matter what she did, Julie couldn't keep Sam's thoughts away from his imaginary children. She tried another approach.

"Sam, the Dave you just described is nothing like the Dave I know. And your Julie is nothing like me. You must know I no longer love Dave, but I do love someone."

Sam looked confused.

"Listen to me, Sam. I'm not the Julie of your universe. I love Keone Boyd. I'll never love you. And I'll die before I let you touch me."

Sam reacted as though she'd punched him in the gut. His face went blank, and he stared at the wall.

When he hadn't moved for a full minute, she rose and padded to the door. She slipped the latch and eased the door partway open without making a sound.

Glancing back, she saw that Sam still hadn't moved. This might be her one and only chance, and she planned to take it.

Chapter Fifty-Six

Where is Keone? He should have reached the cabin by now. Angela needed to think about something else. She'd never met Julie. They never showed up for that party when she and Linda redecorated the condo. But Keone had told her how smart she was.

She'd asked Carvell how Sam managed to get her to the cabin.

He'd replied, "As I was leaving, I smelled chloroform. But Julie was completely attentive when I spoke with her."

"Did she seem calm?"

"Oh yes. Even when she asked me those questions that made me realize she was in jeopardy."

Good for her. Keone's girlfriend was playing this just right. If she kept doing that, Keone could get here, surprise Sam, and take him into custody, without anyone getting hurt. But she knew Keone wouldn't risk Julie's safety. If she had a clean shot at Sam, Angela would take it. She didn't care how crazy the bastard was.

Suddenly, she saw movement. The cabin door was opening. It was Julie. Angela watched her silently close the door and run barefoot toward the shelter of the dense jungle foliage. The welcome darkness was a few steps away when Angela saw Sam appear behind Julie, grab her hair, and jerk her head violently backward, before she could take a clear shot.

Idiot! Took my eye off the damn cabin!

JULIE'S BUTT STRUCK THE ROCKY SURFACE SHORTLY before her shoulders. Pain messages assaulted her brain. She'd instinctively tucked her head into her chest, which kept her from being knocked unconscious, but it still snapped back into the hard ground. Sharp rocks pierced the backs of her legs and buttocks. Then a huge weight dropped on her hips and chest. It was Sam. He must have come to his senses, caught up with her, and grabbed her by her hair just before she reached the jungle.

"If you can't love me, you can at least give me back my children. I'll be gentle if you let me. Don't fight me or I'll have to hurt you."

She couldn't believe the calm, quiet man who had spent so much time and effort trying to convince her of his sanity was about to... She looked into Sam's eyes and saw a rage that threatened to petrify her.

KEONE APPROACHED FROM THE BACK OF THE CABIN, looking for a window to slip through when Sam wasn't looking. It had taken longer to reach the cabin than he'd expected, but he knew the pilot had to drop him off far enough away to avoid being detected. Peeking in a window, he saw the cabin was empty. *That can't be good.*

He heard a yelp from the front of the cabin, drew his weapon, and eased around the corner of the building. What he saw, made him freeze.

On the ground in front of the cabin, Julie was pinned under Sam and struggling to get free. On the other side of the clearing, he saw a rifle pointed at Sam's head from the jungle. He knew it must be Ange. He also knew she had the best chance of hitting Sam, without hitting Julie. He had to let her take the shot.

～

SOMEHOW, JULIE KEPT HER VOICE CALM AND ASKED, "Are you going to rape me now, Sam?"

Sam's face transformed from the bestial sneer of a wild man to a look of utter surprise and confusion. He froze and stared into space. Julie didn't pause a second, this time. She summoned all her strength and jammed her knee into his groin. "Get off me, you crazy son of a bitch!"

As Sam crumpled and fell off her, Julie heard a shot. With Sam writhing on the ground, Julie crawled a few feet away, then saw movement at the corner of the cabin. Before she could react, Keone ran toward her with his gun pointed at Sam's back. "Your kick saved this bastard's life." He pointed to the other side of the clearing, where a policewoman laid down a huge rifle, took handcuffs from her belt, and walked over to kneel beside Sam. "Samuel Loftus, you are under arrest for the kidnapping, assault, and attempted rape of Mrs. Julie Walden. You have the right to remain silent. If you give up the right to remain silent, anything you say can and will be used against you in a court of law. You have the right to have an attorney present for any questioning. If you desire and cannot afford an attorney...."

Julie struggled to her feet and started to follow Keone.

"Julie, I want you to sit here and wait for me. I'll be right back. I promise." His voice was as gentle as it was caring.

Julie painfully lowered herself onto a tree stump, clutched her knees in her arms, and waited patiently for the man she loved.

Keone was back in moments. He lifted her from the stump and cradled her against his chest. When they reached the ATV, he set Julie down in the middle of the front seat and climbed in beside her.

"Julie, the wonderful woman guiding Sam over here is Sergeant Angela Beyers. Without her, I would never have made it in time. The shot you heard was hers."

Angela gave her a nod as she placed Sam in the back seat next to Brad Carvell, then climbed in front beside Julie. Then this woman she'd never met hugged her, stroked Julie's bruised head, and gently eased it down onto Keone's lap.

Feeling safe in Keone's lap, dizzy from her slam against the ground, and exhausted, Julie let her eyes close for just a moment.

~

ANGELA BEYERS' ATV BOUNCED FROM THE DIRT PATH onto the highway. Julie's eyes popped open. "Where's Keone?"

"He's right behind us driving Sam's car with Sam in the back seat. He'll follow us to the station. I guess he told you I'm Angela, yeah? You must be Julie"

"I think so." Julie rubbed the bruise on her head. "Thank you for saving me."

"Looked to me like you saved yourself. You were truly amazing. Keone told me you could hold your own, but..."

"I'm just glad you were there."

"I know that pillow's not as comfortable as Keone's lap, but you were out of it when I dropped him off at Sam's car."

"How did he find out I was kidnapped?"

"Keone went to the observatory then Carvell's house to confront him." She turned her head towards Carvell. "But you'd already left to come here, hadn't you?"

"How did Keone discover where Sam took me?"

"Luckily brainiac back there neglected to delete Sam's voice-mail that explained what he'd done and where to find you. Keone was going to break the land-speed record getting here before I arranged for a chopper. That boy loves you, you know."

"I know. That's what kept me going. How did you get involved?"

"You must have made an impression on the good doctor. He drove right to our headquarters in Hana and confessed. Just in time, as it turned out."

"I really don't know if, at the end, Sam would have raped me, but I couldn't take the chance. Did I do the right thing?"

"Hell, yes. Keone wasn't kidding back there. If you hadn't kicked Sam off, my shot would have blown his psycho head off."

Julie heard vomiting from the back seat and smelled the rank result.

Angela glanced back and then at Julie. "Nothing I love more at the end of a long grueling shift than cleaning up some lolo haole's puke."

Chapter Fifty-Seven

Friday, June 7, 8:00 a.m.

S am Loftus and Brad Carvell fidgeted uncomfortably on metal chairs bolted to the floor. The table in front of them was the only other furniture in an interrogation room at police headquarters in Wailuku. Keone and Julie gazed through a one-way mirror at the two troubled men and waited for Dr. Evan Drayton and Dr. Martin Hasselbach to arrive.

By the time they'd finished with all the paperwork, treated Julie's minor wounds, and provided Sam an ice bag for his groin, the sun was about to rise in Hana. Keone began the drive from Hana Station to Wailuku in Sam's car while Julie slept on his shoulder and Carvell snored on Sam's. Along the way, without waking any of his passengers, Keone called both Drayton and Hasselbach at their homes and asked them to meet him at the station at eight.

Now, watching Sam and Brad squirm as they awaited interrogation, Keone glanced at Julie and marveled at her strength. During the past twenty-four hours she'd been chloroformed, kidnapped, assaulted, and spent hours enduring indoctrination in a wild theory by two madmen—before one of them tried to rape her. Despite all this, she looked so beautiful he could hardly contain his desire to take her in his arms and comfort her.

Drayton arrived and was ushered into the viewing room with them.

"Morning, Sergeant Boyd, Mrs. Walden. I can't tell you how terrible I feel that I misjudged Sam's condition so completely. Julie, I'm so sorry this happened to you."

"Evan, none of this is your fault," she responded. "Sam and I talked a lot in that cabin. He had accepted his delusions and wanted to create a new life for himself with Jan. But the dreams of his children continued to haunt him."

Drayton shook his head. "I knew all of that, but I thought I could help him through it."

"You might have succeeded if it hadn't been for Carvell," Keone said.

Drayton looked through the glass at the scientist who had derailed his carefully constructed treatment plan. "How?"

Keone stepped in. "I want you to hear it directly from him. That's why I asked Dr. Hasselbach to join us."

Hasselbach had just entered the room. "Hi, Evan."

"I guess I screwed up, Martin."

"We both did."

Keone took control of the conversation. Pointing to the two men in the interrogation room. "Doctors, I asked you here to have them describe to you, in their own words, what they believe is happening to Sam. I want you to listen and ask clarifying questions, but not contradict or challenge what they have to say. After you're done, we'll excuse them, and Julie and I will tell you what we've observed.

Keone led the two doctors from the viewing area and into the interrogation room. An officer followed with two folding-chairs.

"Mr. Loftus and Dr. Carvell, I would like you to honestly tell these two gentlemen everything you told Julie and me about your understanding of the events that have taken place from the moments before the collision on March fifteenth to the present. Your openness and honesty in this session may well determine what actions this department takes in your individual cases.".

Sam and Brad nodded.

"Please be seated, everyone. I am going to leave the room. Standard procedure requires that we record this interview. When you've finished, either Dr. Hasselbach or Dr. Drayton can knock on the door, and I'll rejoin you. Is everything I said clear to everyone?"

Four nods signaled it was time for Keone to leave the room.

~

AFTER TWO HOURS, OF SAM AND CARVELL PROVIDING forthcoming answers. Sam described his attempt to prevent Julie from escaping.

"I shouldn't have pulled on her hair. But it was the only way I could see to keep her from disappearing into the jungle. I was shocked when she hit the ground. I'm relieved it ended there."

"But it didn't end there. What happened next, Sam?" Drayton asked.

Sam's eyes stared into space. "That's the last thing I remember until we arrived here at the police station."

Hasselbach looked at Carvell.

"I was in the back of an ATV at this point. I didn't see Sam until they put him in beside me. He appeared out of touch with his environment at that point."

Hasselbach and Drayton exchanged glances before Drayton walked to the door and knocked. Seeing Drayton approach the door, Keone hurried to be on the other side by the time he heard the knock. He waved two officers into the room with him.

"These officers will take Mr. Loftus and Dr. Carvell to a holding area so we can discuss what you've heard." Once Sam and

Brad were gone, Keone beckoned at the mirror and Julie joined them.

"Before either of you say anything, Julie and I need to provide our testimony of the same period. Some of this will be redundant for each of you, but, as I mentioned before, we're recording this entire session and we need all of the testimony."

Drayton and Hasselbach nodded.

Keone began the retelling of every interaction and investigation related to Sam Loftus. Julie joined in with her own impressions of various interactions at the appropriate times. Keone only touched on Dave Walden's actions as it directly related either to Julie or Sam.

WHEN THEY WERE FINISHED ANOTHER HOUR HAD passed. Drayton had the first question, "Could someone explain to me whether these parallel universe speculations have any basis in established scientific fact?"

Keone knew he couldn't and was grateful when Hasselbach spoke up. "I can answer that one."

Hasselbach then spent the next fifteen minutes explaining the theoretical basis of Carvell's obsession to Drayton in much the same way he had to Keone at the observatory, but with a bit more scientific detail. Keone noticed Julie paying very close attention as well.

"What about the energy fluxes?" Julie asked.

"The wavelengths Brad used to support his hypotheses were in a region with extensive noise. None of the events he identified would have survived peer review," Hasselbach said.

"Do you think he was seeing what he wished to see?" Drayton asked.

"Almost certainly. After his sessions with you, he came back to us in a much more objective state of mind. His work with his colleague Radha was faultless after that. At least it was until Mr. Loftus visited the laboratory." Hasselbach replied.

"Other questions?" Keone asked.

Drayton and Hasselbach exchanged glances, before Drayton spoke. "No more questions. But I must compliment you and Mrs. Walden on how you handled every aspect of this dangerous situation. Sam Loftus had what we call a psychotic break. We could have lost him for good if you two had performed any differently."

Then it was Hasselbach's turn. "I can confirm that Dr. Carvell's home lab was licensed and violated no safety standards. After he began his sessions with Dr. Drayton, he allowed observatory staff to inspect it. Most of the equipment was analytical in nature and represented no inherent danger," Hasselbach added.

"If I may, Martin, I'd like to give the sergeant my psychiatric evaluation of your colleague."

"Of course, Evan. We both know he needs help."

"Sergeant Boyd, I'm sure you heard me ask both Dr. Carvell and Mr. Loftus if they would allow me to share my observations from our sessions with you."

"Yes, I did, and we have their statements of consent on tape. We're continuing to record as we speak. Please proceed."

"Dr. Carvell is displaying a pronounced obsessive behavior. When he and Sam encountered each other in my waiting room, no damage was done, because they didn't realize their connection. At the observatory, their shared discovery of the details of Sam's car crash derailed each of their recoveries.

"To put it simply, they reinforced each other's delusions. That is what led to the extreme actions of the past twenty-four hours. Both men are mentally ill and require treatment. Having worked with the police, I know what's required to establish that an individual needs to be held for a period in the Molokini ward of Maui Memorial. Both men meet these requirements. I believe this is the best course of action for the present. The decision is yours of course, Sergeant Boyd."

"What prognosis would you suggest at this point for each man?" Keone asked.

"Carvell's prognosis is very good, I should think. The fact that he confessed to the police in Hana is a good sign. I would expect him to be completely functional in a month or two with outpatient sessions to follow."

"And Sam?"

"I'm afraid Sam has a long difficult road back, even to where he was when Carvell intervened. I can give you a better idea in a month or so," Drayton said.

"All right. Here's what we're going to do. Since no charges have been filed against Carvell, I'm going to get his wife down here to talk with Dr. Drayton. I'm sure she'll co-sign the commitment papers with you, Dr. Hasselbach. As for Sam, I've arranged a meeting for Dr. Drayton and me with Judge Fernandez at 1:00 p.m. It's eleven-thirty now. This officer will show each you where you need to go." Keone said ushering everyone into the viewing area.

When everyone else was gone, Julie wrapped her arms around Keone and kissed him long and hard. "Lindsay offered to take me home, so you can get everything wrapped up. As for me I'll be taking a shower and bath and another shower. Then I plan to fall asleep, knowing I'll be safe—at last."

Chapter Fifty-Eight

Friday, June 14, 2:30 p.m.

D r. Evan Drayton watched through another two-way mirror as Sam Loftus sat silently in the consultation room of the Molokini ward of Maui Community Hospital waiting for the door to open.

"Hello, Sam," he said, as he entered the consultation room.

"Hello, Dr. Drayton."

"Do you know where you are, my friend?"

"I'm not sure anymore," Sam whined.

"I'm not interested in irony today. Answer the question." He was forced to use a firmer approach with Sam these days.

"Okay. I'm in the consultation room of the Molokini ward of Maui Memorial Hospital, in Wailuku, Maui, Hawaii, USA, Planet Earth, in this version of the universe."

Drayton found this version of Sam more annoying, but just as precise. "I saw Brad Carvell a little while ago. He wanted me to tell you how sorry he is about everything. He's making excellent progress in his treatment."

"I'm glad. I guess I didn't set back his recovery that badly then."

"Sam, we're going to get you both back to where you were before you met in my waiting room, but to achieve that, in your case, we have to use the two tools that helped us last time, your journals and Janet."

Sam stiffened. "No. I've hurt her enough. I'll re-read the journals, but I won't let Janet down again."

"Sam, she's been here every day. It hurts her when you turn her away. She is the best friend you have in this world."

"This world." The irony in Sam's words was evident.

"Sam, you can't go on believing that theoretical fantasy that Carvell was spouting. Even he doesn't believe it anymore."

"But it isn't personal for him. I want to believe it. I need to believe it, or Cindy and Timmy won't exist."

"But you realize you can't get back to them, or recreate them here, right."

"I do. I'm stuck here, for the rest of my life, without them."

"Now answer me honestly Sam. Knowing you can never leave this world and return to the one from your memories. Would you rather spend the rest of your life with our Janet or our Julie?"

Tears filled Sam's eyes. After a long pause, he whispered, "Janet."

"Okay. Then you need to let her visit."

"Not yet. Maybe someday. We both need more time."

"That's reasonable, Sam. But don't wait too long."

Sam didn't respond, so he decided to change the subject.

"I want to introduce you to someone, Sam." He left the room and returned with a young African American man of about thirty.

"Sam, this is Doctor Jude Miller. Dr. Miller will be filling in for me for a few days over the upcoming July Fourth holiday."

Miller stuck out his hand and Sam shook it, "Nice to meet you, Doctor. Maybe we can watch fireworks together from the roof."

Miller didn't acknowledge Sam's sarcasm. "For now, I'll leave you and Dr. Drayton to continue your session."

~

Keone, Julie, and Janet sat around the dining room table of the Loftus home drinking champagne and enjoying luscious appetizers in celebration of Julie and Keone's engagement.

"You two have made me happier than you can imagine," Jan said.

"I knew you would be." Julie said.

Keone decided to change the subject before these two started crying again. "Jan, these *pupus* are fantastic. Are you sure you don't have some Hawaiian blood in you somewhere?"

"I wish I did. Our neighbor, Mrs. Kanaloa, taught me everything I know. But I'm looking forward to having you and your brothers teach me how to do real Hawaiian barbeque, Maui style."

"We'd be delighted."

"You'll taste the best in the world at our wedding. We're holding it in the morning so all the boys can compete at the July Fourth rodeo." Julie added, giving her sister's hand a squeeze. "I'm afraid you may need to lend a hand with preparations,"

"Try and stop me."

"Would you like one of my handsome brothers to accompany you to the wedding?" Keone said.

"Very tempting, but I have someone else in mind to take me."

"You can't be considering...," Keone couldn't finish the sentence.

"Don't worry, Keone, Sam is where he needs to be and will remain there for a long time. I loved my old Sam. I even learned to love the new one, for a while. But he grew out of his love for me. If he can continue to grow as a person, why can't I?"

A long pause followed Janet's statement, but Julie decided to clear the air. "Dr. Drayton told you long ago that you have grounds for divorce from Sam. You helped me get my divorce from Dave. I'd be happy to return the favor."

"Thank you, dear. I may take you up on that. After what Sam did to you, I no longer feel obliged to live my life ruled by his treatment plan. And Sam lied to me. I know there was a time during his recovery when he'd honestly decided to learn to love me. I know Carvell derailed his recovery, but after that he lied to my face, pretended he still cared. How can I forgive him for that?"

"The lying was the worst part with Dave, too," Julie said.

"Julie, you're the one person who truly gets it. Sam learning to love me isn't enough anymore I'd need to be someone's first choice, not a consolation prize."

"You deserve to be." Keone said. He recognized the similarity between her situation with Sam and Julie's with Dave. They both deserved better.

"Now. Tell me about this cruise you have planned. And don't you dare spend it all in bed." Jan's expression morphed to something that looked suspiciously like a leer.

Chapter Fifty-Nine

Wednesday, July 3, 4:00 p.m.

S am was surprised when Dr. Miller told him he had a bit of good news for him, during their session.

"Sam, your wife Janet has accepted your invitation to visit," Miller said. "She will be coming by tomorrow afternoon."

Sam was speechless. It had been so long since Janet refused his belated invitation to visit him. *Maybe I didn't wait too long. Maybe it took her that long to forgive me.*

After a long pause he asked, "Did she say anything about me when you two spoke?"

"I don't want to raise any false hopes, Sam. It was just quick phone call. She asked if it would be compatible with your therapy for her to visit at this time."

"What did you say?"

"I told her that you were making progress, and a visit would be fine. She was a little concerned when she realized Dr. Drayton would still be away, tomorrow, but said, 'No. It's time. I've kept him waiting long enough. Tell him I'll come by at four.'"

300

Sam left the session with a kaleidoscope of thoughts in his mind. He had so much to do.

Over the past month Sam had let himself go, growing an unkempt beard and letting his hair grow long. In preparation for Janet's visit, he decided to get a shave and haircut and dress in his best suit.

~

WHEN SAM RANG HIS CALL BELL, THE ATTENDANT TOOK his time answering, but Sam was used to the different pace of care here in the Molokini ward.

"What is it, Sam? Was there something wrong with your snack?" Sam was glad Louie was on duty. He was one of the good ones.

"Louie, my dear friend, the snack was perfect. But now I feel like a shower and a shave. My wife is coming to visit tomorrow, and I need to look my very best."

"Sam, you know I love ya, but it's after 10:00 p.m. We do showers right before the morning shift."

"Then the shower shouldn't be busy, and you probably have time to take off this beard. Look, it will be two less things you have to do in the morning. Come on, I really need this."

Louie stared at him. Sam saw the wheels turning in the young man's head. "OK, Sammy, just this once. Consider it a going away present from me. Tonight's my last night here. Next week I start a new job where I don't have to work nights."

"That's wonderful. I bet you won't have to work with nutcases like me either," he joked. "And bring some scissors. I could use a haircut, too."

Chapter Sixty

Thursday, July 4, 2:00 p.m.

Dr. Martin Hasselbach waited anxiously in the visiting area after notifying the attendant in charge that he wished to see Mr. Sam Loftus. Although he enjoyed his discussions with Sam, he found his unkempt hair, beard, and body odor distracting. Fifteen minutes later, a clean-shaven man with a short haircut entered the room and sat down across the table from him.

"Dr. H., I'm so glad you picked today to visit. I always enjoy seeing you. But today is very special for me. My wife, Janet, has agreed to visit." Sam's excitement was obvious but so was his anxiety.

"I'm happy to hear that, Sam. But I've asked you to call me Martin," he was pleasantly surprised by this new grooming and let it show.

"Sure, Martin. Did you visit Brad today?"

"Yes, I did. It's a special day for him, too. He gets to go home."

"I'm happy for him, and for Diane. They're such nice people. Is he cured?"

"He's well enough to go home. He's hoping to teach this fall at UH Maui College."

"That's great. I'm going to ask Janet to forgive me. I've decided I want to live with her again. It's the right thing to do."

He suppressed a frown, disturbed by Sam's rapid change of topic. He preferred the quieter, more thoughtful Sam he'd experienced on previous visits. "Is everything all right, Sam? You seem a bit hyper."

"Just excited. Do you realize today is Independence Day? I think Brad's release today is auspicious."

Hasselbach remained silent.

"Well, I need to get changed for Janet's visit. But I'm so glad you stopped by. Even though Brad's going home, will you still visit me, you know, on weekends like you've been doing?"

"Of course, Sam. I'll see you this weekend. I hope your meeting with Janet goes well. Aloha."

"Aloha."

AT PRECISELY FOUR P.M., SAM WAS BROUGHT BACK TO the visiting room. He had washed his face, combed his hair, and applied deodorant and after-shave before donning his sharply pressed suit. He just wished he could wear his favorite wingtips instead of hospital slippers.

Sam entered with a spring in his step and a smile on his face. Janet was already seated on the other side of the table and had a manila folder in front of her.

"Hello, Janet. It's wonderful to see you. I'm sorry it took so long to pull myself together enough to let you visit."

"Sam, we have to talk."

Janet seemed tense, but that was natural after the things he'd put her through. He began softly, "I know, Sweetheart. I hope you can forgive me for all I put you through and understand it was this crazy illness that made me do what I did. I'm ready to begin again. We made so much progress before Brad sidetracked me. I was never faking my affection for you. Please say you forgive me."

"I do forgive you, Sam. I know you're sick and can't control what you do. I also believe the closeness we achieved before you went on that tour of the observatory was real."

Tears came to Sam's eyes. "I won't let you down this time, Janet. I promise."

"I believe that you believe that, too. But a couple of events of have changed our situation." Janet paused to summon the strength to continue.

Sam jumped in, struggling to salvage the moment. "I've decided we can adopt. We can have the family I dreamed of together. We can learn to love each other as much as we used to —more."

"No, Sam. We can't. There was time when I might have been able to forgive the pain and suffering you caused me. But I can never forgive what you did to my sister and how you lied to me to help make her vulnerable. You hurt her, Sam, physically and mentally. You behaved like a monster. I can't love someone who could do that. I was in her wedding today—to Keone. I've never seen her happier or felt prouder to be her sister."

"I didn't know about the wedding, but I chose you, not this world's Julie."

"Do you even hear yourself? You said, *this world's Julie*. You're performing again, for Dr. Drayton, for me, maybe even for yourself. You will never get better until you realize there is only one world. And, in this world, another man has entered my life, a wonderful man, who makes me happy. His name is Michael, and he loves me for who I am. He doesn't need to learn how."

Sam's face fell, but he didn't try to escape from reality this time. He knew his offensive to win Janet back had little chance of success but had still hoped. "Too little, too late. You do deserve better. Your forgiveness will have to be enough. I hope you understand that I do want what's best for you."

"I do, Sam. I hope you find a path to happiness as well." She looked down at the folder in front of her. "There's one more thing."

"You want me to sign some documents, right?" Sam's voice cracked.

Janet nodded

"You probably didn't need my signature to get a divorce given my condition. But it means a lot to me that you're asking for it anyway."

"I'm glad you understand."

"May I ask you one last favor, Janet? Could you give me tonight to come to terms with this before I return these to you signed?"

Janet obviously hadn't expected this and hesitated.

"I promise I'll sign them. Swear to God. Just give me the time I need to grieve over this lost opportunity."

"All right, Sam. I owe you that much. I will be here at ten a.m. tomorrow to pick up the papers. But we won't meet again."

"I understand. Thank you. Goodbye, Janet."

"Goodbye, Sam."

SAM STUMBLED BACK TO HIS LITTLE ROOM, CLUTCHING the divorce papers to his chest. He knew Janet needed her freedom. He couldn't pretend he was the best possible husband for her. Still, what were the implications if he found a way to return to his world someday? Would signing the papers here mean his doppelganger in the real world did the same for Julie there?

She was right. Once again, he'd convinced everyone, Drayton, Hasselbach, even himself to some degree, that he accepted his memories as delusions. But inside he never really had. He knew Brad's conclusions were flawed, but so were Drayton's. Not everything could be explained by mental illness. He could never completely let go of the belief that his memories described his real life in another place. Cindy and Timmy were real.

He struggled with his thoughts, alone in his room, for hours. It was nearly midnight before he finally did what he knew was best for everyone and scratched his name on the documents. He even made the point of writing in the manner of this world and not his own. As he changed for bed, he felt a sense of relief. The covers seemed warming as he pulled them over his chest and sleep came gently to wash his remaining concerns away.

Chapter Sixty-One

Friday, July 5, 2:00 p.m.

S am awoke refreshed, though he could tell by the darkness that dawn was still hours away. Lying on his back, he gazed up at the ceiling and wondered at how blurry it appeared. It was like...

...like looking through a soap bubble. The portal had returned and looked just like it did when he was in the car. The bubble moved ever closer to him until it enveloped him and produced a loud pop.

Startled, he jumped from his bed and ran to the table where the divorce documents still lay. Was he finally back home? One look at the documents would tell him, but he was afraid.

Finally forcing his eyes to scan the pages, he smiled broadly. The words were no longer in mirror writing and the plaintiff's name was Julie Loftus.

Somehow, he'd made it back home.

He had a huge task ahead of him. He would have to convince Julie, who would surely be the wife who came this afternoon, that he was himself again. She must have spent as many days with the mirror-Sam as he'd spent in the mirror world.

He tore the divorce papers to shreds and banged on his door to get the night attendant's attention.

"What is it this time, Sam? Hey, where's your beard?" Sam was not surprised that the attendant was a stranger.

"I'm a new man. Yesterday I decided to return to the real world. Now I feel like a shower and a shave. My wife is coming to visit tomorrow, and I need to look my very best."

"Sam, you know I love ya, but it's 2:00 AM."

"Then the shower shouldn't be busy, and you probably have time to give me a fresh shave...."

~

AFTER A FULL MONTH, WHICH INCLUDED EXTENSIVE tests and a period of re-acquaintance between Sam and Julie, it was finally time to leave the hospital. Dr. Drayton was there. Sam and Julie gave him big hugs and their eternal thanks for making Sam well again.

As they pushed through the clear glass doors, Keone and Dr. Carvell were both waiting for them.

"Dr. Drayton knows I'm sane, now. According to Julie, you two always knew. I can't thank you enough. I want to get to know these versions of each of you."

Dr. Carvell gave him a hug and showed him a printout displaying the energy flux that occurred in the wee hours of July fifth.

Keone shook his hand, leaned in, and whispered, "I knew we'd solve this mystery."

Sam and Julie left their two new friends behind and walked to the car. The kids were standing beside the car and Sam swept them into his arms for hugs and kisses. After placing everyone in their appropriate positions in the car, Sam allowed Julie to drive them home.

"Do you think Janet came back for mirror-Sam in that other world?" Julie asked.

"I'm afraid their relationship was beyond repair." *Thanks to me.* Let's just be happy that you and Cindy and Timmy and I are all together again."

He looked outside of the car to see everything was written in the way he found normal.

He looked at Cindy and Timmy in the backseat playing "I touched you last" and laughing.

He noticed Julie's medical bag in the backseat before she brought his attention forward. "I've invited Dave and Janet over tonight. I hope it's not too soon."

"You know I love those guys. I can't wait to see them again." *The real them.*

"Were they that different in the other world?"

"Dave was horrible there. But Janet was pretty much the same."

"What was I like?"

"Still beautiful, of course, but tougher. Dave was hard on you." Sam didn't want to talk about the other Julie. He felt guilty about what he'd done to her.

Sam gradually noticed his wife was running red lights. Then when they neared home, a red light changed to yellow, then green, and his wife stopped dead.

"Why did you stop?"

"I always stop for green lights, silly."

From the back seat Timmy and Cindy sang, "Green means stop, and red means go. The yellow light means go real slow."

Sam realized he wasn't quite home after all, but it was close enough. Some changes you can live with, others...

He wondered if the other Sam had been as fortunate, then smiled broadly and relaxed back into his seat. Satisfied to explore this new world with those he loved.

Chapter Sixty-Two

Saturday, July 6, 5:00 p.m.

Dr. Drayton peered through the small one-way window into Sam's domain. Sam sat in the farthest corner of the tiny room, where he had remained, motionless and gazing into space, since yesterday.

As he continued to observe his patient, life returned briefly to Sam's face. He didn't move or speak, nor did he seem aware of his surroundings. But his eyes were bright and the expression on his face serene.

A voice behind the doctor asked, "Why is he smiling?"

"I'm not sure. But it might be a good sign."

"Or maybe, in his mind, he's returned home."

"Sergeant Boyd, I didn't hear you come in. How was the wedding?"

"Wonderful. Julie was so happy that Jan was beside her, as we said our vows. Jan is a different person since Sam agreed to the divorce. Her boyfriend came, too. I really like him. He's part Hawaiian, you know."

"Did you finally solve all your mysteries?"

Keone stared at Sam's peaceful face. "In our own way, I guess each of us did."

Evan Drayton patted Keone on the shoulder and left to see other patients. Keone continued to gaze at Sam until he heard someone come up behind him.

"Pitiful, isn't he?"

He turned to find Martin Hasselbach standing behind him.

"Oh, I don't know. He seemed to be smiling a minute ago. I just told Evan that I think Sam may have made it back to his own reality, in his mind, at least."

Hasselbach seemed to ponder this. "In his mind, yes, or..."

"What?"

"Oh, I don't know. Sam needs better hygiene, don't you think? How long do you think it's been since he's been shaved?"

"It looks like at least a few weeks. I'll talk to the orderly about giving him a shave and a haircut, too."

"Good idea. Oh, And congratulations on your wedding. It was very kind of you to invite me."

"Julie feels that we all shared a common experience. We look forward to keeping in touch going forward." Keone smiled.

"Shouldn't you be on your honeymoon?"

"We leave tomorrow for a cruise of the Greek Islands. I just felt I needed to see Sam one more time, before we left. Julie understood." *At least she said she did.*

"You know, Keone, you're a special kind of detective. Something you said when we first met got me thinking." Hasselbach paused.

"I said something that got you thinking? I find that... uh... surprising." He couldn't imagine what he might have said.

"In our discussion of scientific rigor, you provided the

example of someone calculating when a comet will reappear then testing to see if it does. Do you remember?"

"Yes." Keone shifted his feet. This topic made him uncomfortable.

"I went back and reviewed the data on the energy surges that Carvell reported."

"You said he'd misinterpreted his data." Keone's discomfort grew.

"Oh, yes. I saw nothing in the range he'd measured."

Keone relaxed. "You had me worried for a second there, Doc."

"Your comment made me realize that I had a bias, too. I had Dr. Rathnachalam go back and analyze a broader spectrum of electromagnetic radiation than Brad had."

"Go on."

"Just as I'd suspected, there were no surges on any of the dates and times he'd recorded—except one."

"Don't say it."

"The one on March fifteenth, shortly before your collision. Radha also discovered one surge since Carvell ended his study."

"When was that?"

"Precisely two a.m. on the morning of July fifth."

"Just a coincidence."

"Of course, you're probably right." Hasselbach smiled.

"Damn right I'm right."

"I'm sure you're unaware, but I've been visiting Sam every weekend and holiday for almost a month. I first stopped by out of curiosity but found I really enjoyed talking with him. He seemed to enjoy my visits, as well. On every other visit he seemed perfectly lucid, always expressing his deep regret for the actions that got him committed. Now he seems catatonic."

"The nurse said he's been like that ever since he signed the divorce papers. No cosmic influence required to explain that."

"No. That would be heart-wrenching for anyone. But when did he sign those papers?" Hasselbach asked.

"She thought it must have been after midnight on July fourth."

"Hmm. So, before two a.m. on July fifth. I wonder which Sam we have in there?"

"What do you mean which Sam? Sam Loftus, of course." Keone had heard enough of this.

"Oh, yes. But which Sam Loftus?"

"You're not considering Carvell's crazy parallel universe idea, are you? You're the one who told me it was extremely theoretical and impossible to prove."

"I know it's not possible to prove. It's just that I visited Sam two days ago, on Independence Day..."

"So...?"

"He'd just had a shave."

Acknowledgements

I began this novel in 2013, and the Maui it describes is the one I experienced at that time. A few things have changed since that time, but I decided to keep it set when it was written, because this was the Maui I experienced at the time. The cane fields are gone now, as are a few of the restaurants, but the spirit of this blessed island remains the same.

I've been blessed with a multitude of wonderful people who read and commented on this book during its multiple incubations and incarnations. Ken Andrus, Elaine Gallant, Doug McLellan, Laurie Hanan, Bill Bernhardt, and Christy and Jennifer Ludwig plowed through the original version of this book and provided valuable feedback. Dr. John H. Draeger provided information on psychiatric conditions. Detective Lieutenant Audra M. Sellers, Maui Police Department and Chief Scott Fleuter, Ashland, Oregon Police Department, (Ret.) provided valuable input on Maui Police Department structure and law enforcement procedures. Any errors that remain are mine.

For this completely re-written and revised book, special thanks to my beta readers Ken Andrus, Jenny Ludwig, R.J. Johnson, Doug McLellan, Audra Sellers, Deyna Puckett, and Lara Bernhardt. Thanks also to the great authors in Maui Writers, Ink and the William Bernhardt Writing Seminars for valuable input. Their talent inspires and encourages me every day.

The Maui, Hawai'i, and Aloha Writers Conferences gave me the chance to meet and learn from several authors, editors, and agents. I especially thank William Martin, Yvonne Medley, Julia

Loren, and Les Stobbe for their early and continued encouragement. Participation in the Rose State, Red Sneaker, and WriterCon Conferences in Oklahoma have further stoked this author's fire.

I'm forever indebted to William Bernhardt, a fantastic writer, teacher, mentor, and friend, who has taught me more about writing than anyone deserves to learn. His recommendation that I completely rework the self-published version of this story and submit it to Babylon Books was a godsend. How often do you get a second chance to do something right?

Many thanks, as well, to Ally Robertson for her conscientious editing of the revised manuscript. I learned so much from that. It's rewarding to continue to learn new things at my age. Finally, I am indebted to Maria Novillo Saravia and her colleagues at BeauteBook for the mysterious and enticing cover. It's so exciting to see Sam Loftus in flesh.

My wife Christy, son Jonathan, and daughter Jennifer teach me something new and wonderful every day.

About the Author

James R. (Rick) Ludwig, Ph.D. spent forty years in the academic, health care, biotechnology, and pharmaceutical disciplines. Rick also maintained a writer's journal since his junior year in high school and populated it with short stories, poetry, and essays throughout his career.

Although a published author of multiple scientific papers and textbook chapters, writing for a popular audience presented a unique challenge. Rick spent the first year of his retirement (2008), converting his writings, including his original writer's journal (1967-2008), to digital format. Since then, he has written full-time, completed four manuscripts, and published three novels. *Eyes of the Beholder* is the first novel in the Maui Mysteries Trilogy. Rick's other completed manuscript is an autobiography of the first forty-four years of his life, which he presented to his children at Christmas last year.

Rick participated in the 2009 Hawai'i Writers Conference in Honolulu, Hawai'i and served as Volunteer Coordinator for the 2013 Aloha Writers Conference in Kapalua, Maui. Rick participated in best-selling author William Bernhardt's Level 1, 2, 3, and advanced writers' workshops between 2010 and 2016 and presented seminars as part of the Rose State Writers Workshop in Oklahoma City (2015), the Red Sneaker Writers Workshop (2018), and WriterCon (2021).

Rick is married with two grown children, Jonathan and Jennifer. He and his wife of forty-one years, Christy, divide their time between Maui, Hawai'i, and Southern California.

You can contact him at rickludwigwrites@gmail.com.